Moss on
the North Side

Moss on the North Side

SYLVIA WILKINSON

HOUGHTON MIFFLIN COMPANY BOSTON
THE RIVERSIDE PRESS CAMBRIDGE

Part I

Chapter One

CARY NEVER FELT she was completely asleep; each time her thoughts faded, her body jerked awake again. The night bugs were screaming outside, but when she crawled down the bed and shut the window, she could hear her father breathing in the other room. She felt her body tighten as she waited after each gasp for him to gasp again. When she opened the window again, the bugs screamed in her face until she fell back in the bed and twisted the sheet around her. Later she opened her eyes to find a gray square of light forming in the window and the bugs silent. Her father was coughing loudly now and she could hear him strangle then muffle his coughs in the pillow. As the gray square of light slowly turned a thin green, the whole room became light and she could not try to sleep again.

The animal sounds outside the window grew louder and more frequent. She remembered the sounds that the night animals had made before she went to bed, the faint rustle and dash through the leaves. On spring nights she could hear the slow hum of the petals falling in the fruit orchard. She would look out the window to find the moonlight spots on the path where the leaves and moths went against the writing-spider webs, sliding and tangling in the threads. As the sun came up, the dew drops in the webs would sparkle then fall away. But now as fall came, she could hear animals walking in the light dew, the leaves sucking under their feet until the sun dried the dew away and the leaves crackled and broke. The chickens fluttered from under the house and walked silently across the moss beneath the shade tree. There they lifted the moss in clumps with their feet and pecked and scratched for the hard-shelled gray bugs that rattled in their beaks.

The sheet over her had begun to get sticky as the heat came through the window and she kicked it away from her body. When she sat up on the edge of her bed, she saw through the open door across the room that her father's body was drawn up into a knot and the bed covers had fallen onto the floor. She walked over to him and watched his sides go in and out quickly, his breath gurgling into the pillow.

"Papa? Papa, it's morning."

He exhaled a long breath and began to jar against the bed but did not answer her. His undershirt was wet and stuck to his skin and little beads of sweat were on the backs of his arms.

"Papa, aren't you any better?" When she spoke, she touched his hair. It had stuck together in tufts and seemed gray and dull and unfamiliar. He turned over suddenly and she started backwards as he looked up at her with a steady blank stare. Cary saw his eyes and felt her heart tighten in her chest and begin to beat heavily. His body was wet but his face had dried during the night; his lips were cracked and his eyes had crusted around the edges.

"Cary . . ." When he spoke she quickly sat on the edge of the bed and placed her hand on his forehead. It was hot and the hair she pushed back from his eyes seemed to get wet at her touch. As she moved her wet fingertips down onto his cheeks, they felt dry and swollen. She held her hand still but felt no movement beneath the surface of his skin.

"You still have a temperature, Papa. You're awful hot."

Then he began to shake his hand and rub his eyes. "No, no,

I'm much better . . . much better. I'll cool off soon as I get out of this hot bed."

His voice was dry and she could feel it hurting his throat as he talked. He gripped the edge of the bed and she watched the veins rise in his hand as he lifted his head slightly from the pillow. He was steady a moment before his grip loosened and his head fell back heavily against the pillow. Cary watched his eyes close and his body become still. His lips were parted but his breathing seemed to have stopped.

She squeezed his hand and spoke, "Papa! Papa!"

He began to speak slowly, "It's all right, Cary. I won't get up just yet. I'll rest today."

Cary felt her eyes begin to burn, "What can I do? Please tell me what I can do. I don't know any more. I just don't know."

He was silent again and she jumped from the edge of the bed turning her back to him. She looked across to the window and the leaves were blurred, the sun turning the edges light green. As she watched, the wind began to move them, they overlapped until they were dark green in the center and she had forced her eyes to focus on them.

She spoke again, still staring out the window, "Are you hungry yet?"

"No. But I'll get myself something later." She could hear him still trying to talk but she could not turn around and look at him.

"You can't. You can't get up." Then she stopped, hoping he hadn't heard her. She turned quickly to him and he was looking at her. "I'll go call the doctor, Papa. I'll call him at the station."

He shook his head slowly until she spoke again. "Mrs. Strawbright will pay for it. I know she will." He did not answer so she turned and went back in the other room. "I'm gone, Papa."

"Don't forget to take a dime for the phone. There's one in the dish in there."

She walked to the table by the stove, took a dime and walked to the door. Cary stood on the edge of the porch, and as soon as the fresh air hit her face she realized how stale the house had become during the night. She found herself looking down the path that led to the pond, thinking of the water and how she would like to go swimming. The garden in front of the house was spattered with the color of morning glories, brilliant against the green. She thought of watching them after sunset as they slowly twisted shut and how she always planned to mark one to see if the same one opened the next day but she never did. A little colored boy appeared coming up the path dragging a burlap sack, and when he looked up at her she started off the porch. He skipped through the yard, watching her come down the steps. When she spoke to him, he ran out to the road and began to walk slowly again. The chickens clucked and ran under the house, while she walked across the yard and into the road.

She walked down the dusty road by the tobacco fields, following the grooves where the tobacco sleds had been dragged earlier that morning. In the ditch by the shade tree were the cookie wrappers and lunch bags where the colored tenants ate their lunch. She climbed down in the ditch and picked up a faded pop bottle. When she looked up to see if anyone was coming, she heard a sled in the field, the tobacco leaves slapping against its sides and the leather of the mule's harness sliding in the sweat on its flanks. She went back up the side of the ditch and started walking again when she heard her name.

"Cary, where your old man been?"

Cary stopped and saw Otis dropping the reins of the mule and coming towards her.

"He's sick, Otis. Got some kind of fever."

Otis stood on the other side of the ditch looking at her with his head turned to the side and the sun filtering through his white lashes. His hands dangled at his sides and he moved his fingers, the sticky tobacco juice sealing them back together.

"Can't get a damn thing out of them niggers," he said absently.

"He'll be back in a couple of days. Never seen him sick in the summer before."

Otis pulled his thin hair away from his forehead and said, "Too hot to be sick. I got a fever all the time." Then he turned and looked down the row, calling to one of the Negroes, "You take this one on in. I'm leaving for a while."

He edged himself slowly down the side of the ditch, holding onto the vines until his feet rested in the bottom. "You going to the station?" Cary nodded and began walking again with Otis walking beside her in the ditch until it grew shallow and he walked out onto the road. She walked ahead of him and felt the dust sting the back of her legs when it caught under the soles of his shoes.

Cary stopped and waited for him to catch up. "Otis, do you think you could check on the barns for Papa tonight?"

Otis began to mumble and look at his feet as he shuffled along. "I'll get one of the niggers. It's all I can do to make it home at night, all I can do."

"Don't bother. I'll ask someone else," she said angrily and began to walk away from him.

"Wait up, now. Wait up." As he spoke she stopped suddenly and watched a broken pine limb batter its way from the top of a tree. When it hit the ground, he was beside her again and giggling softly to himself.

"What's so funny," she said and began to slow her pace so he could keep up.

He continued to laugh and she heard the sticky sound of his hands pulling against the worn fabric of his overalls as he slid them into his pocket. "Just thinking about what your Pa was telling on you the other day down at the station."

"What?"

"We was telling stories . . . well, I can't tell you about them because a kid ain't got no business listening to such."

Cary glanced at him but turned away quickly when she saw him grinning and saw his eyes roll sideways at her under the white lashes. She waited for him to begin talking again, but she could feel that he was waiting for her to ask him what they had talked about. She thought about how she had seen the men on the bench in front of the station look up at her and laugh and how she had not been able to hear what they were saying. While she had waited for her father, she had skipped rocks down the railroad tracks, trying to get them to bounce three times on the iron before they fell off.

Suddenly Otis began speaking again and she felt her heart jump inside of her when she heard his voice.

"He said you was getting eggs out of the hen house and he come in on you and you just looked up at him and said, 'How do chickens do it?' and he said 'Do what? Lay eggs?' and you said, 'That's sort of what I meant.' "

Cary looked straight ahead, feeling the yellow of the bitter-weed on the side of the road slide by her eyes. They were almost to the railroad tracks and she could see the top of the station at the bottom of the hill. Otis was giggling again, but she could not turn around when he started gasping, trying to stop laughing and start talking again.

"He said he couldn't help but get tickled because he had to admit it used to bother him when he was a kid because he had seen dogs and cows . . . said he saw a dog come right in the church when he was a kid and didn't pay attention to any of the people . . . just chased that old bitch right under the pews and gave it to her right there and how his mother tried not to notice and kept right on singing and shoved the hymn book right in his face. And he said after you said it about the chicken, you was afraid he might tell you and just went running off like your shirt-tail was on fire."

"He never told me about the dog in the church but I don't have to ask him to find out things." Cary felt her anger coming and bit her lip so she could stop talking. Otis began laughing every time he stopped talking and walked faster to keep up with her.

" 'Member when you asked him about them frogs riding piggyback?" he said, losing his breath. Then he began to cough when he tried to laugh. "Said you'd keep right on asking questions, and every time you knew you'd asked one like that you'd just scoot off so fast no one could catch you," he said and strangled again on his words.

"Otis, I've got to get on into the station. I can't wait up for you any longer." Cary ran to the edge of the highway and stopped for a car coming under the railroad trestle. She glanced quickly at it before looking straight across to the station, waiting for it to go by. In the corner of her eye she saw the color of the car with its rusty fenders and a man lean out of the side next to her with his arm hanging down the door. Her hair lifted and blew across her face as it went by and she listened to the sound of the tar bubbles breaking under the tires. Then the hand banged the side of the door and she looked up without thinking into the face of the man inside. She held her neck stiff and the face went by, his lips puckered and his eyes resting on her body. When the car was past, she ran across the hot pavement and into the phone booth in front of the station.

Her heart was beating fast when she dialed the number, and as she listened to it ring on the other end she watched Otis stumble across the road. A woman answered and asked her to hold until Dr. Jason was free. Otis crossed the highway and sat down on the end of the bench where two men were leaning together and talking. Then she heard Dr. Jason's voice as he picked up the phone.

"Dr. Jason, this is Cary out at the Strawbrights' place. We need you to come out here."

The men on the bench all looked up at her and she glanced at the folding door, pushing it together tighter.

"My daddy has some kind of fever real bad and I don't have anything to give him . . . No, he hadn't eat in two days and he's got a bad temperature . . . I was really hoping you could come before tonight. He didn't get no better last night . . . Then you'll try to come tonight. I'll be looking out for you in case you can't find the place."

She put the phone back on the hook, listening to see if the dime would fall back down, but she heard it fall into the coin box. She knew the men on the bench were still watching her so she began to turn the pages in the telephone book that hung by a chain in the corner. When she leaned back against the door and it cracked open, she heard a hissing that had begun in the leaves. What she had thought was the sound of someone stacking lumber behind the station was the rumble of thunder. The daylight dropped suddenly and the leaves all became an intense green. As the lights in front of the station began to flicker the men got up and went inside. The air coming in the door was cooler so she cracked it open more and the sharp flashes of lightning seemed to come in with her. When the scattered raindrops cracked in the dust in front of the station, she jumped watching the drops start smashing against the glass on the side of the phone booth.

The screen door on the station opened and blew out of the hand that had opened it.

"Cary, come on in here out of the storm."

"I'm all right in here," she called without thinking; then the hand pulled the door back shut and hooked it on the inside.

As the rain came harder the wind died down and the thunder became more distant. The leaves glistened in the dim light, the water running down their center veins and wetting the ground under the thick branches. Over the station, the gutters filled up and the water ran off the edges in a thick sheet, blurring the green of the trees. Cary played with the chain on the phone book, turning the links inside out in her fingers. When the water came sweeping through the station again, impatient to be outside she opened the door letting the rain smell come into the phone booth.

The sudden chill in the air made her remember the fall days last year when everything had turned yellow and orange and brown, making her restless and uneasy about winter coming. The leaves and weeds were all breaking apart and shattering, the bare stems and stalks had started to show. The animals had gotten restless too, moving in the air and under the leaves, and all of the fields were woven together with spider webs. One evening she had walked through the leaves on the way home collecting the colored ones, stopping and looking under the big maples trying to find the yellow leaves that didn't have the circle spots on them before they fell. She had gone into the house with her hands full of leaves and sat down on her bed, stacking them so they went from small to large and yellow to orange.

She had looked up and her father was standing at the door watching her. Smiling up at him, she had pressed the leaf stack together tightly in her hand.

Then he had spoken softly to her, "I haven't seen you do that since you were a little kid. You remember when you used to take them to Sunday School with you?" She nodded and looked back at him. "Your teacher told me you were a little artist; that she could tell by the way you put the colors."

When he had spoken she had looked back down at the leaves, and suddenly they seemed strange and unfamiliar to her. She had let them loosen in her hands and the colors all blended into one. She had taken the leaf from each end of the stack and put them beside each other and saw they were very different in color. Her hands had felt warm and alive around the leaves as she ran her fingers across the smooth surfaces, following the leaf veins to the center. She had looked up again to see if her father were still there and he had smiled down quietly at her.

Chapter Two

"Now scoot on back unless you're going to spend your two cents."

Cary slid the two pennies into her pocket, watching him walk over and tap the pop bottle on the side of the crate in front of the station. After the dirt on the bottle had slid off in a chunk, shattering and melting into the wet earth at his feet, he dropped it into a square in the crate. She felt the air get hot around her again and dry away the scattered raindrops that had fallen on her from the trees. She thought back to how he had spoken to her and her eyes began to burn.

"I ain't no little kid," she said and asked loudly, "Why do you run me off? If Papa was here, you couldn't talk like that." After she had spoken, she was surprised that they had been her words and she watched as the man stepped back in surprise too.

He turned and she had not moved from beside the bottle crates. "Now look, I've got no fight to start with you or any of the kids around here. I just don't want you hanging around."

"I like to leave when I'm ready." Then she went in the store, slamming the screen behind her, and walked down beside the bread counter with her hands clasped behind her. As she walked she stopped at each of the candy boxes picking up the candy and dropping it back in. He had come in with her and she could feel him standing behind her. Then she turned slowly and looked through the window.

"Customer out front," she said.

He hesitated a moment, then went towards the door, his eyes on her until he backed through the screen. When he had gone she left quickly by the back door of the station and stepped into the tall, unmown grass around the walls. As she walked she pressed the grass on its side with her feet, looking down through the stalks until she saw another bottle. When she picked it up to take inside, she saw the neck was jagged and it scraped across her hand. The two men in front turned when the bottle hit the side of the oil tank on the barn beside the station.

As the service station man put change in Otis' hand, Cary watched from the side of the building while he opened the bottle on a nail. Then a dime clanged against the water can beside the gas pump sending a green haze of flies into the air. When the dime hit the concrete base below the pumps, the flies dropped back on the can like little green weights and settled silently around the waterdrops. Cary saw Otis slap his pocket and turn to see where it rolled, looking towards the sound and not the coin. The dime rolled along the edge of the concrete before it wobbled and fell off into a crack in the pavement. She watched him shrug his thin shoulders before he walked back towards the station.

"Getting so damn rich you won't get your fingernails dirty picking up money?" A man in overalls had spoken from the bench outside the station.

"Hell, I'm getting so damn old if I bent I couldn't straighten out again."

When Otis went inside she heard the cap fizz off another pop bottle and the chairs scrape against the wall as they sat down. Tugging out a broom stalk, she walked from behind the station, slipping behind the car beside the pump and rattling the stalk along the chrome. Sitting beside the water can, she poked the dirt from between her toes and glanced over her shoulder to see if everyone were inside the station. Then she quickly flipped the dime out of the crack and picked it up before it rolled.

When she slipped the dime into her pocket, it clicked lightly against the two pennies she had got for the drink bottle. As she started across the highway, the pavement was hot and the wet tar bubbles crunched beneath her feet. Walking through the stubbles on the other side, she felt grass blades pull loose and cling to the tar on her flesh. Heading up the dirt road to the railroad, her feet grew warmer than the wet sand. The dirt stuck in the tar that pushed up black between her toes. When she got to the tracks she bent to her knees, laying her ear against the iron runner. The hot runner vibrated back until she sat up and felt her ear popping deep inside.

In the tough grass beside the tracks, the heavy dry smell of the bitterweed made her dizzy. The last few drops of rain were falling off the grass and the cross ties were dry except for the dark puddles in the shade under them. Beside her a green snake weaved around the rocks, rolling like a liquid in hot glass until the grass pulled it in and it disappeared. The air around her was filled with the restless murmur of the farm animals that were slowly moving into pasture and heading for the shade. A bird began to scream from the tree by the road until she heard it flutter down and the sound disappeared in the tobacco field. She could see no one around but everything was moving and alive, even the snake made the grass tremble above him though he couldn't be seen. She pressed her index finger against the track where the vibration made it tingle as her feet had in the hot tar. While she waited for the train she found herself rubbing her finger quickly up and down the rail until it felt smooth and hot. Then she touched it against her cheek.

"That's how you feel if you're dead," she thought. As the words went through her mind, she looked at her hand and it seemed no longer to be part of her body. She quickly pressed her finger against her cheek again and could only feel the throbbing in her cheek. The finger was like her father's face, remote and far away, and seemed to have no life under the skin. She felt a sharp pain inside her chest, closing her eyes tight but the bright sun came through her lids. She held them shut while she dotted her finger up and down her arm and the life began to move back into it. When she licked it, the skin was rough again and tasted like tin foil.

"For a minute my finger was dead," she thought and her head jerked up as the wooden ties beneath the rail began to wobble and the rocks rolled down into the grass. The green snake poured out of the grass, slipped across one rail and into the gravel between the ties where it lay motionless. Cary quickly put her dime and two pennies on the runner, straightening them up as they jumped on the rail. Down the track she could see the smoke where the train was on the next to the last bend before the straight stretch by her. Then she stopped to look at the snake.

"Get out of there, you stupid snake."

She bent over to reach it with her hand, but her arm broke out in chill bumps and she couldn't touch it. It was like the spider drowning in the spring that she fished up on a leaf, but when it began to run up the leaf she dropped it back into the water.

She looked up when the train whistled at the lower crossing and quickly picked up a clod, smashing it between the rails. The snake slithered down into a crack beside the cross tie and left only its green pointed tail above the ground. The train was rumbling towards her now. She looked up and saw the train light, strange in the daytime, as the black engine got closer. She turned and ran back to the edge of the field and stood up to her waist in broom sage until the train got in front of her. The man in the front waved at her; always it was the same man and he always yelled something and winked with ugly, wrinkled eyes. She never waved back but smiled, because his train carried him on away from her and she would never have to see him in the filling station or in the fields because his train took him along with it.

"Hey, sugar!" he said and his voice was too high and shrill for the dull rumble to kill.

She thought of the great train wreck her grandmother had told her about. Right there a thousand hoboes were dead and burning who had been stealing rides in the freight cars. The big train had left the track and dumped the cars and men in the fields and caught on fire. And the train burned up and let the engineer out. She never had to fear him because the train would not stop there and she would never have to see him out of it. When she thought of the hoboes, she always felt her body shiver until the train was past. No one had come to claim the bodies and they were all wrapped up without names and taken away. The rails shook now and dirt sifted from the cross ties as they wobbled back and forth under the strain. As the cars rumbled by, the train jerked and heaved on the tiny wheels. A flash of light came in the space between each box car as she walked closer, the cars darkening the sky in front of her and drowning all the farm sounds. She clutched her fists while the train moved, afraid the cars would leap from the track, not knowing if she were afraid because of the hoboes or because the engineer would get out. She saw down the track that the end of the train was near and knew the old man in the back sat with his arms crossed and would nod. He never waved at her, and as the train passed and began to grow smaller she watched the white dash of hair on his head rock back against the dark wall. The white hair lifted slightly in the wind and broke apart like a thistle before the train disappeared around the bend.

When the train was gone and the rumbling sound became faint, she ran back to the tracks. The rails were blistering hot while she looked for the money, and gravel still slid down the slope. She found the two pennies inside the rail and they were untouched, where the clod had broken and knocked them off.

"You damn stupid old snake, look what you did! You son of a bitch!"

She poked into the crack where he had gone with a stick but he wasn't there. Then she looked back on the track and smiled as she saw the dime spread into a silver oval that curved with the rail. She took from her pocket a string that tinkled with copper ovals.

"That makes seventeen copper and my first silver."

She reached in her pocket again and took out a nail. Putting the flattened dime against the track, she took a flint rock and beat with a nail until a hole went through it. She pulled the nail out of the dime, ran a string through the hole, and let the silver oval slide down with the pennies. After she picked up the two pennies, she slid them under the cross tie before walking down the track. Stepping from cross tie to cross tie she could watch her feet slide over the wood, because it would be five hours before the next train came.

When she reached the crossing, she stepped up on the rail until she reached the other side of the dirt stretch. Beside the tracks long runners from the watermelons in the field reached up the side of the cross ties with curling green feelers twining around the dark wood. Across the field watermelons lay like striped whelks bursting above the vines.

Cary held the string stretched tight between her hands, watching the ovals slide down the string. The silver oval was smooth and thin, with no trace of the engraving, but the pennies were marked with the spread image of Lincoln. She stood for a moment with her toes grasped tightly to the rail, remembering when she had the chain of coins on the table trying to polish them smooth and her father had stood watching her.

"The Government would really get after you for doing that," he said.

"Doing what?"

"Defacing money. It's against the law for putting holes in money because they're no good any more and can't be spent."

"I know they can't be spent," she answered quickly.

He walked to the side of the table and looked at her. "You're proud of making them so they can't be spent?"

She stopped polishing the coins and looked up at him. "I don't know that I call it proud." Then she looked back at the coins and began to arrange them into flowers with the ovals for petals. "You never said nothing to me about messing up money before. Does it make you mad because it can't be spent?"

"Now, that wasn't what I was saying at all. You get it on your own and it's to do with as you please. It's just a drop in the bucket. I wasn't trying to make you mad. I was never even trying to make you feel bad about messing it up." He placed his hand under her chin and turned her face up to him. "I should have thought before I said something. It's just like you to collect pennies and put them on the track. Just like you to think of that." He let her chin slide from his hand and she began to string the coins again.

"There's never enough to buy anything worth keeping." She began to tie the chain around her neck, "so this way I make them mine to keep. Do you see?" She turned and looked up at him, the ovals sliding together on the string down her chest. "I see you made them worth keeping," he said softly.

Chapter Three

CARY DROPPED from the rail to her knees below the level of the watermelon vines. She crawled into the thick foliage making a ripple in the vines as she moved through. Each time she stopped, she made two short thumps on the melon in front of her. About ten feet from the tracks, Cary thumped a large green watermelon and it echoed with the sound of ripeness. Then she pulled the sticky stem from its end and began to roll it towards the tracks.

When her thin brown body moved under the vine, the leaves swelled and parted like dirt when a mole crawls below. At the tracks she raised her head from the ground. There was no one in sight but a Negro woman who hung out a tub on the porch of her brown house and disappeared inside. Then Cary jumped up and scrambled to the other side of the track where she slid down the gravel with the watermelon under her dress. The sunside of the melon rolled across her bare skin but she turned it to the cool dirt side and sat there while her body warmed it. She cupped her hands beneath the melon, struggled to her feet, and began walking towards the road.

As she walked along the road the watermelon felt gritty against her stomach. Ahead of her she saw a car stop by one of the little Negro children who ran into the cornfield just as someone inside the car spoke to him. The car started moving and stopped again, this time beside her.

The lady inside rested her arm on the window and leaned out squinting at the sun. She looked at Cary a moment, then turned back to the man driving the car and said impatiently, "I guess she's white. Somebody around here should be intelligent enough to talk to." She turned back to Cary and said, "Young lady, do you know where I can find a Missess Strawbright that sells white Leghorn eggs?"

Then the woman stopped speaking as her eyes came into focus and she saw the protruding belly beneath Cary's dress.

"Young lady! How old are you, child?"

"Fourteen."

"Fourteen!" she exclaimed and then repeated it in a disgusted tone. "You're just fourteen and in that condition."

Then Cary began to laugh and said, "Oh, don't worry none, Ma'am. It's the second one and I'm used to them by now."

"Where is the other child?"

Cary looked absently at the cornfield and said, "Oh, I don't know. We gave it away."

The woman drew back in the car like a turtle in a shell and clasped her hands tightly across her own stomach.

Then she looked up and spoke again in a weak voice, "And what does your husband do?"

"Oh, I haven't got one of them yet. Can't rightly say which one it was."

The car motor began to race and Cary noticed for the first time the man that was driving. He was frowning and she knew he hadn't believed her.

Then he spoke gruffly, "Do you know or don't you know where the Strawbright place is?"

"Turn around where you came from and take the second dirt road on the left beyond the mailboxes," Cary said.

The car wheeled around and Cary began to laugh as she

watched the car go past the Strawbrights' road and turn down the old sawmill road that went deep into the woods behind the farms until it dead-ended at the sawdust pile.

The car had disappeared and she found herself still standing, looking at the road. The pavement had begun to burn her feet and her stomach was sore from the gritty watermelon. Suddenly she started running into the field and sat down under the cornstalks, watching for the car to come out again. She heard the bottom of the car begin to hit the stumps on the road, then the slow whine as it went into reverse and started out again. When she heard the wheels spinning in the mud, she drew tighter under the stalks. The watermelon scratched her skin but she held it tight under her dress. She lay back in the row and tried to remember how, when she was little, she would lie in bed at night and have her soft pillow under her dress. They would stuff things under their dresses when they played under the trees but pull them out and hide when they saw the older people coming, then hide and do it again and laugh at each other.

A flash of light came through the stalks as the sun hit the headlights of the car before it turned back onto the road. She sat up slowly when it started by the field and could hear the voices of the woman and man as it went past. She walked back out of the field, her arms itching and sweaty from the corn. She began walking quickly down the road towards the Strawbright place, turning down the path that went through the woods to the pond. She stooped to her knees in the woods slipping the watermelon from under her dress. After she lifted the watermelon to her shoulder, she walked to the clearing and looked out across the pond. The pale skim of pollen stretched in an almost unbroken pattern across the water, trembling in spots as the fish raced underneath. A frog hit the water like a rock as she began to walk towards the edge. The frogs stretched once in the air before they fell on the water, breaking the skim apart in spots when she walked to the pier. At the end of the pier she threw the watermelon in, raising a tall shoot of water before the melon bobbled to the surface, rolling and shining in the sun.

She walked to the edge of the water and felt her feet sink into the soft mud. Rolling white side up in the water the tadpoles swam frantically for a moment before they squirmed into the clear water beyond her feet and disappeared into the depth of the water. The water spiders crept about on top of the water as if they were walking on glass. Cary began to feel the sticks and stubbles of the water reeds under her feet and her flesh began to crawl with all of the tiny life around her. She raced into the water and when it reached the top of her thighs, she plunged into it, wetting her dress and hair at once as she felt the water slide over her head. When she came to the top her long hair spread out behind her, as if it were all combed straight back to bare her forehead. She paddled along on top of the water, not wanting to feel her feet touch the slimy bottom. When she rested one hand on the end of the pier to hold herself up, she looked across the water and saw her watermelon still rolling and heading towards the center of the pond.

She swam to the melon and grabbed it, clasping it across her belly and floating on her back in the water. When she looked into the sky the sun began to hurt her eyes, so she squinted and rested her attention on one little ragged cloud that hung practically motionless. As she looked at the cloud longer she realized it wasn't motionless but the frayed edges were moving and the shape of the cloud was changing. Soon she saw it thin in spots and become a little face. First it was the face of a balloon, characterless and laughing like a fairy tale person. Then it stretched into ears like a cat still laughing at her. She shut her eyes and began to feel the water again, then she moved herself with her hands so it would feel cool again and not the same as her body. When she opened her eyes, the face had changed completely and was long and thin and its eyes were hollow. It had no mouth but its nose and jaw appeared hard and white as if they were carved out of soap. The sun glare made the cloud begin to encircle in black and the mouth in the face opened and closed as if it were breathing. The face gasped for breath a moment before the cloud began to move again and spread out like a white shapeless rag.

Cary drifted to the center of the pond, her eyes following the light coming through the trees. Water still fell through the leaves and flickered in the air, the trees restless though there was no wind. Her body became nervous as she spun in the water, looking down all the paths to the pond. Then Cary looked up on the dam and saw a figure dart behind the inkberry bushes.

"I see you Johnny Strawbright, and you're not going to find my clothes."

The boy walked out from behind the inkberry bush and stood motionless on the dam.

"I've got them on this time," she called.

Johnny didn't answer. He sat down on the bank and tossed rocks into the water.

"Why did you come down here?" Cary asked.

"I was just walking."

"I bet."

She jumped backwards as a rock bounced off the watermelon.

Johnny got up and walked back towards the woods without speaking. As his back began to be hidden from her by the green branches, she wanted to call out to him, but before she could think of anything he was already gone. She splashed a moment in the water, shoved the melon towards the edge, then let her feet rest on the bottom. She banged her fists in the water, but she still felt angry because she didn't know why Johnny had come down to the pond. At the edge of the water where she got down on her knees to pick up the watermelon, her dress sucked against her body and the chain of coins thumped against the melon. Although no one was there, she looked up quickly, the sound of the coins still in her ears.

"Papa," she heard herself whisper as she climbed up the slippery bank and then let the watermelon drop from her hands onto the pier. It split open and the inside was red and grew white and pulpy near the center. With the large half that held the heart sticking jaggedly out, she walked to the shade. There she sat down and picked out the seeds with her fingers, biting deeply into the spongy center before pressing it in her mouth until the water ran down her throat. Coughing until the melon fell out of her mouth and onto her arm in thin red stains, she pushed the melon off the end of the pier, watching it splash and sink, its striped side turning over and rising near the surface of the water. Then she lay face down on the pier, trying to turn her face away from her hair that smelled stagnant like the water as it dried stiff and stuck to her skin.

Chapter Four

THAT NIGHT she sat watching the lantern in the house. In two crisp globes that hissed softly like a teapot reaching a boiling point, the lantern light spread outward to the walls of the room. Its white-hot light masked the two faces there and left dark caverns below their cheek bones and in the sockets of their eyes. One face, lying flat, projected against the wall three profiles; each as it rose in tier upon tier identical in shape to the one below, yet larger and fainter. Each profile had a great bottom lip sucking inward and outward as the chest of the man in the bed trembled and expelled the air. In the face that spread the shadows, two eyes lay, one half shut, the other open, yellowed, and running in the corners. From the mouth there was a faint hissing sound, then a quick sucking sound, then the hiss again.

"Papa?" The suck of breath stopped and the hissing of the lantern hummed smoothly across the room as the tired lungs held the air. "Papa, you can still hear me?" The breath came out, hot and wordless, and filled the air over the bed with the smell of sickness.

"Papa, I don't know why he hasn't come. He said he'd run on out before dark. He told me that." Her words were choppy and self-conscious as the man lay silent. "He knew we were needing him in a hurry, that I could tell watching you how you been doing since morning that you won't getting a bit better. I don't know why he hasn't come. I just don't know." Her words faded as she leaned back; the white light sliding around her hair and across the yellowed eyes on the bed. The iris seemed to be breaking apart in the center of his eyes and oozing into the white like the yolk of an egg settling in the bottom of a bowl, its shell gone. When she had watched him that afternoon, the eyes had come apart like the old eggs that had begun to fill with the red string veins of the baby chick that was forming. Those eggs she had dumped away, never telling Papa that she had made the mistake of taking them from the nest. He had always said it was written on the outside of every egg which to leave and which to take, that the fertile eggs were slick with a hard light-brown flesh worn from the daily squirming of the mother hen on top of them; and the fresh eggs were rough like sand rock. She left the wrong eggs while the chickens were feeding, and after weeks of lying cold in the nest or under a setting hen, the chickens rolled them out and smashed them on the floor. While gathering the eggs, she remembered, the yellow-eyed faces clucked like an old lady's laugh as she held the bottom of her apron and her nose with one hand and clumsily picked up the eggs with the other, sliding them into the apron. She remembered the dry heaves all the way back to the house as she tried to wash out her lungs in the wet night air, the sound of the chickens still in her ears. She turned her head as the thought of the egg smell brought the sick smell back into her nostrils.

Glancing back quickly at the man who sucked again for breath, she saw he was a living rotten thing that was not at all the egg with the red veins. He had become like the other egg without its shell, only the sickness had eaten the shell from his body and the inside was coming outward, spreading on his face and down his arms. She had watched the eyes, the mouth, because they had remained even when the sickness had taken the smooth brown skin; But they were sinking now and being tucked in their sockets by the red rotten inside that had fed outward on his flesh until it was formless. As she sat by the bed, she could only think of decay; the corn smut in the rainy season that swelled the smooth kernels out of their rows and popped and blistered them until they were dull, black bubbles on the ear, or the pale yellow mold on the compost pile.

Then Cary shook her head until everything left her mind for a moment, and when she realized it was the smell that made her think of these things, she moved away from the sick bed. She walked to the other side of the room and stood in the wet draft blowing from the front door. She looked at the dry Indian corn beside the door, three ears tied together by their shucks with two red ears and one freckled ear with white grains scattered in the red, that caught the lantern light like polished glass. Papa had told her that the ones with white grains were cross-pollinated, that the wind from the Strawbright garden at the main house had brought pollen and it went down the silk and turned the grain white. He used to laugh at the pale and sickly white grains crowded among the lush maroon of the Indian corn; "like an albino nigger," Papa said. And then he would say, "See, the wind ain't snooty, it don't think that hybrid stuff of the Strawbrights' is a bit better than that we shelled right off the ear. It just breezes around, kicking a little here and there and them grains get squeezed into rows like the commonest corn." He found out about pollen and eggs off mash bags and seed packets, saying: "There's a use for educated folks." He would sit down at the filling station and snatch anyone who might come by and say, "Would you mind telling me what it says here about the best time of the moon to build tomato boxes and get them started with this kind of seeds; I done forgot my glasses." She smiled faintly as she thought of his anger when she said, "Papa never had any glasses nor had he any need for them because he could see a gnat in your eye and pick it out on the tip of a handkerchief."

She rattled the corn and the corn weevils flew out sending a little stream of dust from the holes drilled in the grains. They flew across the room and thumped against the lantern. Watching them until the two globes hurt her eyes, she closed her lids and saw the white circles traced on the inside. As she opened her eyes, black spots began to dance before them in pairs and in the oval shape of the lantern globes. They spotted on the wall among the tiny moving dots of the weevils reflected by the lantern. But as the globes disappeared, the three profiles appeared again with the lip still moving up and down. She turned her face quickly back to the lantern.

If nine weevils hit the lantern before I count to twenty, my eyes will turn to brown like Papa's like Aunt Sadie's baby's did, she thought. Then she began to count to twenty softly and raise a finger each time a weevil thumped against the globe. On seventeen, the ninth weevil bumped the lantern and she balled her fists and laughed.

The next time it must be harder so the wish is worth more. She looked around the room and thought, If ten weevils go through the loop on the top before I count to twenty I will meet a boy and he'll pick me up so fast my hair will come loose and he will hold me in his arms while we ride double on his horse and the wind will blow my hair across his shoulders and he'll hold me tighter when it starts to run . . .

Then she thought of Johnny Strawbright and heard him call to her from the back of the stallion.

"Cary, come on up and ride behind me. He can carry double."

She had stood by the edge of the barn looking at Johnny who held his hand down to her.

"Come on up."

"How can I hold on?"

"Well, you can hold on to me I guess. I don't hold on to anything. You don't have to hold on when you ride."

A strange chill had gone through her body. As she watched the black close in the green of the sky behind him, she felt that she had already seen everything before her that was taking place now take place before. She had stood, afraid to move, almost as if a spell would be broken if she stepped from the spot she was in. Then she had shaken her head and dropped her face, looking at her arms barely visible in the pale light and stared until she made colored dots move before her eyes and until she heard Johnny ride away on the horse. As the colors flickered across, she remembered what it was, her arm, thinner then and the colored lights running through the light golden hairs and across her dark flesh. She was under the ferris wheel and the lights and clatter were running over her head. The seats were twisting around and stopping one by one as couples got in and closed the bar across their laps. Then they inched up one by one until all of the seats were full and the wheel began to spin, making her dizzy.

"Want to ride next time, Cary?" I'll take you on our last two tickets."

Her father held the two tickets that were sealed together in a strip in his hand.

"No," she said quietly.

"No? Why not? I won't let you fall."

"No! It's too fast."

"Now I've never seen you scared of anything before. You don't have to be afraid and you may never get a chance to ride again. Come on."

Cary watched the wheel turn and listened to the people scream as it swooped down towards the ground. The bars connected to the wheel that turned in the motor creaked and rattled, and the tiny motor rocked back and forth on its resting place. The wheel turned faster and faster until the band on the motor was a blur under the flashing colored lights and the cries of the people melted into one piercing sound. It went on and on until the man by the motor moved suddenly and threw the lever by the wheel. The scream reached a peak and then began to melt away into a slow droning laughter as the wheel turned slower and slower until it came to a stop letting people begin to step dizzily out of their seats.

Cary watched them all leave before she turned to her father. He held the yellow tickets up in her face.

"No!" and she ran back against the picket fence that went around the merry-go-round. Tears began to fill her eyes as the people rushed into the line to be counted for the next trip on the wheel. She watched her father hand the tickets to a little boy who snatched them from his hand and ran to the ferris wheel. As he put them in the man's hand her throat began to ache and she wished the tickets were hers again.

Now the colored lights were gone from her arm and she was looking at nothing in the darkness out the door. Johnny had turned the horse away and left her standing there, unable to talk to him any more. She had heard him come back from riding and go into the barn with the horse. She waited a moment and when Johnny did not come she began to walk towards the barn. She walked through the cornfield and the leaves that were drying on the stalks rustled as she walked. They slipped across her shoulders and rattled against the stalk behind her as they slid back in place. When she came out of the field beside the barn, she listened for a moment but could hear nothing inside the barn.

Her body felt chilled and stiff when she stood in the silent grass afraid to walk across the dirt to the barn. Then she began to move lightly across the soft dirt with her eyes on the ground until she came to the door. She pressed one shoulder against the door and looked through the crack that Johnny had left open. The inside of the barn was darker than the outside where she stood. Slowly she moved closer to the opening away from the door so it would not creak as it moved open. She stopped again with her face beside the opening. Now she could hear Johnny inside; he stood against the door frame in front of the mare's stall with his forehead against the back of his arm. She slipped through the opening in the door and began to walk towards him. Then she stopped in the middle of the barn, afraid to move any farther. The coolness of the barn seemed to close in around her as dry dust fell softly on her face from the cracks in the floor of the loft.

He looked up, seeing her for the first time. He stood without speaking and as her eyes became used to the dark, his tall image became clearer. His eyes were shiny now and flickered with dashes of white across them. She had run from the barn, before he could speak or walk towards her and Cary remembered going back and staying in the house the rest of the day, wondering about the strangeness of his eyes as he looked at her.

She watched her fingers now, still moving to count the dead weevils, but her thoughts of Johnny Strawbright faded quickly from her mind. Her father moaned and startled her, and when she looked up he raised his hand, shooting a long narrow shadow up the wall.

Then she turned her head back to the lantern thinking, If ten weevils are dead on the table, Papa will be well in the morning. She walked to the table and began to rake the weevils to the side with her finger. She counted to eight and on the other side of the table she saw a wiggling bug with burnt wings still spinning in a circle. As she crushed it with her fist and picked it away from her hand, she shivered and a chill ran down her back that was turned away from the warmth of the lantern.

I should have made it eight, ten was too much, and I didn't do fair on the ninth one. Something else, maybe I can think of something else. There's nothing new inside that I haven't counted already and that wouldn't be fair because I'd know. If it was light, I could go outdoors; I could find something or go tell him again. What if he forgot I told him to come; I didn't say it enough times maybe, but I told him and he said he would come. It's much later than he said. He wouldn't have forgot I don't think.

Then she ran to the side of the bed, "Papa, I'll take the lantern and see if maybe I can find him or show him where the house is or something in case he's lost. You won't mind the dark a little while will you, Papa? I'll be needing the light." The sick man raised his hand slightly so she took the hissing lantern and went out across the narrow porch and down the steps. As she moved across the packed earth in front of the house and through the tangled flower beds, the dew wet her feet and trickled in droplets down her legs. Then she remembered what Papa had said about the dew infecting and she looked down in the thin moonlight at the sore on top of her foot where the hot water had splashed when she was scalding jars. The dew shone on her foot, and seemed to creep into the opening and move inside her legs. She began running through the wet plants, stopping in the road where the dirt stuck to her feet and the lantern hissed slowly back to normal after the run. It was a wet quiet, the bugs were quiet and the air stirred only slightly, enough to sway the broken silk webs of the spiders that brushed against her skin. The lantern sound was hoarse in the night air as her voice broke the silence.

Her circle of light from the lantern that always seemed to protect her was small tonight as the light reflected off the water in the air and fell back to her. She began to call, "Dr. Jason! Dr. Jason!"

She repeated his name over and over, and each time the air would awaken with the cry of the bugs, louder and louder until her voice was a small thing. Again she looked at the sore on her foot and she thought of Papa with his smooth brown skin bursted and oozing with sickness and she did not want to think of him or of anything he had ever told her. She just wanted her mind to be empty and quiet, but her stomach crawled with nausea as she saw the sores coming up on her leg and taking her skin. As she ran her hands up and down her arms, feeling the smoothness, her foot heated with fever and she longed to drive it in the earth and scrape away the sore. She began to rub the sore with her other foot until the rough dirt on the bottom of her foot began to tear

away the scab and send pains up her leg. Then the scab broke
and the top of her foot was wet and stinging.

The bug sounds died away except for a few lone jeers, embar-
rassed and alone after the chorus, yet she jerked her head in the
direction of the sound after each jeer. She began to run down
the road and call Dr. Jason again, but suddenly she stopped and
the lantern dropped at her feet. It had gone out. The air was
quiet now except for the slow death creak of the twisted limbs in
the orchard as the bugs stopped crying.

She was afraid to look up because the night was directionless
and lightless, and the small enclosure the lantern had made
around her was gone. Without the circle of light, she felt she
was no longer in a place but lost and falling in a shapeless and
enormous world with her body never bumping against anything
that was solid. She grabbed her ear . . . a bell! She heard a
single ring of a bell, then it was gone. It was the same sound her
grandmother always heard when the last breath of someone
nearby was drawn — but each time Cary heard it, it struck her
with more force than before and seemed a new thing, since she
knew that it came from no real iron bell; it was from beyond
anything that had a weight or was suspended in a church steeple.
The sound brought her back to herself again and with her hands
she felt the hard smallness of her face as someone still half
asleep, waking from a nightmare, searches across her features
until she is sure of their warmth and firmness. She grabbed the
dead lantern and ran back down the road to the house and stood
in the doorway, nausea swelling in her throat and her face dry
and parched against the wet air.

"Papa . . . ?" There was no sound. She ran into the room
and lifted the matchbox from the mantle. Then she pumped the
gas back into the lamp and held the match inside; it flared
brightly until it settled into the two globes.

"Papa, he's not out there! There's no sign of him, Papa.
Papa?"

She walked to the bed with the lantern and held it in his face. The lips were not moving up and down. She ran to the window and pulled a broken pane from the frame, then held it over the sick man's face.

"Papa said the breath would show . . ."

She held the glass in front of the light and a gray circle of moisture slowly vanished. Then the glass slid from her hand and clattered beside the bed.

"Papa." Her voice echoed through the house. "I'll run to the Strawbrights' and use the telephone. Don't you worry, Papa; I'll call him out here right away."

Chapter Five

She ran back to the road, this time in the other direction; this time without the light. The house they lived in was the first of the Strawbrights' scattered tenant houses, and since she tended the chickens at the main house twice a day, the way was familiar. The moonlight shafts between the trees flickered like the ghost of a picket fence that fell without resistance as she ran. Running through the orchard she held her face down from the webs that dropped between the trees like tightropes. She clinched her fists so the spider fear would not stop her tonight and she would not think of how in the daylight she would have fallen to her knees and searched her hair, afraid of the lone spider that was in every web.

The house was in sight when she reached the other side of the orchard; she saw lights in the windows. Mrs. Strawbright would be in the kitchen washing the eggs and crating them. As she started to go up the steps, a figure rose from the porch chair by the post and she stopped short at the bottom of the steps. Sam and Johnny Strawbright were sitting in the chairs and it was Sam who came to the edge of the porch.

"Hi, Cary. Haven't seen you in a couple of days."

Then from the other chair, she heard Johnny shuffle his feet. He said, "What are you doing up here so late?"

She answered, "It's Papa who's sick. I was wondering if I might use the phone to make a call into town. Dr. Jason must have forgotten I told him to come out, and we're needing him bad. Papa is awful sick."

Johnny Strawbright watched her in silence at the bottom of the steps. She looked back at him and said nervously, "Johnny, I ain't got time to stand here; Papa's on to dying and it's my responsibleness to get him some help." She did not want her words to sound like that, like she was no better than a Negro, but Johnny's silent stare had thrown her into nervous speech.

Then she turned quickly to Sam, "Sam, you'll tell your mother for me. Johnny, you make me so damn mad sometimes!"

After she had gone up the steps and stood on the edge of the porch, Sam turned and looked at her before he went in the door.

She said, "I don't know what to do for him, Sam. He's really sicker than I've ever seen anybody."

"You know what he's got?"

"No, I don't know. He's just all swollen and broken out and I do know he's getting much worse."

"I'll get Mother," and Sam went in the door.

After he had gone, she stepped back in the shadow by the porch post and looked away from Johnny. He began to whistle loudly then got up, scraping the chair backwards on the floor.

A voice came from the kitchen. "Be there with you in a second, Cary."

"Please hurry, Mrs. Strawbright. It's important."

A heavy woman with her hands in her apron appeared in the door.

Cary said quickly, "Mrs. Strawbright, Papa's awful sick and ain't coming out of it a bit, been getting worse since I come to tell you he wasn't up to getting that fodder and Dr. Jason ain't come out like he said he would."

Then Johnny got up and walked down the steps, passing by Cary who stared down until he was beside her. He brushed her shoulder when he walked by and she snapped her head around to look at him, but he walked on into the darkness. Then she followed Mrs. Strawbright, who pushed open the door for her, before they went into the electrically lighted kitchen with scrubbed walls and cabinets heaped with egg cartons.

"You come on in here and set down by the phone. I'll ring him up for you and you can tell him."

"I'd be obliged if you'd tell him for me, Mrs. Strawbright. He ain't realizing how bad off Papa is."

"I'll call him then. You come on in." Then she called into the darkness, "Johnny, you go lock up like I told you to," but he did not answer. "Sam, you better go make sure he doesn't leave the crib standing open again." Sam walked slowly to the door and glanced quickly at Cary before he shut the screen.

Cary turned away from the door and said, "Tell Dr. Jason his skin is all broken out and swollen and he can't get his breath good and he ain't got a bite of good food down in three days . . . and his skin's hot as fire."

"Sounds like pox of some kind. Has your Pa been skinning those swamp rabbits in the kitchen?"

"Seems I remember he has. Yes Ma'am, I guess he always was prone to bring them in to clean them up."

Mrs. Strawbright looked at the girl and shook her head, "They're filthy little things to look so otherwise. I've heard of them carrying fever before, though it ain't often it gets out or there'd be a vaccine I guess. Claude ought to know better than to bring them in where food's prepared. I wouldn't think of eating one of them things." She picked up the phone and began to dial the doctor's number that was written on the wall in front of her. Mrs. Strawbright watched Cary as she listened to the phone ring, then Cary began to talk again.

"I wouldn't eat a rabbit. I don't see how nobody could eat them, but Papa said he liked them better than chicken. I never have liked eating no kind of wild animal cause it just doesn't seem right to kill something that wasn't raised for eating. I couldn't never watch him skin them. They get so limp and wet looking when they're dead. Papa never took a shot of no kind that I can remember, so he could have got it from them I guess. He thought it was pretty much foolishness sticking pins in folks and making them swell up and hurt when they were healthy to begin with . . ."

"Hello, Dr. Jason? Mae Strawbright. Cary is up here telling me that her Pa is pretty bad off, rabbit fever or something worse I'm supposing, and she needs you to come out here and look after him right away . . . Yes, tularemia, I guess . . . No, hasn't come out of it at all, just steadily worse since Tuesday, has a high fever." Then she paused again as the doctor spoke and Cary moved closer but could only hear the grating of his voice. "Yes, I'll take care of it. Put it on the bill with Johnny's tooth. Oh, I see . . ." Then there was a long wait as Cary leaned against the wall and tried to get a word of what he was saying. "Yes, thank you." She put the phone back on the receiver and Cary looked up into her face.

"He'll be on out as soon as he can. He's got a woman there in labor and he has to stay until the baby comes because there's no one in town that could watch over her. Now you better be getting on back to your Pa. Can I get you some soup or such for him?"

"No, thank you, Ma'am, much obliged though, but he couldn't take in what I fixed him tonight at all and vegetable soup was always a favorite of his."

"Well, you see if you can't get something hot in him and the doctor will be on out directly." She walked with her to the door and said as the girl ran off down the steps, "Now don't you hesitate to call me in the night if you need something, just come on up to the house and yell under the upstairs window."

"Yes, Ma'am, you've been mighty kind, Mrs. Strawbright. I'm hoping he'll sleep quietly tonight, but I'll feel better after the doctor comes. Much obliged, Ma'am." Then Cary ran towards the road; her face burning with embarrassment, the same shame that she always felt when she had been at the attention of a superior. She had felt many times that Mrs. Strawbright was being too nice, and trying to establish too much of a connection since they were just her tenants. When Cary had been in the house, she felt Mrs. Strawbright's eyes following her, making her talk constantly until she was outside of the white-plastered walls. Cary thought of how she always got restless at night and would start talking out on the porch with her father and would stop to see if he had been listening and he would always ask her a question so she could go on.

Suddenly Cary stopped dead still in the road as she saw eyes, mirroring all the light of the night, motionless in her path. They stared straight ahead in circles of iridescent green like dew droplets on a violet leaf, glassy yet with velvet softness beneath. The eyes turned quickly to the side and the lights went out, the black rabbit form appearing. Its smooth body was a funny roundness with no interruptions for fangs and claws, a roundness sitting nervously there, its heart beating furiously beneath its fur, its muscles tight, waiting for a movement. Cary stepped forward, the rabbit darted and disappeared as quickly as it had appeared. It seemed the rabbit was never there.

After it ran, she felt strangely alone for a moment, wondering why it had been more afraid than she. She always wanted to walk up to them slowly enough so she could touch them, but they sat nervously there and ran as soon as she reached out.

She stood by the road waiting for its cry as she heard a twig pop in the undergrowth, but it had safely vanished without even awakening the night bugs. She remembered how the birds would scream at the cat in the chinaberry tree outside her window with an endless repetition of cries before flapping upward to the thin branches, yet she could not place their sounds in her memory as a single sound. She only knew they made noise, leaving it impossible to distinguish one noise from the other. Her memory seemed to hold only the single sounds that would come back at first in a muffled distant voice, then grow into an intensity they never had in life, and they would throb in her mind over and over until she could force herself to forget them for a while. She knew why she had listened after the rabbit had gone into the undergrowth. Her father had been riding the hay mower and she was watching the sheets of green lespedeza fall to the side when suddenly she heard a shriek from below the hay. As she dug into the soft hay, a baby rabbit began to burrow in deeper, dragging its hind legs. When she lifted it in her hands, she saw the reason for the cry; its back was broken and half of its body was lifeless.

They, her father's people and she, had been in her grandmother's house when the old woman moved towards the fireplace to roll the log and stopped suddenly, her hand to her ear and her eyes deep and hot with fright. Cary on the floor by the hearth with the rabbit at her knees, listened as the house began to rattle with the horrible gong, the windows shook in their sockets and the soot tumbled with flat sizzles into the fire.

Then the voices of the other people in the room had begun again, but the bell had left a space in her ear like the seconds after the lightning until the thunder begins to roll. Her ears seemed to be huge gaping spaces and the sound of the bell had buried itself deep into them.

"Mama's heard another death bell, death bell, death bell, who will be the next to go, to go, to go . . . the chariot is through the sky and who will be the next to go, to go . . ." Their voices echoed in a monotone that had no meaning in itself, but the sounds kept pouring into Cary's head and pressing against her forehead.

"Cary's rabbit it will be, Cary's rabbit gets the honor of the chariot because it died in a God-fearing house."

And her rabbit had dragged its legs across the hearth and

rolled into the cup of her hands. She had taken its back legs and tucked them under and lifted away her hands like a magician. The rabbit sat with its smooth gray body motionless and its ears flat to its head; eyes black and clear and looking up into her face. And then it moved against her body, spreading its hind legs limply across the floor.

"Should have knocked its head on a tree; should have given it to the dog; should have put it out of its misery."

And the tears had streamed into her face and she had looked at the floor without taking her eyes off the rabbit, before going into her bed and putting the rabbit against her chest. She looked up as a black figure walked to the door of her room and pushed the door shut; the voice fading into a hissing and crackling that was no more than the fire. Then a little later, the echoing voices came back into her ears and her hands pressed against the sides of her head. It was the single sound, the death bell and the rabbit cry from beneath the mower blade that she wanted to hear, not the scolding and laughing voices of the adults that went up and down like keys on a scale. The rabbit pressed its warm nose against her chest stretching its full length against her warmth.

The door began to open slowly and the light that slid in was broken by the huge form that walked inside and ambled to her bed.

"It'll heal, little Cary, it'll heal its broken back and hop away from you back to its woods, don't you worry none about it. Your old Grandmama's bell weren't for it. I'm sure I must have been hearing it for that old bloated cow up the way or some of them old people at the church."

"But I was hearing it when you was, Grandmama," Cary had said, "and I wanted my rabbit to grow big and stay with me."

"But it's only with you because it's a sick thing. When it's a well thing it will go back to the woods where it belongs."

More tears had come into her eyes as the rough old knotted hand lay against her face, and she knew it could feel the tears and wanted it to go away, but when it did she wished it were still there.

"Did they hear the bell too, Grandmama?"

"No, little Cary, they don't hear it."

And the next week while she was in the yard getting clover for it, it had died, and she had buried it under the chinaberry tree beside the fish and the biddie. She could not stand to look at it dead and had wrapped it in catawba leaves and dug a shallow grave with her hands. Still on her knees she had looked up and seen Johnny Strawbright digging fishing worms under their compost pile. He had stopped and watched her put it in the ground, and her face burned and ached because then he knew where the others were too, but it was too late to move them because they were in the ground already.

Later she had fitted over all the graves squares of moss that she had dug up down at the creek bed. For a few days the green moss spread smoothly across the mounds, but it dried up in the heat, curling up and shattering away. When the moss had died, she went out one morning and took it off the graves, throwing it into the woods, then she pushed a stake in the ground at the head of each grave, but she never saw Johnny Strawbright down there again.

The air was still silent around her now as she stood in the road, and she knew the rabbit would not come back out. She heard the hum of a mosquito that silenced when she felt him settle lightly on her arm. The air echoed with a popping sound as she hit her arm and she felt a tiny wet place in her hand where the mosquito had broken and his blood had come out.

"How could Papa kill a rabbit?" She heard her own voice thin and frail in the night air. She thought of all the animals that ran when they saw a human and how she had seen the children throw rocks at the squirrels and chipmunks that ran under the house. Her rabbit had looked so clean and soft, yet Mrs. Strawbright called them filthy little things. But she remembered that even though she kept it in a box full of shavings and it never went out in the weeds she had found gray ticks swelling behind its ears.

She walked slowly back towards the house trying to understand where the fever had come from.

As she walked up the path to her house, she felt no need to hurry now. In the dark the umbrella tree looked like a giant mushroom speared with moonlight, with the house huddled beneath it. As the house appeared from the road, the lantern she had left inside glowed yellow-white through the oilcloth in the windows and the house became a jack-o-lantern with too many misshaped eyes.

Suddenly she heard a soft thump and felt dirt spray the back of her legs. As she turned, she heard Johnny Strawbright laugh and then the sound of his footsteps as he ran towards his house.

"Son of a bitch! I knew you were out here somewhere," she screamed and she scooped up a clod from the flower bed, but his footsteps had disappeared. She was in her own yard now, and as she turned towards the house she crumbled the clod in her hands.

When she went up the steps and into the mouth of the jack-o-lantern, the yellow glow from the oilcloth disappeared and it was dull brown on the inside of the windows. The room was filled with odd-shaped objects shadowed with the white light of the lantern and there was not a child thing in the room. The floor and the walls were bare except for a hook rug by her bed and the Indian corn in the corner. She heard the bed rattling in the other room, and when she took the lantern to the door she saw her father shaking in the bed, the covers slid off on the floor. She held the lantern over his back and saw that he was covered with chill bumps. Then she set the lantern on the floor, picking up the covers and wrapping them around his body, holding them tightly around him. She leaned against him trying to make the shaking stop but he tried to struggle out from under the covers.

"Papa, stop. You've got to get warm. The doctor will be here soon."

The man did not speak but began to gasp and pant like a hot animal.

"Papa, can you hear me?"

He continued to fight from under the covers, his arm waving wildly in the air. She felt his hand shove her back from the bed so she stood up, and watched him tremble weakly with his face in the pillow.

"The doctor says you've got rabbit fever; that you get it from skinning wild rabbits."

She walked to the door and held the light behind her so she could only see the thin white light on the edge of the bed sheet.

"Papa, do you think the reason that they always run from you is that they don't want you to catch the fever? I don't see how a rabbit could mean to do anything bad. But you killed it. Do you think maybe that's why he did it to you?"

She heard her own voice, thin and childlike, as she walked into the front room. Her body trembled when she set the lantern on the table and said, "That was a stupid question. He's so sick he can't even hear me." Then she shook her head. "He's so sick, he doesn't even know it's me."

Walking to the door of his room again, Cary held the lantern up, but turned away when she saw the bed covers piled back on the floor. She saw her bed in front of her and the black square of the window with the curtains sucked through.

Chapter Six

As she walked to her bed in the corner and saw her shadow rise on the wall, it was as though the bed had begun to grow taller and she must get in before the sides were raised. She sprang into it, and as she lay on her back the clicking sound of the crickets under the house began to click like the sides of the beds being raised . . . all the way down the row . . . the outgrown baby beds . . . click . . . goodnight, Ella . . . click . . . goodnight, Lyndie . . . click . . . goodnight, Belinda . . . and she had waited, looking to the right side of the bed for the face in the white starch to bend over her and pull the covers up around her neck, then the sudden click as the side of her bed locked.

Did she pull the others' covers up? she thought. I don't think so but it is dark. I'm glad it's dark because the others can't see her pull up my covers.

And then the nurse had said, "Goodnight, Cary. We will miss you tomorrow night, but we will pray and thank God for giving you a family back and maybe your new home will have a grown-people's bed for you to sleep in."

She could not say goodnight to the nurse that night as she had always done. This was to be her place for one more night and the nurse had taken it away. She looked up at the ceiling and in her corner was the crack and Elsa would get the bed because now

Cary would have to give up the bed with the crack over it. It split out like a pair of pants, like the ones the boys had to wear with short legs; and in the summer when it was dry the plaster would crumble down and sometimes in chunks big enough to throw at Elsa's bed and Elsa would have to wait until Cary threw the plaster chunk before she had any to throw because she did not have a pair of pants over her head or even a crack.

And Elsa wiped boogers on the wall because she was proud of how many she had every night after playing kickball on the dusty playground and how many she could get in a row reaching through the bars of her bed in the dark. Cary remembered how Elsa had laughed when, awaking one morning she found one of her boogers on the lollypop by the train on the wallpaper. Cary had clawed it off with her fingernail while Elsa was in the bathroom and Elsa had gotten mad and told the girls not to let Cary get in the jump-rope line at playtime. Cary could not reach the wallpaper from her bed, but she always told Elsa she could and that, even though she could, she still didn't think it was nice to put boogers there and she ought to put them under the bed where they didn't show.

Elsa knew about things. She talked with the boys during playtime when they were all together on the field. One day Elsa had come up laughing and squealing, the sweat popping out on her face, and would not tell them what she was laughing about. They all knew she would tell them but it had to be when she chose to do so. Finally after they had followed her around all day, when they were getting their supper trays, she said she would tell them if they all sat at her table. Elsa had sat there with her lips puckered and her elbows on the table and watched them to make sure they were listening before she began.

"You know the twins, the ones that came in from Archdale when they shut down . . . ?"

Everybody knew the twins, she knew that, and how they did not look alike when they came because they had on different clothes, but when they got their clothes issued no one could tell them apart.

Then Elsa went on, "Well, we were down at the gardener's shed and they said they wanted to look under my dress."

A groan went over the audience and their eyes opened wide as she leaned back in her chair. Lyndie was the first to speak. "You didn't let them, did you?"

Then Elsa laughed. "Of course not, stupid, but I really fixed them." Then all the girls began to laugh quietly and waited for Elsa to speak.

"I told them I'd let them see mine, if they'd pull down their pants first and then they pulled them down and I looked and ran before they could get them up to chase me."

They all laughed and the boys' table looked up and the girls put their hands to their mouths and laughed louder after glancing sideways at each other. Then the boys turned around and someone made a dirty remark because you could tell by the way they laughed. And the twins laughed too but their faces turned red because they knew what the girls would talk about tonight.

The next morning Cary's parents had come for her at the orphanage. Her mother wore a flower-covered hat with blond curls hanging from it like tentacles from the bulbous jellyfish that wobbled on her head. Her father had walked behind and she remembered how she wanted him to be in front but always when the woman was with him he lagged behind as if he were the child and she his mother. As they came up the walk, Cary stood in the dress she wore two years earlier and the buttons gapped open down the front and she wanted to clasp them together with her hands. The nurse came for the uniforms to put back into stock, the two summer ones and the two winter ones that had already been packed away when spring came, as Cary got ready to leave. No one ever came there, to this section anyway, because the older children did not leave until they graduated to the third section when they were twelve. People only came for the babies

that were fresh and new and not the ones that already knew they
were orphans and always would be. And they had already told
Cary goodbye and been told to go back to the table where the
modeling clay was and Elsa would get Cary's because Cary had
not let hers get all mixed together like Elsa's and each lump was a
separate bright color. But Cary knew that she had not gotten the
clay yet; she knew they would be at the window watching to see
her mother in the bulbous hat with her big breasts creasing in the
front opening of her dress where the heavy glass pin only seemed
to lower it and expose them more. The nurse began nudging her
towards her mother from the moment they started up the walk,
but Cary had stood at the top of the steps with her shoulder
turned to the side.

When Cary was lying in bed the night before, she had heard
Elsa telling Lyndie and Belinda what boys looked like but she
knew Elsa was making it up and didn't get that good a look before she ran. But last night Cary had heard Elsa talking and it
was even louder than usual. She was talking about how she had
been fed with a bottle when she was a baby because she had been
brought to the orphanage right after she was born but that the
babies that had mothers weren't fed with a bottle. Cary heard
the beds creak and knew that the other girls were moving to the
sides of their beds. Elsa began to talk softer and the beds rattled
with the pauses at the end of her sentences as they got closer.

Cary lay there looking at the pair of pants on the ceiling and
wished for a piece of plaster to fall, a big piece that would hurt.
The girls crawled back to their pillows as the door cracked at the
end of the room and the nurse looked in. After the door had been
pushed shut again, Belinda crawled to the side of the bed next to
Cary.

Then she spoke loud enough for the other girls to hear her.
"Do you remember when you nursed your mother's breasts,
Cary?" Cary still looked at the pair of pants in the corner of the
ceiling and hoped for it all to fall and hide her beneath it.

Then she said, "Why you asking me?"

"Because Elsa said your mother brought you up from a baby before you came here and you never lived in the nursery part where the nurse carries the bottles in but that you lived with your mother and anyone who lives with their mother lives off their breasts till they're old enough to eat food just like the kittens in the shed, and she said it's true."

Cary's stomach rolled over and over, and as Belinda's last words faded from her consciousness she went to her knees and dropped her head over the side of the bed, vomit splattering on the floor. The nurse had rushed in and Cary was still strangled as it poured from her nose and as the nurse carried her into the bathroom holding her face over the commode. But it was all out and the dry heaves seemed to bring her stomach up into her mouth while her head was held over the commode.

"There, there, it's all out now and you're going to feel better. You were just nervous about going home and our stomachs don't like us when we're nervous."

"I don't want to go there, I don't want to go there where she is!" But she didn't want to stay where she was either. After the grumbling janitor had left with his mop and she lay half-awake in the night with the taste of the vomit still in her mouth, she could not think of any place that she wanted to go.

Cary looked at her father coming up the walk to the orphanage and he stood a whole head shorter than her mother, but beside other men his dark skin and smooth, muscled body seemed to be cut from cedar wood. She noticed some men looked pulpy and soft but yet not so bad as her mother with her white skin showing at her throat and chest and down her heavy arms. Cary ran down the steps and put her head against her father's side, closing her eyes and clutching his shirt in her hands. When he stepped from behind her mother, Cary looked up and wanted them all to know — the nurse, the ones in the window; she wanted them all to know that the man was the one she loved and think that the woman with him was not her mother. Cary glanced back at her mother and saw that her skin was red and raw where the pin hit against her chest.

She watched her mother turn and walk towards the wagon while her father walked over to talk to the nurse. While she waited for her father, she watched her mother panting and climbing into the wagon, the mule shuffling his feet while the single-tree jingled up and down. They walked to the wagon and Cary turned around when they got in, though she had not wanted to turn around, and when she saw the nurse in her white starch with the Red Cross pin at her throat lift her hand and wave as soon as she turned, she was sorry she had looked back. The front side of the building seemed so strange now with its paint-chipped sign and unkept shrubbery. It seemed to be hiding itself from anyone who might come near, and seemed as if no one lived there and it would grow up in weeds. The bricks were covered with red-tinged vines that faded between the trees and disappeared as the wagon pulled away.

She turned in the seat and saw her father's wrists on the reins, the veins rising in his hands as he held the mule back; then she put her own wrists across her knees in the same position seeing the same razor sharpness and the bronze skin only slightly lighter than his. And in her pleasure she never heard the voice of the woman on the trip home and it became a murmur no more meaningful than the steps of the mule in the soft ground. She thought about the others at the orphanage and how they would never see a wrist like their own until they had a family of their own. Then they would be old and their wrists would be wrinkled and not really like their own anyway. As the fields crept slowly by, she watched the sharp wrists on the reins so she could forget the vomit of the night before. She kept her eyes to her father's side of the seat so she could not see the bulbous breasts swelling from the dress beside her. She could never be sorry for the others because of that night.

Chapter Seven

THE LANTERN light began to grow fainter and she heard the gas hiss and sputter, but her body felt too heavy to move from the bed to get the gas can from the mantle. Her eyes were sore, and each time she closed them she felt her body begin to sink and fall. When she opened them she looked up into the gaping rafters of the ceiling that went into the darkness in criss-cross shadows. She spread her legs on top of the covers and moved her feet up and down, trying to stay awake.

When the lamp hissed smoothly again, she listened for breathing in the other room, but her father was silent now. She found herself looking for shapes in the rafters, but she could only see the horizontal shafts of wood hanging with dusty webs.

She remembered when she had told Papa then about the pair-of-pants crack in the ceiling at the orphanage and he laughed and told her that a girl her age should not imagine seeing a pair of pants on the ceiling. She had taken over the house, and at night when the work was done and they were tired, they would sit on the porch with their feet on the railing and talk and laugh until bedtime. She told him of the nights after the beds were locked and the room was dark how she could see rows and rows of colored dots moving across the ceiling. They would pour across in front of her eyes and, when she would concentrate, they would go faster in reds, blues, and whites. Then when she closed her eyes they were there the same and as pretty and she could think of green pinwheels and there would be green pinwheels — and she could get red stars and yellow stars, anything she wanted to get to stay there and go across until she fell asleep, but you could only see them at night or in the shade if the sunlight had been too bright and you closed your eyes under a tree.

She told Papa how she thought that since the earth was round that the people were on the inside like fish in a bowl, and at the bottom of the globe was the ground and at the top were the sun and moon and stars stuck on the blue ceiling that would turn black when night came so the people could rest their eyes and it would be so black you could not see the sun. Then one day in the playroom the nurse took a globe out of the closet and showed her all the countries and they were on the outside and she had to come look at it every day before she could decide where the sun would have to be and understand that on the inside of the ball were dirt and rocks. It was all very strange and she still could not see where the air on the outside all ended; before it had seemed so simple because she had put everything on the inside of the ball and not scattered in space.

"And when I started thinking about how I'd put everything on the inside, I started wondering why I never thought what might be on the outside. Then you got to think what the ball might be made of and you know you're wrong because the way the sun and moon move. There's a lot about that I got yet to figure. Why the moon changes and all."

"I just ain't fit to answer any of that, honey. I'm thinking that come fall you should go to regular school at the district Indian school and maybe take the bus and go if we get ahead this winter. Don't see why we couldn't ride in one day on the bus and find out what grade you could start in." Then he paused and said, "You know, Cary, the way you talk about that orphanage, I wonder if I was wrong letting them put you there or not, or maybe I was real wrong bringing you back here."

Cary sat in the stream of light from inside the house, sorting out the red stocking tops from the stack in front of her. "Why you wonder about that?" she said without looking up, her hands running a red hoop over and under the white ones stretched on the frame in front of her.

"I can't answer none of what you ask. It's been so long since my mother sent me to school and it didn't do me no good anyway. There won't no other Indians there and I couldn't see how nothing the teacher said meant anything to me so I just didn't listen I guess. Did you know they tried to teach me to read?"

"No, I didn't know you ever went to school."

"Yeah, they tried to teach me. It's hard to remember right now whether I just didn't have the sense or just didn't care whether I learned or not. Just couldn't get interested. My brothers were all bigger than me and they were learning to farm and I wanted to be out there with them. None of them ever stayed in school long enough to learn how to write their names and I guess Mama was sort of counting on me to get educated. You knowed she could read, didn't you?"

Cary began to pop the loops off the metal frame and weave them through each other as she nodded her head. "And she used to stick everything she read right under her nose and acted like she had to look over the top down into it before she could read it."

"That was because of her eyes. Before she died she said her arms weren't long enough to hold the book out so she could see it. But she was real proud of you. She used to just rave about how you were better than the whole lot she had and how she would have liked to have gotten hold of you when she was a younger woman. She made me see to it that you got in the orphanage because she was afraid if I raised you, you wouldn't know any more than I do."

Suddenly Cary dropped the iron frame on the floor and her father looked around at her. "Papa, I don't see how she could ever say anything like that. There's not a man down at the station or anywhere that doesn't ask you when he doesn't know something."

"Well, that's because I know farming but not because I know anything else. I listen to you talking about things they told you at the orphanage and you know something; I didn't even know that about the stars and the world. I sit out on the porch every night and look up to see if the stars are out and if it's gonna rain and never thought once how big the stars might be or where they were or what the world might be like, whether they were in or out. I ain't so stupid I didn't know it was round but it just never occurred to me about the stars until you started talking. Just never occurred to me."

"I just ask stupid questions. The nurse used to say that."

"Like I said, it just never occurred ot me, but that doesn't mean they are stupid or that I wouldn't like to know myself. I seen them little dots too like you was talking about. I seen them lots of times after a bright day but ain't got a bit more explanation than nothing for them. I'm real glad to know that about the stars."

He watched as the tips of her fingers tied the loops and her eyes looked up into the sky. "Have you ever wondered about that circle around the moon, Papa? Like it is tonight?"

He scraped his chair up to the edge of the porch and bent over to look under the edge of the roof. "Oh yeah, I seen that many a time. Don't think about it much; I just know it means rain."

"It means rain?"

"Yeah, every time it's like that at night, you more than likely expect rain come morning. But to save me I don't know why."

"You know how it is in the morning when there's a lot of dew before the sun comes up, and like where there's a spray of water and you can see the sun in it and sometimes there's a rainbow."

"I don't know as I follow you."

"I'm thinking maybe it's the same thing. Only it's moonlight instead of sunlight and the water is way up there with the moon but in the morning it'll be down here and be rain."

He leaned back in his chair and looked back down at her. "It's just an education for a man to sit with you and listen to your questions. You been like that as far back as I remember. I told myself that I was going to have to do better so I could afford to keep you and let you go to school and keep you here with me. And it won't just selfishness because you always loved to play around outside and have animals and all."

"They had a lot of things to learn there, Papa. They had a globe and books and a playground and all but . . . Well, it was the same every day, the same people and all and I got so I didn't like it like I did when I was little."

"Well? I don't know what could be samier than this, honey."

"No, it's not. There's always something new because things change. They grow and you plant things and pick things. It's just all different. And women like the nurse, they just don't know much. They try to talk to you and make things better when you feel bad, but you always know that's what they're trying to do so it doesn't help much."

Then her father sighed and pushed his chair back. "I wish Mama was here to talk to us now. You could tell her I won't wrong in bringing you back."

"The others were jealous of me when they found out I had a Papa and I used to talk about you a lot, about how strong you were doing things at the farm and how we did the cooking together and all." Then she paused and said bitterly, "They hated me then, I could tell, because they didn't have anybody."

"You could have had a mother to talk about too. And I think she could have been a good one if she just could have stayed put. She just couldn't stay put on a farm; she was just used to different. I guess I never tried to change her mind much because I was always afraid I hadn't done right by her, bringing her out here with me. Farming was just all I knowed and a man has got to do what he knows. People just kept telling me a thousand stories about how you can't take a city woman to a farm, that a farm woman is different, but no amount of talking my Mama could do would make me look for another woman. I probably done wrong to be that way and was selfish, but I thought she would try to make things work out harder than she did."

"You don't love her much, do you?"

"Love her?"

"I didn't think you cared much for her."

"Oh, I cared a lot. I did. And if she walked up now and said she'd like to stay a while, I would be prone to say stay as long as you can stand it. I won't go get her though. She knows she can do as she wants. I don't know; people say different things about loving. But then some people would say it was loving to go drag her back here, but I just can't do that if she wouldn't be happy. I always did kind of hold it against her not wanting to raise her little girl though, I reckon."

"I don't want her to raise me," Cary said angrily.

"Now, Cary, you don't know that you don't. You just never got to be around her enough to find out."

"I was around her enough. I don't like her out here."

Cary was silent now and her hands had stopped working. Her father turned and looked at her and she had her face turned away from him. She was just thinking of when, just a few weeks after she had come home with them and the woman had gone back into town again, to work she had claimed, and Cary and her father were there alone in the house. She had listened to her mother complain during the canning and farm work while her soft hands and knees grew rough and cracked, then one morning while they were scalding tomatoes she dumped a panful into the water tub in front of Cary and threw the pan against the wall. A spout of the red tomato stain had splashed against her white legs and run over the top of her foot. Then she wiped it away with a rag, tossed the rag on the floor, and began packing up her clothes and things in boxes and tying them with string. Papa was in the field when she told Cary she was leaving, and Cary had watched her go down the road with the jellyfish hat on her head and two boxes under each arm. Then she went to tell Papa so he would not have time to catch the woman if he had wanted to try. But he did not; he just looked at Cary dully for a few seconds when she told him and went back to his work muttering, "Long before now I expected her to go, long before now."

"Those are real pretty," he said quietly to her now.

She jumped when she heard his voice and realized she'd been thinking of when her mother left.

"Those pot holder things you just made. They're real pretty colors."

"You can buy pretty colors. I just can't arrange them right. I've seen them much prettier if you know how to make designs and can run them through with a hook right." She heard the anger and impatience in her own voice and pushed the stocking tops up against the wall.

"Well, I think they're real pretty and I bet lots of people would like to be able to make them as nice."

"I'm tired of doing it. I guess I'll go on to sleep."

"Well, goodnight then, Cary. You want me to bring your things in in case it rains and blows in on the porch?"

"I don't care about them getting wet. You can do what you want to."

She walked into the house, carrying the lantern into his room before she lay down on her bed, feeling the bed sink with her weight and wobble until she lay still. When she closed her eyes, the colored dots began to move across. She held her fists against her lids but the dots only moved faster in transparent red and blue like a thousand tiny birds going across the sky, disappearing in the trees.

"You watch them birds in the tree, honey. You watch them close when the little ones are feeding on the ground." She could hear her father's voice and see herself watching the birds as they tumbled from the nest to the ground.

"See how you can already tell which one is the male. He just stands out bright red and the girl birds are almost like the leaves so they can hide in the nest."

And she could see the one female bird near the trunk of the tree with her mouth open crying for food.

"And you'll see the daddy's favorite, you just watch, you'll see it every time. The males can squawk all day and he'll feed that little girl bird first." And the female bird began to chirp softly as he put the food in her mouth while the two male birds stumbled around with their mouths open. Then from the tree came the angry cry of the mother as she swooped down on the male bird, dropping the food from her mouth.

Cary had watched as they flitted around in front of her eyes and had seen the opening and closing of the colored wings.

"Now if that don't beat all," her father had said and begun to laugh. "That just beats all I've ever seen. If animals ain't just like people!"

He had laughed again and said to her, "I guess you just think I'm crazy, honey, but I can't help but think they're like people. You ought to see your Mama light into me when she thinks I'm petting you too much."

Cary lay in bed and clutched her pillow tightly against her chest as the dots came back in front of her eyes and the birds disappeared and she could no longer hear her father's voice. As she fell asleep she heard him come in the door and put her hoop on the table.

A few nights later when she was still inside scraping out the supper plates, she heard a car door slam near the house, then a female voice before the car drove off.

"Someone's coming here, Papa," she had said.

"Yeah, sounds like it."

She had put the dishes aside and gone to the door of the house.

They could hear footsteps on the path and then in the square of light that spread from the door across the yard, a heavyish woman appeared. Cary's eyes stopped moving and her jaw tightened as she saw her mother; it had been three months since she had left. The woman stopped at the bottom of the steps and spoke to the man who had gotten up from his chair and gone to the edge of the porch.

"Claude, I been wanting to come out and see how you been."

He wiped his hands against the sides of his pants and spoke with a slight tremor in his voice, "Come on up, Elnora; don't stand there in the yard."

Cary had gone inside the door and leaned against the wall as they began to talk. Then her father called, turning in his chair: "Cary, get on out here and speak to your mother." There was a trace of irritation in his voice that was directed at her and not the woman, as it had been before she left. She walked out and stood in front of the woman, leaning against the shelf with the flower cans around the porch. Cary picked up one of the vines that fell from the can and snapped it in two without speaking. Her mother's hands were folded and Cary waited for her to stop rocking the chair and lean in her direction, her dress falling away from her chest.

Then finally she leaned forward and said, "My, how you've grown. It ain't been but three months, three long months mind you, but hardly time to do growing such as that. Ain't she grown, Claude?"

Cary looked down at her and said, "You've grown too."

Then the woman laughed nervously and glanced to catch the expression on Claude's face, but it had already faded. She spoke again. "Oh, I've been eating pretty well to be living in town such as I was."

"Where did you get the money? You didn't take none of ours when you left."

Then the woman rattled her chair back and forth by rocking

her feet. "Oh I been working at jobs here and there, nothing regular, been altering down at the store and waiting on tables some, just nothing all the time. It won't what I had hoped, that I could get us a little ahead to buy up a little land and maybe let you go to school but . . ."

Her voice trembled more and more and since her father had not spoken, Cary spoke again.

"What did you do at nights?"

"Oh, I had to work nights some. Those jobs don't pay the best and I hadn't had no previous experience . . ."

"Did you tell them people you were married? Didn't they ask you? Didn't they want to know why you were able to run out so easily . . . but they didn't have to ask did they, they knew already you hadn't never married Papa . . ." She looked at the woman but she was still seated; it was Papa who hit her. Then Cary's body began to shake as she waited in silence; tears were already rising in her eyes and her throat ached.

"You didn't, did you? You didn't, because they would never have sent me there if you had and when you came back to get me, acting like you had gone and got married, you hadn't then either! You think you can keep on coming back and forth as you please as long as you ain't seen no preacher to make it right."

Then the woman saw the disadvantage beginning to form on the other side. She spoke with a haughty voice as she rose from her seat. "Now where do you hear such talk as that? I just never heard of a child thinking so dirty. Do you want to go back to the orphanage; is that what you want and live with a bunch of nameless bastards? I hate to use such a word but you know where all them children come from I guess, since you know so much you shouldn't. Your father and I thought we'd done the right thing bringing you out . . ."

"They ain't no more nameless bastards than me!" Cary screamed.

The woman spoke again in a sharper tone as Cary looked at

her father. He stood motionless with his fist clasped in his other hand, looking at his feet when his eyes met hers.

"We can get on our feet money wise . . ." the woman continued.

When Cary pushed her father aside, he did not resist her. Then she ran to the door of the house with tears running down her face. A smile began to creep over the woman's face in the thin light as she looked at Cary and said, "Now I thought things over and I come back to try to make things work out comfortable like for the three of us."

Then Cary screamed from the door, "You're just what Elsa used to talk about. You just take up with any man and he gives you money." The anger of her words made her father stumble back against his chair, scraping it across the floor. "Do you think I don't know what you been doing in town," Cary continued. "What you was doing when you got pregnant with me? You was whoring and you been whoring again and you been turned out and he" — her voice trailed off as she looked at her father — "lets you back in the same as before. I was hoping this time it was going to be different and you won't coming back but he let you in the same as before . . ." and she ran in the door and her bed creaked as she collapsed upon it and tried to muffle her crying in the pillow.

The parents sat back down on the porch chairs. When the sobs from inside the house stopped, the woman spoke: "I had no idea we were going to have such a problem with that child, she's been picking up all that vulgarness around them tobacco hands. Claude, she ain't got no reason saying those things about me."

"She ain't never showed herself like that before. Ain't natural for a child to think such as that. I knowed she was smart but that ain't the right way to be smart."

"She was never any child of mine, she was the spitting image of you and even when she was a little baby, Claude, you remember how she would be screaming until you come in . . . ? She

won't no child of mine and here she is growing up and we didn't
know in time to give her some discipline."

"I don't rightly know what to say to her. It's hard to explain
such as that and it's a surprise to me. Why she's just a little
girl."

"I remember when you come down from the hills, Claude,
how I told everyone that I couldn't love no man as little as you
and that you was near about black as a nigger and that if you
didn't look twice you'd think you was, but when I seen you get
mad when they messed with you and I said to myself, 'He may
be small, but he's man enough for any woman and . . .'"

"God knows, Elnora! Shut up so I ain't got to do all of my
thinking out loud. Don't go talking all the time like a fool just to
hear yourself talk."

They sat in silence for a long while, the man still and the
woman fidgeting in her chair hating the long silence. This was
an uncomfortable silence because she knew he had to be the first
to speak.

Then the man finally spoke: "It ain't never entered my mind,
Elnora, that it might bother her about you and me, never entered
it at all that she was old enough to even think about it. I never
thought much about it but it don't mean much when you con-
sider how people are and how they feel."

The woman started to speak but he continued, and she knew
he was doing his reasoning out loud and it was her place not to
speak.

"But I don't reckon marrying you could have made any difference to her because she wouldn't have never liked you anyway
because it's easy to see you weren't alike by no means of speaking. Don't think you did nothing to make her hate you . . . but
maybe that's what. You never did nothing one way or the other."

Then he stood up and looked down at her and his sudden
abruptness made her start backwards. "Damn it, Elnora, damn it!

Don't that little girl mean anything to you?" Elnora sat trembling and for once was speechless. She had seen him angry only a few times; his anger was sudden and fierce, but she had seen it leave as suddenly. Then he would only sit in silence like a dying fire, his temper refusing to carry him on, until the last coals smothered into ashes. He looked at the door of the house and said, "She's a sensitive nature. She knows she's growing up but don't want you to know it like it was something bad that would change your way of feeling and won't talk about nothing but what's already happened. She's taken to noticing things and they been going on in her head but she ain't said nothing until now, been reasoning out the way she thought right. She just had to get mad before she'd tell you what she'd been reasoning out. A sensitive nature and you got to be careful around one such as that."

Cary twisted the sheet around her body and yanked it tight against her chest, but she could still hear them talking on the porch. Then she rolled over and began to scratch her nails through the dirt on the wall by her bed. She began to write letters and, one after the other, she spelled out every cuss word she knew. When she could not think of any more, she looked at the slanted list of words and began to repeat them over and over to herself until they did not sound like words any more but like the animal sounds outside her window. Then she began to claw circles around the words until they were only clean round spots on the wall like white grapes. She thought of the green scuppernong vines on the old place when she was small. She was tugging at the bottom of the vine that ran up the tree and laughing as the grapes tumbled down and bounced across her father's body. His mother, it had been the last year of her life, was picking up the berries and putting them in her apron. She pushed her son in the side playfully with her foot and said, "Think you're like them kings with women dropping grapes in their mouths do you?" She had seen the picture on a cigar box he had given her for her okra pods, and he laughed in surprise at her thought.

"Yeah, and you're one of the beautiful women in them veilly dresses with a cloth over your face and you're fanning . . ."

"Oh hush your foolishness and get up from there before you squash half of them."

He had gotten up and the sky went behind the trees which drove themselves into the ground. When he saw the old woman bending painfully over, he looked quickly at Cary. She stood with her legs apart and her hands bulging with grapes and frowned when she saw his face, because for a moment he had looked old as her grandmother as he caught his balance. Then she forgot about it and raised the grapes to her mouth, squirting the inside across her tongue. Her eyes were bright a moment, then faded to a frown again as she picked the seeds from her mouth.

"I wish they didn't have no seeds."

The old woman had straightened up to speak, thankful for a change in position. "Now that's a fine wish you're making. Did you know if there weren't no seeds there wouldn't be no grapes?"

"God makes grapes grow anywhere he wants to," she said proudly.

"Well, he makes them grow but you've got to get them started with a seed. Same as any plant."

"The grapes is round and pretty and tastes good and why do they have to have a seed inside them?" she sang.

"You shouldn't have never started to try to answer her, Mama. I don't know where she gets them questions from. Got her mind made up before she asks; sometimes I think she knows she's putting you on a spot."

"Well, you got to answer them. You should have heard yourself as a youngun, talking about spots!"

Cary had the sticky seeds in her palm and was looking skepti-

MOSS ON THE NORTH SIDE   65

cally at their pinched, brown cover. Then she looked up and said, "It ain't the truth."

"Well now, aren't you a pretty one telling me it ain't the truth when you ain't been in the world but five years and out of the house getting into mischief but three. Don't you know to listen when you're being told something; that we wouldn't go round telling you what ain't got no truth in it because you'll have to decide between lies and truth soon enough."

The child had a hull on the tip of her tongue and had rolled it around until all the juice was gone, then she spit it at the old woman's feet.

"It ain't the truth," Cary repeated bravely. "God puts the trees and the plants and the people here when he feels like it and a grape don't need no old seed to grow around because he can put a whole plant anywhere he wants to."

"And why do you think your Pa planted that corn out there for me in rows and there're plants there now and you was out there dropping seed for him? It's one thing asking questions and being just plain ignorant is another."

"Well, you can eat corn seed and you don't eat old grape seeds." Then Cary paused and said, "People don't plant no seeds to get more people."

The old woman glanced at Papa and went on, "Well, they do so to speak come from a seed. The Papa plants the seed in the Mama and it grows there until it's ripe and ready to live on its own: it's the same thing so to speak."

Cary threw all the grapes she had picked up on the ground at the old woman's feet. "I didn't grow in no Mama; my Papa asked God for me and he sent me and she didn't even ask for me but he did and I didn't . . ." Her voice broke into sobs as she fell against her father's leg and tried to hide her face in his overalls.

Her father had looked up at the old woman and the sadness in her face told him not to scold her, and it had been a good way to say it he thought, but it was just too soon. He had lifted Cary up and said to her as he held her in the air, "Papa asked for a pretty little girl and God gave him the prettiest one in heaven." Then a light smile had crossed her face but her Papa knew that none of them felt happy. The old woman walked away with her half-full apron clutched against her, and he had followed her with Cary but she was far away from him he knew even though he held her in his arms.

The last time Cary remembered the old woman, she had felt water run from her hair and tickle the skin down her face. It was a light rain and the water touched her face, not hard but slow and soft, just suspended in the air, only beginning to trickle when it touched her skin. She was at the old place in the winter when the mornings were always drizzly until the sun rose at noon. She played in her grandmother's yard alone, filling her teacups with mud and emptying them into little round mounds on a board behind the shrubbery. Her grandmother came out on the porch, stood there a moment with her heavy body rocking slightly until she grabbed the railing and went down the steps. The old woman didn't see Cary behind the scrubs when she walked out into the drizzle, stepping heavily and flat-footed in her ragged bedroom shoes, gathering up her balance after each step. Her gray hair stood in a stiff friz over the top of her head and was knotted in the back with two brown pins. The old woman wobbled out into the garden and Cary saw glimpses of her body through the wire and vines as she walked behind the grape arbor. The dead plants pulled at the hem of her skirts when she wavered in the rows, and a little forked stick hung from the bottom of her dress. Suddenly Cary heard a thump and a deep gasp and saw that the old woman had fallen forward in the row. Cary sat there afraid to move until she saw the heap begin to move down the row again. Then she saw the old woman was not back on her feet, and Cary ran to the end of the grape arbor. She watched the old woman crawl through the dead plants, picking up the rotten stems and flinging them back again.

"Pepper, humph, pepper . . ." the old woman muttered.

Then Cary went to her side and kept pace with her as she crawled along. The old woman stopped and flung her head around to look at her, her mouth drooping open and the corners of her eyes falling. Her cloudy eyes began to shine with water until a tear ran from the corner across her cheek and dulled one eye.

"Soup mixture . . ." she muttered, again picking up the dead stems. "Thought there might be a pepper . . . some were left . . . peppers keep . . . niggers stole them I bet . . . niggers steal you blind . . . take a bite . . . throw it down . . . wasteful things."

Cary looked at her then said, "Pepper? Grandmama, the pepper died, remember, in the dry spell."

"No, no! Your grandpa and I always had the best peppers around . . . green and red ones when they were ripe . . . prettiest shiny things you've ever seen . . . all slick and smooth like they could burst out . . ." The old woman turned up the corner of her lips but the tears still flowed from her eyes. "All swimmy-headed again, got all swimmy-headed . . ." Then the old woman began to try to stand up, reaching into the air with her hands, but they fell hopelessly back to the ground open-palmed in the mud.

"Grandmama, can I help you up?" the little girl said as she watched the broad-backed old woman suck in air, her shoulder blades poking up under the back of her dress.

"No . . . No! Go on back to the house, mind you, go on!" She could hardly understand the old woman whose back began to quiver violently. Cary turned and ran back; watching her grandmother as she started crawling down the row again, no longer picking up the rotten stems. Cary went back to the house and sat on the edge of the porch out of the drizzle that was beginning to fall heavier. She watched the dark old woman with mud clinging to her clothes come around the far end of the grape vine and slowly crawl back toward the house. She started to run to her again to pull her to her feet, but she knew somehow that she should not. She watched her until she got to the edge of the yard, where the old woman crawled over to the wide stump of the oak tree in the front yard and dragged herself across it on her stomach. While she slowly shoved herself to her feet, Cary saw mud clumps fall away from her clothes.

She watched the old woman start to walk, falling across the stump then rolling off onto the ground crawling towards the steps. Her father had come from around the house dropping an armful of stovewood at his feet and running when he saw her coming across the yard. He began to pull at her shoulders and she clawed into the powdery brick of the bottom step with her nails, trying to hold herself down.

"Don't . . . don't . . . go on . . . don't touch me!" she said.

"Mama, look at you. Look what a wet mess you are. You know you aren't supposed to come out by yourself. Mama, you're sick."

She had rolled away from him, pressing her back against the steps and holding her arms in front of her face. Cary walked down the steps to her and looked into her face watching her jaw tighten and the muscles tremble beneath the loose skin of her arms. Her grandmother began to speak, her voice at first only short sounds that Cary could not understand. Then her face stopped trembling and her voice was high and steady.

"Claude, Claude, you hear me. You hear me. The day when I can't go on my land, go in my fields. When I can't walk without leaning on something . . . I plowed and hoed those fields; I lived and worked those fields in the hot sun . . . and Papa never had to tote nothing for me. I lifted and carried the same as any man and don't tell me to stay in that house . . . don't you tell me I can't manage, you hear me, Claude!"

Then the old woman began to breathe deeply and turned her heavy body over on the steps. Cary watched her reach up the steps with her hands and begin to edge her body upward, wheezing loudly as she moved up one step at a time. The old woman crawled across the porch and pulled herself to her feet for a moment there, settling her weight in one of the chairs. Cary watched her sit solidly there, her skimmed eyes blazing at the steps. Cary had run to the old woman then and crawled into her lap, pressing her face against the apron across her belly and breathing in the warm smell of her body as the old woman folded her hands over Cary's back.

"You hear, Cary, you hear? You hear them making me out to be half dead already? They going to try to take everything out from under me, steal away everything I own, because they think I ain't got a mind about me anymore."

Then the old woman had rested back in the chair and begun to stroke Cary's hair, looking out across the steps at Claude.

"Look at you standing there in the rain. Have I got to tell you to get on in the house?" Claude walked up the steps and sat on the edge of the porch, turning his back on her without speaking. "Don't know that I ever told you, Cary, about the man and woman and the stones. There was a man had a great stack of stones to move and when he tried to tote them he found he couldn't pick them up in his arms, so he got angry and went to find some more men to move them with him. Then when he come back with a bunch of men, he found to his surprise that the stones were all moved. And when he went to ask his woman he found she had rolled them, end over end and one by one, until they were all moved."

"Mama, that's a foolish thing to talk about, especially to a child that can't understand anyway," Claude said abruptly.

"You mind your tongue. This is my house you're at and you're to remember that."

"You talk to a grown man like he's a child and to a child like she's grown," he said as he stood up and walked by them into the house.

"You build a fitting home for yourself and find a fitting mother for your child and you'll have the right to be a man and not until."

Cary raised her head from the old woman's chest as the screen door slammed on the house and her father went inside.

"You don't build a house of mud when it rains every day. There're better and harder working men than you that seen all they made go to ruin. You remember that, you hear?"

Cary heard her father's voice fade as he walked to the back of the house. "I ain't got no fight to pick with you, Mama. You just believe your way and I'll believe mine. And I won't meaning to pick a fuss with you over nothing."

Cary turned in the old woman's lap and started to slide down, but her grandmother leaned back and latched her fingers around her.

"I'll get me some peppers directly . . . Soup mixture's flat as rib broth . . . niggers better stay out of my garden . . . peppers is hard to grow, mind you."

Cary began to squirm in the old woman's lap, "Grandmama, let me down." The old woman released her grip and Cary slid onto the floor and ran down the steps. She went under the bushes beside the porch and got her cup and began to fill it with the dry sand at the edge of the house.

"You got no business out there in the rain. Get on back inside." And Cary had crawled under the house and filled her cup with the dry sand where the chickens had scratched. She heard the old woman shuffle over to the edge of the porch and had tucked her feet under her so she couldn't be seen.

"I know you're under the house and the first thing you know a snake is going to get you and carry you away." Cary felt her eyes fill as she listened to the old woman, but she did not move. Then the old woman's voice softened, "You can help me pick out the colors for my quilt. I'm going on in and get to work." The old woman was silent, then Cary heard her walk back across the porch and open the screen. She looked up as she heard her footsteps and dirt fell down into her wet eyes. The rain still fell in the bushes beside the house and Cary held her hand out under the leaves and caught the raindrops. When she tried to wash her eyes they began to burn and the tears ran down her face.

"Picking on Papa. Just leave him alone." She called him and more tears ran down her face. Suddenly she heard him run across the porch and down the steps. She looked up as his legs swished through the bushes and he lifted her out from under the house and held her in his arms. She put the side of her face on his shoulders and the rain began to wash the dirt from her eyes down her face.

"Honey, did she say something to hurt your feelings?" She began to cry harder as he carried her up the steps.

"I got dirt all in my eyes."

"Just don't you mind her. She's so old her mind isn't right anymore or I'd say something back to her."

Cary felt her body draw up tight in the bed as she remembered her father's words, but she could not open her eyes and wake herself up. She thought she heard him get up from the porch chair and walk to the door of the house. She was facing the wall in her bed, drawn into a knot with the sheet twined around her and it seemed he was standing beside her bed looking at the mass of white circles on the wall in front of her and she was watching the colored dots again. She felt like one of the gray bugs that would roll into a tiny knot if he touched her and she would grow small again. The room seemed to shake with a shudder that ran through Papa's body as he saw her there. She had not spoken but she could hear her voice repeating . . . "It is not mine . . . It is not mine . . . It is not mine . . ." as he stood by the bed. She held her lips tightly together but her voice kept on until a voice on the porch drowned it out calling Claude's name over and over.

She tried to open her eyes as she heard Elnora come inside from the porch, but she did not move. She wanted the sheet twined around her body to choke her away into sleep, but her eyes would not open. As she had forced them tighter shut to make the dots go away, nausea rose in her stomach and she felt a dizziness that did not carry her away from where she was but made everything in the room more intense. Her eyes felt large and sore as if all the smoke from the fire that had died in the fireplace was spread across them and was racking their slick surface into rawness. She felt the woman walk into the room and across the house and push the door to her father's room shut silently. The noise from the other room was muffled but the stillness of the night left it alone to fill the air. The bed that had creaked like a huge moaning bear rolling over in its winter cave when her father had come in from the barns, now chattered in succession like a gigantic cage of monkeys mocking her and turning their backs against her ears. Seeping through the mechanical sound, the human voices melted into one but into a oneness that smothered all the sounds of the one as a separate and it was lost; the quiet night was taken away . . . the kind of night when the tiny chinaberry flowers could be smelled and the frogs would cry to each other in aloneness; but always somewhere in the distance, a voice would answer, single and clear and alone but knowing that a voice had called from across the ground and, in the space of stillness after the call, there was a moment saved for the answer. She tried to hear the sounds that were outside the house and even though she knew the chinaberry flowers were drifting down, spinning like lavender pinwheels and settling softly on the ground below the window, she could not hear them glide through the air and brush the grass as they melted back into the earth. The room had become tangled and would not open and let her escape, though she wanted to be flung upon the wet grass and roll until she was wrapped in wetness. Then to lie under the tree and look up at its heavy branches and feel the wetness of the dew seep into her skin, making it soft and smooth again; and hear somewhere again the call and answer of the frogs but they never called again for her to hear. Their voices too were smothered into a oneness that no longer had a name of its own or a sound or a shape, but was the crushing together of two halves, misfitted but driven together by a force that would not let people or animals live in peace. The separate voices of the world called for an answer before and its answer had a place somewhere on the other side, but the gulf between was dark and deep, cut by a stream that would carry along any leaf or moth that fell upon it, yet as the leaf or moth settled upon the surface, it gave up to the stream its choice. The gulf sucked in the voices, so that on the other side, where someone waited, the voice was lost and it seemed that it had never been uttered. Yet as the voice fell into the gulf and landed like the moth in the stream, it did not remember that it had a choice nor did it desire a choice because now it was swept along by a tide that had no control or controller and its self and soul were lost in the stream.

Chapter Eight

CARY OPENED her eyes and found herself looking into the blurred shadows of the rafters. The wood of the rafters began to focus, but her mind was too tired to think of anything around her. She tried to remember what she had dreamed but she could only remember the people and felt her eyes moving around the room, looking for someone. The lantern still burned but the room seemed darker now, and no one was there with her. The weevils were all dead on the table except for one torn-winged moth that floated drunkenly in the inside of the lantern globe. Then she sat on the edge of the bed and watched the moth until it fell to the bottom of the globe and spun in the dust. She stood up and wavered a moment then walked slowly across the room. Standing by the door of her father's room, she held the lantern up and looked at his face but he seemed unrecognizable; he was not as he was in the dream. Now his eyes were sealed together and there was not the slightest tremble in his body. On the floor beside his shoes was the piece of glass from the window, but her body would not let her walk over to pick it up. She went back and sat on the foot of the bed, feeling the damp air through the front door hit her face. She did not know how long she was there until the noise of a car on the road caused her to look up and see the headlights flash across the door and through the windows of the house. As she glanced around the room and at her father's door, she found that nothing had changed.

The front door was ajar and in it appeared the figure of a man; middle-aged, short, with thinning hair and a black bag in his hand.

"This is the right place I suppose," he said as he walked into the room. Cary nodded her head and pointed to her father's room. She stood up without speaking and followed him into the room with the lantern, watching over his shoulder as he sat on the edge of the bed. When he picked up Papa's wrist, Papa remained the same as if his hand was meant to be moved by another and not himself. Cary watched as the doctor laid the hand back on the bed and took off his glasses, rubbing his eyes. "He's dead. He's already dead." Then the doctor shook his head and dropped his hands to his knees. "You let it go so far before you called me. He looks like a strong man. He was a real strong man."

She watched him speak but could not move or speak.

"I'm sorry, Cary." Then he sighed, the dark creases in his face deepening. "I'm not blaming you nor any of you people for not knowing what to do. I would have come out sooner; I'm blaming myself but it couldn't be helped. And today I have been going since five this morning . . ."

When he looked up, he saw no expression of grief on her face but a sort of anger as she stared across the body.

"I'll send someone out for him tomorrow morning early and you can go on back with me tonight if you want to, or go up to the Strawbrights'. It's best you go in town until after the burying and I'll see if I can get you placed somewhere. Just get together a few things that you'll need to wear to the funeral. I don't know what to say. It's an awful thing, putting a little girl through this."

He continued talking but he was no longer directing his speech at her. "Got to tell the Strawbrights to get someone down here to scrub this place out with ammonia and let it stay vacant all winter if possible and give them germs time to settle out. I hope no one else has been in." Then he looked up at Cary who shook her head slowly. "When we get in town, the first thing you've got to do is get off those clothes and scrub good and throw them away if you've got some others, anyway get them washed in something strong."

She looked at him and her eyes were very round and very hard. "Why didn't you come earlier?"

The doctor began to frown again, "I couldn't have helped him tonight. I can't tell you how sorry I am. I'm so tired I can't think what to say. I've been all night with Elnora Carlin in labor and having a bad time of it and it won't until after dinner that she ever started giving birth and then it was born deader than a doornail," he said, then he realized she had not been listening to him.

"Elnora Carlin! Elnora Carlin!" she repeated. Cary's body began to shake violently as she tried to speak, "You been birthing her baby with Papa dying?"

"She's the same as any woman, Cary, once it's started she's got to have a doctor and he has to stay with her. There's nobody else around. It's not the first time I should have been two places at once."

"I'm going to stay here tonight," she said quickly.

"Oh now, there's no sense in that. The body has to stay here and I just can't leave you here."

"Mrs. Strawbright said to call her if I needed her. I'll go up there."

"Well, that's all right. I'll drop you off on my way out and get you settled. I can't leave you in this house."

Cary watched the doctor's hands begin to shake as he dropped his head. "What an awful thing for a child . . . awful." Then he looked up at Cary who still watched his hands. "You don't have a mother?"

"No!" she answered quickly. "She's dead."

"Let me take you to the Strawbrights' on my way out."

"I can walk up. She said to come to the window so as not to wake everyone. I'll get my things and go on up."

"That's fine. I'd feel better taking you but you suit yourself. I got a long night with Mrs. Carlin yet." He walked to the door and stopped when he heard Cary speak.

"I hope she dies!" she said and hit her fist on the table. The light dimmed a moment, slowly flaring up again. She looked up at the doctor who stood immobile at the door. "I hope she dies," Cary repeated. She looked small and very ugly, not like a child or a woman but a dark animal. Then her eyes looked confused a moment as she thought of her words, but anger returned to her face. He turned and walked quickly out the door, glancing at the Strawbrights' house where all the lights were out. Cary followed him and watched him go down the walk and waited until she heard his car start and leave. It was quiet again and she turned and looked at the terrible stillness of the room and through the lantern she saw the last moth dead in the bottom.

She walked into her father's room but did not look at the body in the bed. Then she snatched down the oilcloth curtains and took all the rags by the wash pan and the paper by the stove and piled it in front of the bed where the dead man lay. She took the kerosene can and dumped it into the pile of colorless cloth and paper and the pale liquid ran beneath the bed. Then she grabbed the lantern from the table and ran to the other side of the table, throwing the lantern at the pile. The glass shattered, a huge sucking sound went up, and a flame shot as high as the ceiling all in the space of a second. Suddenly the room was moving with the dancing shadows of the flames on the wall and it was as if night and day were fighting for a hold on the room. The bed covers caught and the man was nothing but a dark mound stretching the length of the bed. As her face began to sting, she backed out onto the porch and ran down the steps. From the yard the house was a jack-o-lantern come to life, a glowing and moving orange in the many eyes and the walls swelled with yellow flames. Then she turned suddenly as she heard voices shouting:

"Fire in one of the tenant houses! One on the lower side! Claude's! Fire! Fire!"

Cary disappeared into the undergrowth, long before the mass of men with buckets ran into the yard. She saw Mrs. Strawbright come up behind them, panting from the run, and stop in the yard as all the men had done.

"It's gone! Forget about that! Just see if you can get Claude out; he's sick in the bed and Lord only knows how he'll live now."

She began to call Cary's name and Johnny Strawbright went on the porch and held his hand over his face as he tried to look in the door. The inside of the room had no shape and there were only a few spaces of bare floor left that were hopelessly surrounded by flames.

"Mama, the beds are burned to the metal!" As he turned the heat left his face and went to his back and legs, burning as the hot cloth touched them.

"Johnny! Johnny, Cary don't answer out here!" His mother ran to the bottom of the steps. He walked away from the fire when the house trembled under his feet and led his mother away from the fire. Cary watched as Johnny began to cough from the smoke and the orange of the flames reflected on the back of his body.

"Mama, I can't go in there; there ain't no floor left even."

As he led his mother across the yard, she saw Sam running towards them.

"Johnny, did they get out of there? What started it?" he cried.

"They aren't here anywhere and it was too far gone, Sam. There ain't no going in there."

His mother still clung to his arm and looked into Sam's face. "He was sick in bed, Sam, and you remember the little girl was up at the house just tonight getting me to call for the doctor."

Sam's face dropped as she spoke and then he said her name as he looked at the house that was in full blaze now. "Cary, Cary? She ain't around here nowhere; you sure, Mother?"

"I called and called but you can look if you think there's any chance."

She watched Sam run to look around the house in the undergrowth while Mrs. Strawbright and Johnny stood and watched the fire. He came nearer where she hid, his shoulders and whole broad body moving like a heavy, powerful animal. She moved quickly away from him, feeling the cool air dash across her face when she turned from the fire. She heard him breathe heavily as she ran deeper into the woods. The sound of the flames still sucked and cracked behind her as she ran to the creek when she heard Johnny call to the other tenants that were gathered. "Go and see if you can get the irrigation pump on a wagon and get it going from the spring and get some hose up here and wet those trees before it spreads." The walls were beginning to twist and fall inward and the blaze was reaching into the chinaberry tree. Cary smelled the singe of green leaves mixed with the wood fire, then looked back towards the fire. It glowed red between the trees and reached in thin red fingers through the chinaberry tree.

She felt her body begin to tremble as she saw the top of her tree sway and snap and its round mushroom top envelope in flames.

"No, don't burn."

Then a great shoot of water went over the top of the tree and zigzagged on the ground below. A stinging sound went through the air as the tree became dark again but the glow of the house showed stronger through the fire-thinned branches.

She walked closer again and stood beneath the tree, the water falling from it on her body. She dropped into the shadows when she saw the Strawbrights were still there and listened when Mrs. Strawbright turned to Johnny.

"Johnny, it's an awful thing! That child was just up at the house tonight, perfectly all right," his mother said with tears streaming down her face.

"Wonder what started it; must have been a stove or the lantern or something like that. It went up awful quick for one without an explosion of some kind," Johnny said.

Sam walked back from the other side of the fire, walking slowly with his head down. "No sign of her, Mother. It must have caught on her or something so she couldn't run."

"Don't talk like that. I won't have it. I just won't have it," Mrs. Strawbright cried.

Johnny had turned to walk to the house and stopped and looked at his brother. "She wasn't dumb enough to get caught afire."

"You can't say that. You don't have to be dumb just to get trapped," Sam said loudly.

Then Johnny turned his face quickly and walked on.

Sam said, "Mother, you and me better go on back to the house and report the fire and all. There's no use standing down here."

"Sam, I'm not leaving until I'm sure what happened to her."

"That fire won't be cooled down enough before morning to go anywhere near it and then there won't be a thing left to tell by, Mother. Maybe she went somewhere else, Mother. Dr. Jason may have come and taken them in town. We ought to go call."

The woman's face lifted as she spoke, "Yes, that may be it. Oh, I pray to God it is." She turned away from the fire and walked back towards the house, saying, "I'll call him right away and see if he's been out. Maybe she wasn't in there at all."

The next morning as she sat in the chinaberry tree by the burned house, Cary still felt the heat of the fire and smelled the scorched green leaves on the upper branches. The whole atmosphere smelled of the fire, but the sharp scent of excitement had gone now and only the dull, dry staleness of the ashes remained. In the night sparks had flared up as a stray bit of paper or cloth that was lost between the ashes blazed anew, but the fire was completely over now and any new spark was lost as the day dawned. The smoke still rose from the flameless rubble with an occasional clatter as the last scraps of metal furniture fell to the ground.

It seemed to Cary that there was a gap in the earth; before, everything had had its place and the flowers had pushed against the house and the house had pushed against the flowers, but now there was only the great gaping hole singed on all sides and blackened to the edge of the woods. The house seemed a great husk that had split open and its insides were rotten or perhaps carried away by the wind. But now, she thought, she had done it; it had not rotted away or blown away — she had done it. She moved higher in the tree until she was wrapped in leaves, and when she bent away from the center of the tree to see the remains of the house, she grew dizzy.

She thought about the moment of the night before when everything was bright and hot and how she had watched from the edge of the woods as the people had run up. When they looked at the fire, she had felt a moment of fright that they would stop it before the house was gone. But they had only stood and watched with Johnny going to the porch, trying to go in, then backing away. Then she had seen Sam begin to look around the house, calling her name, so she ran into the woods towards the creek. She had lain down under a tree near the creek and looked up at the sky. Even there the air was full of smoke and a slow moving haze went through the tree tops dulling the stars. The pine straw stuck in her flesh as her body grew heavier and the wetness seeped through her clothes. She had felt the earth crawling with insects and heard the animals moving about in the dark as if she were not there until she could no longer stand to lie there. Then she had gone back to the chinaberry tree; everyone had gone then, so she had climbed up and sat in a pocket between the branches, where she still sat motionless.

As the sun rose higher she heard the clatter of shovels down the road and in the clearing a mass of people began to appear. They stopped and talked among themselves while Otis and another tenant walked around the edges of the house, talking to each other.

She heard Otis call out to the other man. "How the hell is anybody going to be able to tell if they were here? Have you ever seen one burn down so far?"

"It's most likely he was here being sick; there's the bedstead over there," and he walked into the ashes and they rose in the air in gray flakes among the smoke.

"Do bones burn?"

"Hell, I don't know. I guess so if they get hot enough. It's a bad business; I ain't never been faced with nothing of this kind before. I ain't never occurred to me, but I don't like it."

Otis walked through the rubble, picking up a pan and dumping the ashes out of it. "Here's an enamel pan!"

"Now what the hell has that got to do with anything?"

"Well, it didn't burn."

"I guess it didn't seeing as is you cook in enamel pans."

They scratched in the ashes around the bed with shovel handles.

"Ain't nothing here but I guess we better scratch around a little more to satisfy Mrs. Strawbright."

"I hate it about the kid. Course sometimes these things is for the best; if Claude was to die, it was best for her too," Otis said and threw the pan back into the ashes.

"Well, why the hell was Claude to die any more than her if it happened at the same time."

Cary watched from the tree and realized that they did not know he was already dead. She could tell them the lantern turned over. No, she thought, they wouldn't believe her because she wasn't there last night. They would know why she had reason to run. Johnny would know. The longer she watched the men scratch in the ashes, the tighter she drew into the leaves. She felt that their eyes would look up suddenly and she would have no place to run.

Then she looked into the road. Johnny and Sam and Mrs. Strawbright were coming. Mrs. Strawbright looked tired and her hands were still wound into her apron. The tenants walked out of the ashes and met them in the road.

"Ain't no sign of them, Mrs. Strawbright. No sign left there at all."

Mrs. Strawbright's fatigue deepened as she spoke, "I don't guess we could expect any; if only we could have gotten here a little sooner and could have known."

"There won't no going in there last night, Mama; I told you that." It was Johnny who had spoken.

"I ain't blaming you, Johnny, or anybody. Dr. Jason just shouldn't have gone off and left her like that with her Papa. He sure ought to have known better than that. I just can't stand . . ." She stopped and searched for a word. "I can't stand the mystery of it."

Sam had not spoken but had walked into the ashes and begun to kick things over with his feet. His mother had followed him, but Johnny walked over towards the tree. Cary felt her heart fall inside her as she saw him draw closer to the tree, walking in a straight line that seemed to have directed him to her. Her eyes burned as his head moved almost below her and she knew the slightest movement would tell him where she was. The horror of her discovery flashed across her mind as she saw herself dragged from the tree and in front of them. Then she looked back at Mrs. Strawbright and Sam, wishing only Johnny were there. She watched the back of his shirt stretch over his shoulders when he stooped down and looked at the ground. Her hand moved slightly and she clutched her fist and held tighter to the tree because her body wanted to fall from the tree and have him grab her. She began to feel dizzy as she clutched the tree, wishing he was not so close and would go, but she could hear him breathing and hear sounds in his throat. In a zizzag row in front of him were the weather-worn stakes of her graves, the goldfish, the biddie, and the rabbit. Then slowly he reached out and placed one finger on the stake of the rabbit grave and looked at the cracked mound. With the other hand he pressed the dirt in place. His shoulders moved suddenly as if a chill had raced up his back before he rose quickly and went back to the others.

After Johnny had gone with Sam and Mrs. Strawbright, she waited, watching the mass of people that milled around the rubble during the morning, wondering what they were saying to each other as they walked back up the road. She did not move from the first position of the morning. As the sun rose high at noon, she felt dizzier and hungry and she wanted to wash her face in the spring. A man and his wife were there; they talked a while, wiping the sweat from their foreheads, then nodded at each other and left. She jumped from the tree and landed on the soft turf below where the chinaberry flowers had rotted into the ground. Beside her were the graves and, after looking down the road, she pulled the three stakes from the ground and threw them into the rubble. She then ran back into the underbrush and finally into the woods thick with the smell of rotten persimmons and cedar.

Soon she walked from the woods on the back side of the farm and sat in one of the gullies that slashed into the bank of the creek. The gully came around her body and over her head so she could not be seen unless someone were to walk down the creekbed. She held a handful of the hardest persimmons she had found and chewed on their orange covers throwing the center into the water. Her mouth felt dry and fuzzy inside from the persimmons, yet all their sourness and the hours around the fire had not brought the one thing she felt she wanted, to cry — not aloud, just to feel tears fall and run down her face and cool the stinging in her eyes. Her lips were dry and cracked, and as she ran her tongue across them, the cuts sealed for a moment before they cracked again.

She thought of the time when her cousin had been run over and how she lay in bed and wanted to cry but couldn't. Then when the funeral came, they had come for her at the orphanage, and she had sat silently as her mother and aunt sniffed and shed huge tears all the way to town. As they walked up the hill to the grave where the small crowd had gathered and were waiting for the family, she had taken her place in the row of folding chairs beside the tent and her chair seemed to be in the center of an empty field and the others were not around. She looked at the patent leather buckle shoes on her feet that her mother had put on her after taking off her oxfords on the way to the grave. They had belonged to her cousin, and in the toe of one there was a dent where her feet did not reach the end, so she wiggled her toes until it popped out. Then she looked up and the pallbearers were lumbering up the hill with the casket; it was short and wide, and as she turned, the tear-stained faces snapped back into focus. She looked around frantically for a second, thinking back how her first dog, the one her grandmother had found and given her, had been run over in her own front yard by the tractor. She thought about how he used to come to her bed every morning and bark or lick her hand if it was over the side; how she had lain there and cried the days when he did not come and how his body had been smashed on one side beyond recognition as a body anymore. She remembered the nights when she still thought she heard his bark — days after he was dead — then the tears had come, first just flowing down her face, before the uncontrollable sobs as she jolted her folding chair.

Her aunt had slipped her arm around her back and pulled her

against her and the tears came harder and she was a part of all of the people there. Their tears increased as hers increased and all the eyes of the family had turned to her in red-rimmed sadness.

Her aunt had said softly to her, "We will miss her, darling, but she has gone to heaven and we mustn't be too sad." Then she had said, "Poor little thing!" and cried more as she shook her head at her sister. "It's so much sadder to see a child cry, so much sadder . . ."

She had stayed at her aunt's house that night where her mother was rooming and slept in her cousin's bed, and as she fell back into the pillow, tears began to roll from the corners of her eyes. Then she began to laugh quietly to herself until she fell asleep thinking of how she had fooled them.

But it would not work now, no tears would come even though her eyes burned in their sockets. The creek ran close below but the sound of the water seemed distant. Then she walked to the edge of the bank, and stopped a minute, watching the water. When she went into the creek and sat upon a rock that the water ran underneath, chills went through her body as the cold water touched her feet. As she stuck her feet into the sand beside the moving stream and pulled them out, she heard little sucking sounds before the sand closed in again.

The water began to sting the top of her foot and she looked down and saw the sore she had broken the night before. She washed her foot in the water but the feeling had gone; the water didn't feel cool and the sore didn't sting, the yellow-white skin of the blister spread loose on her foot. Water trickled down the side of the creek and slid into the moving stream carrying the moths and leaves with it that spun and bumped around the rocks. To her side she saw the curved and pointed frame of a dead animal. Honeysuckle vines climbed in and out of the lattice and held together the fleshless bones. The heavy head had fallen to the side, the huge dumb head of a mule, and a third hole gaped above the eyes. Its legs were coiled and wrapped around each other, loosed by the decaying skin. Green clumps of mud-clogged grass grew at the end of each leg, thriving on the rotten hooves, and one front leg lay in jagged slivers. Water still ran through the channel between the ribs. An uprooted water willow began to twine through the cavity, but it stopped and shivered against the water as its roots caught around the sides.

Cary frowned and slipped off into the stream and the water splashed around her legs. She grabbed the muddy roots of the willow, tugging wildly as the mud ran down her arms. She pulled until the tree ripped from the bones, uprooting them and leaving them criss-crossed in the honeysuckle. Then her thin arms swung the battered tree around her body and flung it back into the stream where it tumbled over and over but soon caught between the rocks.

"Go on! Go on! Don't stop!" and she kicked the tree and it rolled over lazily in the stream stopping once more, batting back and forth with foam sliding over its leaves.

"Go, don't stop now! Go on!" and she turned her back and shrieked above the sound of the water. She held her hand to her mouth as she looked at the top of the creek bank where the sun shone through a light mist, but the air was silent and empty. Her breath came hard and fast and her heart beat heavily in her chest, when she felt the silence around her. She climbed the crumbling bank and tears welled in her eyes. When she reached over the top of the bank and felt, open-fingered, she clutched a wet, leafy plant. The plant became loose as she pulled herself upward, before its roots tore away from the earth. She slipped back down the bank, her hand clinging to the stripped green stalks. She watched the last drops of dew slide away then let the stalks fall slowly from her hand, her chest heaving outward as she gasped for breath. She pressed the palms of her hands against the bank waiting for the dizziness to go away, but her head got heavier.

Then she climbed to the top of the bank again and pulled herself over on her stomach. But when she stood up and looked down across the broken cornstalks and the bleached orange pumpkins, she wondered why she was there. Nothing was clear in her mind. As she looked in the sky, there were clouds. When she looked at the trees that moved slightly in the wind, their leaves twisted around their limbs. These things had no meaning; they began to blend together into a pale, colorless mass and the air was empty of sound. She had heard no voice, but as she looked up she saw an old man running towards her, dropping his pitchfork as he ran. His mouth was moving. She heard her name as it shot through the silence and she fell to her knees and wept.

Part II

Chapter Nine

ITS FEET moved up and down nervously on her arm until she frightened it and it went into the air, circling around and bouncing against the walls of the room. Falling under the curtains, it bumped a few times against the window, swooped dizzily across the room, zigzagging between the people, then came back to rest on her arm. This time she jumped from her chair when it hit on her skin, sending it on its way again. When she realized she was standing in the middle of the room, she began to notice all the faces had turned silently to her.

Her mother spoke suddenly. "Cary, please keep still." The woman dropped her face into her hands and said, "There I go talking to her like she's all right. Talking to her like she could understand me . . ."

"The fly . . ." Cary said, raising her hand which dropped again slowly as the words trailed off. The other three faces began to move and look at each other; the sound of a gasp filling the room and hanging in the air. She looked from one face to the other then turned to look back at her chair. In the chair the slight dent she had made remained, and the arms covered with white crocheted doilies reached up around the sides.

As the doctor spoke she looked quickly at him. "Well, she's finally out of it," he said. "I've heard before that some little thing you could never guess would be the thing to snap them out of it." Then he smiled slightly and said, "Like that little fly tickling her arm."

"Cary, honey" — it was Mrs. Strawbright who spoke — "everything's all right now. You don't have to tell us anything about what happened yet, just tell me if you want something to eat or if there's anything I can get you."

Cary still stood in the middle of the room and began looking at the ceiling for the fly. Then she went back to her chair, dropping heavily into the seat, and staring across the room at her mother. The soft plump woman was still the same pulpy white she had been the night she came back to their house, except for the dark red area around her eyes. Streaking down her cheeks and at the edge of her nose, there were red and almost transparent tear stains. Cary still watched her, blurring now the pulpy body in her mind as the red-rimmed eyes set directly in front of her own eyes. Deep-set behind lids that rose like swollen sties, her mother's blue eyes were motionless in their red surroundings. Cary stared at the blue circles, and when they melted into the red, a light smile crossed her face.

Her mother rose and turned her back to her, looking out of the window. At this movement, when the red disappeared, Cary thought of the blue circles again and her own eyes began to burn and push into the inside of her head. She pressed her fists against them and her face fell to her knees.

Her mother spoke again. "Don't know if you paid any attention to or even heard what we was saying before or not, but I told Mrs. Strawbright that we won't up to settling with her for the house she lost if it was any fault of yours or Claude's and she was kind enough to say that we need feel no obligation, that it was an accident of some kind that nobody could have prevented and she was only glad you were not hurt any."

Elnora still stared out of the window, but Mrs. Strawbright pulled her chair up beside Cary's and placed her hand on her arm. As Cary sat motionless, Mrs. Strawbright slid her hand away slowly and rested it on the arm of her chair.

"Cary," began Mrs. Strawbright, "I know it gave you an awful scare, it was a terrible thing, and don't you worry none about it. I don't ever want you to have to think about anything that happened again. The boys can get a new house put up in no time and we can get someone to take your father's place. It won't be easy this time of the year to expect someone to move, since most of them are going to town for winter. But you can go in town too with your mother since she wants you to start school the first of September." Then she smiled and added, "I'm just so glad you're going to be all right. I've been so worried about you."

Cary stared until Mrs. Strawbright dropped her eyes. Then Cary spoke softly, "What day is it?"

"It was the twentieth of August today, honey," Mrs. Strawbright said. "You've been up here for eight days."

"Eight days!" Cary shrieked, her voice loud in the small room.

"Yes, honey. We've had to look after you like a little baby. I was so worried that something had happened to your head and you wouldn't ever be right in the head again."

Then Cary moaned and slumped back in her chair, looking down at her chest. Her cheeks flushed as she began to speak without looking up. "Have I been talking crazy? You know, like I was out of my head?"

"You haven't said one word till today, Cary. That's what had me so worried."

Cary sighed aloud, and when she heard the sound her eyes darted around the room before she looked back at her chest.

"I'm hungry!" she said and looked up at Mrs. Strawbright. Then her mother spoke before Mrs. Strawbright could answer.

"They've been more than kind to care for you until now. You just wait till we get home."

"Do I have to go with her?" Cary said and turned to Mrs. Strawbright.

Her mother flushed suddenly and said, "What . . . what did she say?"

Mrs. Strawbright looked at Elnora and fidgeted in her chair before she turned back to Cary. "You'll have to go if she says so."

"She's not my mother."

Elnora was now in front of her, wobbling on her feet, and glaring through hot, watery eyes.

"Just foolishness, sitting here in this house, embarrassing me. That's all you ever want to do, say things against me."

"You didn't marry Papa."

"I wish you would stop it, acting like a child that doesn't know anything when you know perfectly well what things are." She turned to Mrs. Strawbright. "We'll be getting on in town now; I'm not on my feet good yet."

"Well, I'll send some soup mixture by you. She's been eating fine so I don't think she lost any strength for it."

"Oh, much obliged, Mrs. Strawbright, but don't you bother. I have some vegetables cooked up."

"Well, as you please. And don't you worry about Cary; she'll be all right again as soon as she gets over the shock. Once she gets herself busy again, she'll be all right."

Cary walked to the door and slid out between the screen. She squinted as she looked out across the yard and the air felt wet as it hit her face. By the barn she saw old man Otis squatted with a plow handle lying across his knees. She walked down the steps towards him and the barn rose up ahead of her like a gray block. She opened her eyes wide again as she got closer seeing that the old man was whittling down the end of the handle. It was new wood, white and babyish looking, and the chips were scattered in the black dirt. He did not look up as she watched him; he merely picked up the rusty plow blade, scraped away the dirt clinging to it and thrust the handle into the top of it.

Cary clapped her fists against her knees and cried, "Look up, goddamn you. Look up!"

The old man raised his head slowly, his eyes remaining the same until they fixed on her, then they opened wider and a snarl crossed his lips.

"Talking kind of big, ain't you?" he said, looking back to the plow, but he did not resume whittling.

"You told them where I was, didn't you?" she said.

"I told them where you was. They was thinking you was dead."

"Old man. Old ugly man!"

The old man began peeling away tiny chips at the end of the plow handle, cutting towards his fingers. Then he spoke softly, "You ain't got no call to be mean to me. No call at all," and he whimpered softly on the last word.

Cary looked down at him and at his skinny neck that poked from the back of his collar. His skin was red and dry until it reached the collar level where it fell loose and yellow down his back. As she watched his tired old skin move awkwardly across the bones of his hand, her chest began to hurt and her legs tensed beneath her.

Then she stepped back a step and said, "I'm being sent away from here."

"Ain't no interest of mine," he said gruffly as he dropped his head lower and began fitting the plow blade into the handle again, driving it clumsily at the blade before it finally slipped into place.

Then Cary heard the low rattling voice of a goat from the inside of the barn. She looked up and saw it standing in the door with a loose rope hanging around its neck.

"Nannie, you come loose," and the plow and blade clattered to the ground as the old man went to the goat. The goat began to hop around on her small feet as he went near her, rolling her eyes around wildly beneath their sleepy lashes. Otis snatched the rope and held it in a shaking hand as he watched Cary.

"I didn't know that was your goat," Cary said.

"Why . . . why you ask that?"

"Oh, I just seen it out one day headed down the road. There's a billy down a mile or so."

Then Otis wound the rope around his hand until the goat wobbled on her front feet. The muscles stretched tight in her throat as he pulled up on the rope.

Otis began to speak gruffly but his voice trembled away from him. "Why didn't you tell me? I didn't know she went running off. Why didn't you tell me? She's got no business running off."

"I told you I didn't know she was yours."

She looked hard at him and darted away towards the steps where her mother was walking down, one step at the time with her hand on the banister. She stopped short as an oily blue car pulled between her and the steps. Then it was thrown out of gear and the brake pulled up before Johnny Strawbright got out.

"Johnny, will you take Cary and her mother into town?" Mrs. Strawbright said.

Johnny stopped at the bottom of the steps and turned, noticing Cary for the first time when she stood in the center of the yard. Her face was still darkened around the edges from the smoke, but across her nose and cheeks Mrs. Strawbright had scrubbed her dark skin until it was shiny.

Johnny looked at her and said, "Where were you the night the house burned?"

She drew in a quick gasp of breath and looked up into his eyes. When she started to speak, no words came out and her breath stung her cracked lips.

He spoke again, "We thought you must have been in there and looked all over. What did you do anyway, get scared and run away?"

"Johnny, you leave her alone. She's had a hard time of it." It was Mrs. Strawbright who had spoken. Dr. Jason stood in the doorway, looking round and weak beside the broad-shouldered body of Mrs. Strawbright.

Johnny turned quickly to Cary who had her head bowed and was looking at her feet.

"I'm sorry." Then he turned towards his mother. "I'll take them in for you, Mama. How far in do they live?"

Cary's mother spoke. "We live just outside Ellis Grove near the colored section. We're going to move in further soon but it's the best I can do for now."

Dr. Jason said, "You rest up, Elnora. I got to run on down the way for a call but I'll be checking in on you from time to time. You got no business being up already and you can get Cary to cook for you." He looked down at Cary, remembering her words to him the night of the fire and was sorry he had spoken. Cary turned her face from him quickly when he began to frown at her.

Dr. Jason pulled open the front door of the car and Elnora let her body settle heavily on the seat. Cary waited until Johnny got in the car before getting in the back seat behind him and sitting close to the door. She looked up and saw Mrs. Strawbright brush the top of her cheek with her hand then turn away and go up the steps. When she got to the top, she turned and looked into the car for Cary's face. After she caught Cary's eye, she lifted her hand slowly to wave, but Cary ducked her head behind the seat and pretended she did not see her.

They drove on down the dirt road away from the house, past the fields, yellow and brown with grass. The barbed wire and cedar posts whipped past the window rhythmically until Cary turned her face away. She watched the back of Johnny's head as he stared straight ahead. The hair on the back of his neck grew in three long points, going from dark brown to bronze at the top of his shirt collar. His skin was smooth and brown beside the blue shirt; the shirt looked collapsed and limp against his tight skin. She saw his chin tip upward, and as his eyes appeared in the mirror she turned back to the window. The fence posts were gone now and there were acres of broken tobacco stalks with pale green shoots coming from the rotten mother stalk. She thought how Papa had always ridden over the stalks with the cutter after the others had left them standing, so the second growth would not come and draw from the soil before frost.

Cary looked back from the window as her mother turned to Johnny and pointed to a road up ahead. Her face began to burn when her mother spoke and she hoped Johnny would not turn at the road. But he slowed the car and swung wide around the mailboxes, the car bumping into the patch of cracked pavement down the center. The side of the road suddenly began to be filled with houses with yards of packed dirt, swept as smooth as a floor. The houses were closer to the street than the farms they had left behind, and among the gray, unpainted boards was an occasional new plank or a yellow-white timber propping up a sagging porch. A mixture of colored chickens ran in the yards fluffing into the dirt. The sun had begun to set, making the chickens fade into red, white, and black speckled spots against the sides of the houses. The out-buildings all leaned slightly with the curve of the land rather than towards the gray houses to which they belonged. On the side walls facing the road were peeling posters, two for the new State Fair and one for the motorcycle races. Tiny black children of all sizes sat in the dirt in the yards or rolled tires around the trees. In the dead garden beside one of the larger houses was a baseball game. One boy tossed up a round object and hit it into the air with a flat plank, then a squash flew above them, falling in orange and yellow flakes.

The car stopped suddenly and Cary fell forward against the back of the seat. She leaned back again and the color rose in her face as she took hold of the window handle. The car was rocking methodically while Johnny edged it forward, trying to get out into the highway traffic. Cary was looking towards the other window when suddenly she saw movement in the ditch beside the road. In the bottom of the ditch, ducking his head out of sight, was a tiny little boy. He raised his face slowly. It was a pinkish-white and his hair sat in scattered tufts on top like little clumps of bleached grass. When his head rose higher, looking into the face in the car window, Cary saw two huge ovals surrounded by short white bristles — the eyes of the little boy in the ditch.

In the center of his eyes were two pink balls that were a deeper pink than his skin. At first they had glowed as though a pale light was behind them. When she looked longer, the eyes began to blend in with the skin. His nose was flat and wide, scaling away where he had been sunburned. His lips dropped shapelessly down his chin.

Her mother turned quickly and said, "Look at that little albino nigger! I seen him when I came through before. If he ain't a sight!"

When she spoke the little boy crawled from the ditch, sensing her notice of him, and ran. He moved across the field on spindly white legs that looked tender and young as the shoot of a plant not ready to support any weight. She watched the child, stumbling and falling through the field — his dark clothes a blotch on his white body — until he finally disappeared behind one of the gray houses.

Her mother laughed and said, "Look at him run! Funniest looking thing I've ever seen. Looks just like a nigger then's white as a ghost at the same time."

Cary's chest began to ache as her mother spoke and she thought of the little boy tripping in the rough stubbles. She felt the stalks cut into his white skin like a knife in butter. While her mother kept talking about the little nigger, Johnny turned into the road. Cary crawled to her knees and looked out of the back window toward the back of the gray house. She saw the little boy leaning against the house, his skin glowing pink in spots as the setting sun reflected on his body. His thin little arms and legs trickled from the mass of dark clothes. As their car moved further out of sight, he looked like a baby bird plucked of all its feathers and pinned against the wall of the house.

Chapter Ten

SOON THEY REACHED the house, and Cary felt strange when the car stopped in front of it, not sure it was theirs, because it was like all of the others on the street. The house had a straight dark front that rose directly in front of the sidewalk except for a narrow patch of uncut grass, and it seemed that too many houses had been packed into a small space. When they got out Cary heard the car radio come on, then fade, as Johnny drove away. She followed her mother into one small room with a kitchen and bath and listened to her mother introduce her to another woman, younger than Elnora, with a small child in her arms. Cary sat on the foot of the bed, her knees bent up to her chin as she dropped her legs over the metal bed frame. Through one of the front windows, she saw a few streaks of red left in the sky that showed between the two houses across the street. Uncovered electric bulbs with pointing rays of light circling around them began appearing through the long narrow panes in the windows across the street. Overhead she heard the heavy shuffling of a man's footsteps as he trudged across the room, and the scrape of chairs as the family sat down to dinner. In the back room the other woman's baby was crying while she talked to it in a rasping, monotonous voice. Finally the crying stopped and Cary could hear only the clicking of the dishes from the room above. The window was open and the mixed smell of cabbage and fish floated in.

"Cary, you wash up while I warm us up something," her mother said as she turned to watch Cary. When she saw she had not moved, she walked in beside her and put her hand on the bed post. "A lot of people live here. There'll be some of them you'll like to meet, though most of them aren't worth much or the kind you'd want to associate with."

Then she walked over to the window and spoke again. "I've seen a number of children playing around over there under that tree where the tire is hung but I suppose they're too young for you. You're almost fifteen now. It's hard for me to believe."

Elnora turned and rubbed her hands together and patted the sides of her hair, her mouth still parted as she looked into Cary's face. Cary's head was down, but as she felt her mother's eyes on her she raised her face and looked at her. Cary's eyes were crimson from the sun and were liquid and bright against her dark skin.

"Your eyes are shining like two little coals. Claude's eyes was bright like yours but black as tar." She spoke simply and rubbed her hands down the sides of her apron. "Think you could eat some squash? I could fry them up in some onions in no time."

"Yes." As Cary spoke Elnora's body eased suddenly and she dropped her twisted apron from her grip.

"Oh, that's good. I'll get right with them so we can get to bed early."

Cary glanced up at the ceiling and said, "Do they move like that all the time?"

Her mother stopped in the door of the kitchen and said, "Yes, pretty much until about eight when they get the children down. But you get used to it soon so you don't even hear it."

"I don't like having someone over my head, I don't think."

"Well, when it's that or climbing up three flights of steps every time you go out and come in, I'll take the first floor. Course then you have to worry about people on the street at night but we haven't had any trouble yet."

As her mother disappeared into the kitchen, Cary began to walk around the room. She reached up and pulled the string hanging from the light, but when the light came on the room seemed as empty as before. There was only a dresser with a three-sided mirror beside a bureau, pushed awkwardly in the corner. The room had the appearance of one that was packed up ready to be vacated. She stood in front of the mirror and her image was elongated and warped. As she moved it rippled across the glass as if she were boneless. Walking closer she picked up a mirror with a porcelain back that was painted with a scene of a woman under a willow tree looking in a mirror. When Cary turned it over and saw the image of her face from the chin up, her eyes and nose seemed to be placed in a row. Her black hair grew in soft fuzz around her ears and she noticed for the first time the long braid lying across her shoulder. She began to pull the rubber band off and unwind her hair.

"Who did my hair like this?"

"I didn't. I guess Mrs. Strawbright did it to get it out of the way," her mother called from the kitchen.

"Well, I don't like it like that." She shook her hair loose and looked down. In front of her on the dresser there were two tubes of lipstick, one with pink caked down the tarnished gold cap. When she picked it up it stuck to her fingers and she dropped it with a soft thud on the dresser scarf. As it hit she moved quickly away from the dresser to the window, wiping the lipstick from her fingers on the inside front of her dress.

"Cary! About ready! Wash up!" Cary walked heavily to the sink where she plunged her hands into the dish pan. She dried her hands against her dress and sat down across from her mother in front of a plate of brown and yellow squash. They ate without speaking, the pain gradually building in Cary's sides.

When she finished she pushed back her plate and said, "I don't feel so good." Her head began to swim and she squinted her eyes under the heavy light of the bulb dangling over the table.

"You go lie down. I'll clean up the dishes. Been too long since you ate last, that's all."

Cary went back into the bedroom, pulled the light cord, and balled up in the bed facing the wall. The bed sagged irregularly under her weight and continued to vibrate as she lay there. She thought of her hard bed in the old house and the swaying bed beneath her seemed to let her down gradually, suspending her in the air. Yet the noise of the slats and the springs sounded like her father and his rattling breathing in the bed across the room. She heard a heavy bump on the floor above her head that made her raise her head slightly before lowering herself deeper into the mattress. A child's laughter and another bump came from above and her mother's voice hummed from the kitchen. She felt all of the noises in her stomach instead of her ears, and as she laid her hand on it, she found it trembling and beating like a heart. Across the room in the dark, the two front windows were cut in perfect squares of the gray-blue night outside against the blackness of the room. The whole room was built only of vertical and horizontal shafts that ran straight across the room stabbing into the wall or driving themselves into the floor without wobbling. She rolled her head but the room would not become angular, nothing would slant, and as she closed her eyes the windows became orange squares. Then they faded and multiplied into a checkerboard of squares of light and pushed upward and outward until the checkerboard became all black with only the feeling of the lines driving up and down and from side to side.

Chapter Eleven

SHE AWOKE the next morning, hearing the baby crying in the back room and the voices of her mother and the other woman as they moved about in the kitchen. She rolled over on her chest and saw that the bars of the bed were linked together with little white skulls and each end post was clasped by a handlike piece of iron. The paint had peeled away in spots and beneath it was a bright blue. Sitting up she saw her dress hanging across the foot of the bed. Then she found that her legs were under the covers. She shivered as she thought of her mother undressing her while she was asleep, but she could not remember it. When she crawled to the foot of her bed and began pulling her dress on over her head, she heard her mother's voice from the kitchen.

"Cary, you getting up?"

She jumped onto the floor and pulled the dress down across her hips.

"I'm up."

They ate breakfast with the other woman who mashed up food in her plate and pushed it in the mouth of the baby in her lap. Cary's mother got up, taking a hat from the cabinet and pinning it on. "I guess you're free to do as you please while I'm at work. There's nothing I want done here," her mother said.

Elnora put her plate in the sink and ran water over it, before going out through the bedroom. Cary waited until she heard her mother going down the front steps before she put her plate in the sink and pulled open the back door. It led through the other bedroom, and the woman at the table turned and looked sharply at her. Cary then slipped through the door, across the bedroom, and pushed through the screen that led to the back porch.

The air felt damp and little droplets of water sparkled in the streaks the sun made through the trees. Into the rain barrel under the gutter drops fell with a deep metallic echo. As she stood there she heard a splashing in the bottom of the barrel. When she went closer to it, she could also hear a dull thumping against the sides between the splashes. She tipped it over and saw a wet and oily black bird that was suddenly swept under the water as she rocked the barrel. She stuck her head into the dark cylinder and scooped out the bird that pecked at her wrists and hands with its bright yellow bill, shaking water on her from its wings. She tried to hold it in her hand but the bird squirmed and fought, its wet feathers coming loose in her hand. When she set it out on the ground it tumbled over and over in the dirt before righting itself and walking away with slow wobbling steps and dragging its muddy wings. Cary watched the bird until it disappeared into the grass, squawking in a long, hoarse voice.

In front of the house she heard a car come to a stop, its wheels grating in the rocks. When the door slammed and she heard footsteps, Cary turned away from the grass where the bird had gone. She heard someone go to the front door of the house and knock, then the steps of the woman that had been in the kitchen as she shuffled through the house. A masculine voice disappeared into the house and, in a few minutes, the door to the porch was opened.

"Cary, someone here to see you."

Cary looked up and saw Sam, who was dressed in dark pants and a white shirt, walk to the edge of the porch.

"Cary, hi. Stopped off to see you."

Cary turned her face back to the grass and spoke quietly, "Hi, Sam."

He walked down the steps taking his hands from his pockets and rubbing them down the sides of his pants.

"You better stay on the steps. It's muddy out here," she said quickly. She walked over and sat down on the bottom step. As she did he sat down above her. She looked out across the yard when he began to speak.

"I was really glad when Mother told me you came out of it all right. You was really out of your head for a while."

She turned and looked up at him and he glanced downward again. His hair had been combed with water and was beginning to come unsealed from the back of his head and standing up in tufts.

"I was coming in to see Mollie Stallings today and Mother let me have the car. Johnny told me where you was so I stopped by."

He looked down at her, but she stared across the yard again. "I was awful sorry about your Pa. I always liked him and I know how you'd rather live with him . . ." His words trailed off and an embarrassing silence followed.

"Feels so stupid being here, walking out in this yard where you don't know where nothing is," she said. Then she got up from the steps and walked over beside the porch, her back to him.

"Guess you lost all your things when the house caught fire."

She turned to look at him when he said the words "caught fire," but his expression and voice had not changed.

"Nothing to lose," she said hastily, pausing a minute. "Did Johnny say anything to you about the fire?"

"Nothing except he and I got to stay home and build it back before school starts. I don't see no sense in it myself because Mother knows good and well no one's going to move in before seeding time."

Then they looked up suddenly as the bird began to squawk loudly in the grass.

"That old bird sounds madder than heck at something," Sam said.

"I pulled him out of the water barrel and he got madder than heck at me."

Sam looked at her and the black smudges on her skin were still unwashed from the fire. Her hair was oily and dull at the roots but grew shiny and black down her back. On the back of her dress was a little tear and her shoulder blade showed through smooth and bronze only a slight shade lighter than her sunburned arms. He listened as the squawks grew louder and the bird thumped deeper into the grass.

"Cary?" His voice had changed to a more cautious tone. "How old are you now?"

"Fourteen," she said absently.

"You're awful little."

"Well, I'm fourteen just the same."

"Will you go to regular school? With us, I mean."

Cary turned her back to him. "I don't know. I guess I have to go to the Indian school."

"Are you all Indian?"

Cary began to pull a honeysuckle vine off the bricks, and when it snapped loose she said, "What did you come over here for? To ask me a bunch of dumb questions?" Then she paused and said, "Can't you look at my mother and see she's not an Indian? She gets sunburned and peels, but I'd rather go to the Indian school if you really want to know."

"Their teachers aren't as good."

Cary pulled the leaves from the vine and thumped them on the ground. "I don't care one way or the other."

"What are you going to do during the day now?"

"I don't know," she said loudly. "I haven't decided."

He was silent for a moment before he said, "When Mother lets me have the car again sometime, can I take you out riding?"

"There's nowhere I want to go around here." She stopped, listening a moment before she said, "Do you hear that bird crying? He sounds like he's hurting."

"It's just a starling. They always sound like that. They aren't anything but little crows and they're dirty."

"No, I think he's hurting. He doesn't sound the same as he did before. You hear over behind the garage; like something's got him?"

"Well, there's nothing you can do if something does." Then he stopped and said, "There are a lot of places to go on the mountains if you've got a car." Cary had walked out into the yard. "Are you listening to me?"

She turned and walked back to the steps. "I'm listening. You said you wanted to ride up on the mountains."

"Well, I didn't mean that necessarily. I just said we could go somewhere if you wanted to."

"I know," she said quickly. "I know where I'd like to go. Will you take me to see the little white boy that lives out on the road near here? Do you know which one I mean?"

"I don't know what you mean at all," he said, his face twisted into a frown.

"The little albino nigger. Like the white grains on the Indian corn, that's what I mean."

"Now I really don't know what you're talking about."

"You know what an albino is don't you?"

"Sure, I've seen them before. The only ones I've ever seen were crazy. Animals too."

"What makes them white like that?"

"Something's wrong with their pigment in their skin so they just don't have any color. There's other things wrong with them, too. They're just like any other freak I guess."

"Will you take me by to see him?"

"If that's what you want to do. We'll talk about it later but I better go now. I think I can be back in tomorrow."

She nodded her head as she watched him walk around the house, but she was still thinking about the little white boy that had run from the ditch. When Sam was out of sight, she got up and walked toward the grass where the bird was. She stopped suddenly, the damp grass was around her bare feet and a short distance in front of her was the bird. It was on its back and its breast had been ripped open from the throat to the base of its wings. The squawk was a distant creaking sound in its throat and its black oily wings moved slowly up and down around the bloody red chest that was half eaten away. She looked up when the grating wheels of the car in front of the house took off and before her was the angry snarling face of a cat, its yellow, furred chin spotted with blood.

She ran at the cat and yelled at it as it disappeared around the garage, "You get out of here, damn you! You dirty bastard cat." Then she looked back at the bird whose wings still moved up and down. When she stooped and touched it, the wings began to move fast again, spattering blood on her hand. Then it flipped over on its stomach and was still. Cary stroked the smooth feathers on its back but the bird did not move.

"I told him. I told him something had got you. I should have known something had got you."

She felt a gust of wind hit the side of her face and looked up at the porch; one of the gallon jugs fell from the shelf to the ground. The bottle hit with a soft clunk then flipped over once and split down the center when she heard glass hit rock. A human voice moaned from the inside of the house; she saw the woman from the house as she shuffled down the steps and stooped by the split bottle. The woman picked up the two halves and stacked them together, the two pieces of glass scraping softly against each other. In a clump of dirt, lying on its side and formed perfectly in the shape of the bottle was the green plant that had been planted in the jar. The woman picked up the dirt and plant that remained in one piece and held it in her hands with the leaves draping over her arms. She silently thumped the plant and its yellow leaves floated away from the stem. She held the glassless clump in her hands a moment before she dropped it to the ground where the dirt split open like the bottle. The plant fell sideways from it, its roots exposed. The woman began to pack the dirt around the plant until it stood straight again in the bare spot of dirt that the rain had beaten smooth from the over-run of the gutter. When she turned and disappeared up the steps, Cary looked at the plant still unable to remember the sound that had made her turn around. Suddenly a quick gush of water came from the porch and washed the leaves to a glistening green. In a flash of memory, the shiny gleam of the leaves and the rain puddles and the cracking sound of the bottle began to fit together for her. The scene in front of her faded from her eyes and she saw on the ground in her memory dark pine straw and she remembered a continual stream of bottles bouncing in it. The bottles bounced, irregularly spaced, and each time before one hit she could hear the crack of a gun shot. She had stood with her feet planted in one spot, knowing that Sam and Johnny knew exactly where she was and thinking that, if she were to move, she would walk directly into the bullet.

She turned to watch the two boys; Sam held the gun and Johnny was hurling the bottles into the air. Sam lifted the gun to waist level with his back turned to the bottle spinning in the air. Then he would quickly turn around and raise the barrel of the gun, firing at the bottle. Cary watched, wishing that she had never come with them shooting. She was afraid to ask them to let her shoot and she had become irritated and exhausted from the monotonous whirr of the bottle going into the air, the gun going off, and the bottle hitting the ground, still whole or cracking open on a rock. Johnny went to the junk heap where the bottles were and lifted up an old gallon gasoline jug by its looped handle. He swung it a complete circle and it went into the air, its weight carrying it much lower than the other jugs. Sam instantly lifted the gun, and directly after the crack of the rifle, the bottle flew apart into shiny chunks of glass with the orange liquid that had remained inside bursting into droplets.

When the bits of glass tinkled to the ground all around her, a shudder ran through Cary's body. Then Sam said, "Boy, I got that one, didn't I? Busted it in a million pieces."

"Who the hell couldn't hit the side of a barn? You can throw up your own damn bottles for a while. I'm tired."

"Why the hell are you tired? You haven't done anything."

"Well, if you're not going to let me shoot the gun you can stay down here all day shooting at the damn gnats for all I care."

Then Johnny looked into the bushes where the last bullet had gone, lower than the others, battering against the trees and leaves until it was silent. He spoke again, "And I just may tell the old lady about how you let bullets run wild. You could have hit someone in the field on the other side shooting that low."

"How the hell could I have hit someone on the other side? You could shoot your butt off all day long at those woods and not get a bullet through them."

"The hell you couldn't. How wide do you think the woods are? Not more than forty feet between here and the cornfield, I betcha."

"O.K. little brother, you're so damn wise. Can you see any light shining between the trees?"

"What the hell has that got to do with it?"

"Well, if you can't see light through there, then it ain't nothing but solid trees between here and the other side, and a damn twenty-two ain't going through a pine tree."

Johnny thought for a moment knowing he was beginning to lose his side of the argument. Then he glanced quickly sideways at Cary who shuffled her bare feet uneasily in the pine straw. She ran her feet under the cool, wet underside of the straw looking down at the ground away from Johnny's staring eyes.

She heard him begin to talk again to Sam, trying to retain the loud voice of the argument and only coming out with a strained sound because of the lapse. He didn't seem to take up where he had left off.

"It don't take a hole between those trees no bigger than a pea for that twenty-two to go through and I betcha that bullet would go a mile before it would fall to the ground and it could still go in somebody."

Then Sam looked into the trees, noticing the pinpoints of light coming through the greenery and brush around the thick trunks of the pine trees.

"You don't reckon it did go through do you?" Then he paused a minute. "There ain't nobody working that field today anyhow. But if it did hit somebody, they'd never have any way of knowing who shot it."

Then Johnny snapped back, as he noticed Sam weakening, "Yep, it could still go in somebody, put out an eye. Bust an eye right on out of their head if they happened to be looking in the direction of the gunshots. And everybody knows you go down here shooting."

Sam leaned the gun against the tree and Johnny continued talking. "Or maybe it would have popped them in the throat, busting right in their Adam's apple or through their windpipe and they're over there now strangling to death."

"Oh shut that crap up! You're getting stupider than hell. A twenty-two ain't going to kill nobody that far away and we would hear them choking no farther away than we are."

Cary put her hand to her throat and felt her Adam's apple, trying to run her fingers across her windpipe.

"Aw, quit that damn crap, Cary. I didn't hit nobody. How come we didn't hear nobody holler? How come?"

Then Johnny began again. "You probably busted their vocal cords all to hell and they are over there lying in the dirt, croaking like a goddamn frog or something, trying to call someone to help them but they can't and are going to lie there bleeding to death because they can't make us hear them."

"If you don't stop that bullcrap, I'm going to beat shit out of you."

"Mama told you not to use that word."

"Well, listen to Mama's boy . . ."

Then the argument was broken off suddenly as a distant cawing sound was heard. Johnny started laughing and said in a melodramatic voice, "See, some poor shot man is crying out there in the woods, a bullet in his gullet, crying out and no one will listen because the bullet in his throat makes him sound like a crow."

"What a big crapmouth you are." Then Sam picked up a clod and broke it into white dust on the front of Johnny's shirt. Johnny dived towards him, grabbing him around the waist and forcing him to the ground.

As they rolled in the pine straw, Sam tried to push Johnny off, saying in a broken voice, "Why don't you quit talking so much? If there is a crow around here anywhere you're going to scare him off and we might have a chance to shoot at something real for a change."

Johnny answered him, "Ain't no damn crow stupid enough to fly anywhere around where somebody's been shooting a gun," and held Sam's face down in the dirt until Sam got his arm around Johnny's waist and dragged him under him.

Cary walked slowly over and picked up the rifle that was leaning against the tree. She had watched as the boys scuffled around the loaded gun and almost waited to hear it go off as one of them knocked against it. She carried it over into the shade and sat down with it in her lap, the barrel pointing towards the ground. She kept her hands away from the trigger and looked at the fingerprint impressions her hands made on the oily blue barrel. Then she began to rub it on the legs of her blue jeans, trying to erase the fingerprints and remembering how Sam had screamed at Johnny about rust and skin oil when he had touched the barrel.

Suddenly through the trees came the clap of wings as though the limbs were falling from the trees as the birds broke out. Cary looked in the direction of the moving leaves and in the corner of her eye saw the boys stop fighting. Sam had begun to crawl quickly towards her, but the birds were already in the air overhead. In her mind ran a flash that he couldn't get there in time and, if she didn't do something, the birds would all escape. She pointed the gun upwards towards the black birds and as soon as her fingers brushed the trigger, the gun cracked sharply. She could not take her eyes away from the seven birds in the air, until one began to descend from the group. Six of the birds began to squawk loudly and disappeared immediately over the trees but one had fallen only a short distance from them.

"Well, I'll be damned; I'll be damned, Sam, look at that! She got one of then black bastards dead center."

Sam walked over to the bird that flapped slowly in the grass. "Of all the lucky things I've ever seen. She don't even know the trigger from the hammer and she picked one right off on the wing. Cary, that's the damnedest thing I've ever seen," he said.

Cary walked over towards them but did not take her eyes from the bird in the grass. It had stopped flapping now and the sun glistened on its black feathers in shades of green and blue as though the bird had been dipped in oil. She stooped to the ground and picked up the bird, dropping it quickly again when she felt its warm feathers beneath her touch. Then she picked it up again, turning it over and over but there was no blood on it anywhere.

Sam began to speak. "You know, Cary, that's one of the hardest things in the world to do, to hit a crow on the wing. They're smarter than hell, lot smarter than people, and they can see a gun a mile away and hardly nobody can hit one, especially with a rifle. I've gone looking for them many a time with my gun in my pants leg and they still seen it."

Cary dropped the rifle from her hand, falling into a heap on the ground and sobbing violently. "I didn't mean to hit him; I didn't mean to."

Then Johnny said, "Well, what the hell did you shoot at him for if you didn't mean to hit him?"

Her shoulders began to shake as her face went between her knees. Sam picked up the gun and said to her, "I wish to hell I could carry a crow back and say I shot it on the wing." Then he lifted her up by the arm and said, "Come on, Cary, let's go back to the house and get something to eat. I want to tell Mother about this." She began to walk back beside Sam, her body limp but her arm stiff where Sam held on to her.

Johnny walked behind them carrying the black bird by one wing. Cary looked back at the bird with its feet curled under its chest. When they got back to the house, Johnny took the bird and went out into the field where they had planted corn and where the thin green shoots had begun to crack the ground. Over one shoulder he carried a tomato stake that he had picked up at the barn and the crow in the other hand. When he got to the center of the field, he pushed the stake into the ground. Then he took the old strip of rag that still clung to the tomato stake from last summer when they strung up the tomatoes and tied the crow to the top of the stake.

"What's he doing that for?" she asked.

Then Sam turned to her and said, "That'll keep the crows out. You won't find a better scarecrow than that. You can string up everything under the sun out there and try to fool them. I seen people string tin cans and mirrors and all kinds of stuff and they'd pull every plant out there up but when they see what we did to one of their friends, you won't catch one of them coming around our field."

Johnny walked away from the field and the black rag of a crow blew stiffly back and forth at the top of the stake. She looked at its shiny feathers, but it had not bled where the bullet went in.

She had watched the crow go through the whole summer that year until it faded to a dull black and then was swallowed up in the green of the tall cornstalks. When the corn had dried and been taken in and the fodder pulled, the stake with the crow remained lost among the dying stalks. Then the stalks fell and the stake with the crow must have fallen too, because she never saw it again and she never went out into the field to see if it was still there.

Now Cary turned back to the starling that the cat had ripped open. A fly had begun to buzz around it and its blood flowed slowly out into the grass. She walked over to the garage, pushing open the side door and looking into the dark inside that moved with spider webs as she opened the door. She walked slowly towards a stack of shovels and rakes in the corner, but as a spider web brushed across her face, she turned and ran back outside, brushing the web from her body. When she bent her head over and began to shake her hair, she saw the dried blood on her hand that had turned almost black. She ran over to the rain barrel, tipped it up and began to wash the blood from her hand. The plant from the broken pot had began to shrivel and curl in the sun and some of its roots stuck up broken through the dirt.

"I didn't kill the bird. I won't bury it," she said softly to herself. Then she paused and said, "I told Sam something was hurting. I told him." She wiped her hands on the side of her dress as she went back up the steps and across the house into her bedroom. The shades were still down and the room was dark as she waited until she could see her bed clearly across the room. She lay down on the bed, and as she clutched the pillow in her hands, she felt tears begin to run slowly down her face.

Chapter Twelve

SHE LAY in bed that night, her mother already asleep and breathing heavily beside her. Cary looked up at the ceiling where flakes of light danced across each time a car passed by on the street. When she closed her eyes, she saw the little flakes of light swirl and flicker and tumble over each other below as in the crystal water at the old spring. After the rainy season the water poured over the top of the terra-cotta pipe. Soon the flow slowed down and a steady stream came from the overflow valve. She and Sam and Johnny had been sent by Mrs. Strawbright to catch the salamanders that had washed over the top and put them back in the spring. The little wet lizards slipped through her fingers and fell into the water, squirming back into the deep pools.

"Sam, look at that. Look at that gold!" Johnny exclaimed from the thin stream below the spring. He was shorter than Sam then, two years behind him in age. Sam was the same square-shouldered boy he was now; his thick back accenting his brother's lean narrow one.

Then Sam said, "That ain't gold." Cary had crawled over to the pool beside Johnny and looked down into it. In the bottom of the crystal-clear water, flakes of gold flickered on the sand. A salamander ran across the bottom and the gold flakes exploded into the water then began to float back onto the sand.

"See, you can tell it ain't gold, it's too light or that salamander wouldn't have kicked it up."

Johnny looked up frowning. "How do you know it's not gold? They've found it around here before. It could be sure as anything."

"It's not, I tell you. I forget what you call it, but it ain't gold. I seen it many a time."

"You can't know so much. It could be gold."

"Well, if you're so smart, why don't you start prospecting and take it to town by the sackful and make an ass of yourself?" Then he stopped a second and said, "Mica, that's what it is. Mica!"

"Aw, I've seen mica before. It don't look like gold. It's sort of shiny but it comes in big chunks and you can peel it apart. I know what mica is and that is not mica!"

"It's little pieces of mica. Anything that can come in big pieces can come in little ones."

"Why don't you shut up!"

"You shut up yourself dammit, or I'll knock your head off."

Johnny and Sam rose to their feet when Johnny said, "You're just full of big talk. Always have to show off when there's a girl around."

"You're the one that's full of big talk. I can knock your block off any day."

Cary, who had crawled up on the back side of the spring, called loudly to the boys, "Look over here. Come here quick and look!"

Johnny and Sam stared at each other a moment, then Johnny shrugged his shoulders and went over to the spring where Cary was on her knees in the pine straw. She was uncovering a spongy plant with short blunt tentacles on it. "Look here what's coming up. A real funny kind of mushroom." The mushroom glowed pink, and as she crawled around on her knees she flicked the pine straw off a cluster of orange ones just like the pink one.

"Gee, I've never seen anything like that growing before. They don't look real." It was Johnny who spoke, as he stepped down and lifted up a clump of straw. "Think they'd live better if we left the straw on them? I wonder if they grow anywhere else."

"I know what they are, they're coral mushrooms and they are found in dark, damp places," Sam said as he walked up behind them.

Johnny stood up and stared at Sam's face. "You're just too damn smart for your own good. You think you're smart as some goddamn scientist."

"Well, it was in my biology book and when you get in high school, maybe you'll learn something."

"Oh, Mr. High School, he's so damn smart."

Then Cary walked beside them and said, "Why don't you both shut up. I'm sick of hearing you. I don't see why you have to fight about everything." As she spoke Johnny shoved her in the chest with his hand and she fell backwards in the pine straw.

"Johnny, you shouldn't have done that to a girl." Sam reached down to help her up but she had run over against a tree.

"She's not like a girl! She'd hit me many a time if she hadn't known I'd hit her back!" As he spoke his voice trembled and color rushed into his face.

"The heck she's not a girl and you don't hit a girl there."

Johnny's face grew hotter until he turned and walked back towards the house. Sam then looked to see where Cary was, but she had disappeared.

She remembered walking quickly back towards her house, starting to run when she saw the side of the house in the clearing. She went up the steps then dropped into a chair and watched up the path so she could run into the house if Sam had followed her.

She still looked at the ceiling from her bed watching the golden flakes and waiting for another car so she could see them again, but the cars were fewer now and the street was silent as it grew later. Finally she could stay awake no longer, and before she fell asleep she began to hear Sam's voice just as she had heard him today, but he was saying what he did before she had run away from the spring, ". . . you don't hit a girl there."

When Cary awoke the next morning, she heard her mother's voice and that of a man coming from the door. She stepped onto the floor and chill bumps swelled on her arms when she heard her mother's laugh. She leaned over and saw the man at the door. His skin was dark brown like a Negro's but his hair fell in a straight chunk over his forehead. Then the door closed and she could not hear him anymore.

"Who was that?" Cary asked.

Her mother started back at her voice. "Oh, I didn't know you was getting up. That was Maurice. He fixed my coffee pot handle that broke."

"He looks like a nigger."

"Well, he is part nigger I think. Seems to be so, but sometimes when you look at him he don't look like one."

"Is he the one that shoes horses?"

"Yes, he's a blacksmith but he'll do welding and fixing if you ask him. In fact he told me once he'd rather just give up shoeing altogether and that to be truthful he was scared of horses and I said I didn't blame him."

"Mrs. Strawbright said he was sorry." Her mother walked into the kitchen and Cary tried to watch her face. "He is a nigger too. That's what she said. If you're part, you're a nigger," Cary said.

She heard her mother open the oven and set a plate on the table.

"Your food is here. I've got to go now."

Cary walked into the kitchen and her mother quickly shut the cabinet door and turned around.

"What's the matter?" Cary said.

"I just put the money up, the change. I got the change from paying Maurice. I don't much like keeping money stuck around in the house but I don't like to carry it around."

"Well, you don't have to be afraid of me taking it. I don't want your money."

Her mother sighed and walked towards the door. "I wasn't hiding it from you. You don't have to say things like that. I just feel like you ought to be careful about money around a place like this."

"I saw Maurice give you the money and you hadn't given him any so I know it wasn't change," Cary said loudly. Her mother turned quickly without speaking and walked into the back bedroom.

The back screen slammed and Cary hit her fist on her knee and snatched back the chair and sat down at the table. As she ate her breakfast, her throat tightened when she thought of the greasy face of the man at the door. His skin was pitted and swollen and sweat ran in the ruts in his face. She remembered his eyes that seemed set in their sockets looking straight in one direction as he talked, unlike most people who looked at your face. While her mother had talked to him he looked down at her breasts. Thinking of Maurice's eyes she remembered faintly the time that the children from the orphanage had been in town selling paper poppies they had made in the playroom. They were red crepe paper and on wires with green tape wrapped around them. They had all come into town from the orphanage and each one had a cigar box with twenty flowers to sell before lunch for ten cents each and the money was to go for a new bathroom at the orphanage. The people in the town were tall, and when she walked down the sidewalk she felt small and lost, because she didn't know any of the people or the buildings along the street. Most of the people were moving fast and didn't stop or notice her, but when they did look she had moved up against the building and wouldn't look at them.

Elsa had come running up to her when she was on the corner pretending to look in the window.

"I ain't got but seven left to sell and it's only ten o'clock."

Then she reached over to look in Cary's box which Cary snatched back and held against her chest. "How many you got? I bet you got more than that left," Elsa said.

Then Cary turned her back to Elsa and ran around the corner, towards the street that ran parallel to the main street. There weren't as many people there and the store windows were dusty and not as pretty as the ones on the main street. The things in the windows didn't look new; they were old and someone had used them before.

She stood up against the window of a store where she could smell food. The window was full of paper plants that were stuck in pots. Then she looked in her hand at her box of paper flowers. She didn't want to look inside the box, and when she shook it, she felt them all hit the top.

"There's another one. Ain't she cute."

Two Negro women walked by with shopping bags in both hands and sandals and colored socks on. They both had paper flowers pinned on their blouses. As she watched the people pass she realized they all had on flowers and she hadn't sold any of hers. She began to feel all jumpy inside as she watched them go by and into the restaurant.

"What you got there?"

She jumped and tears came into her eyes as she realized there was a man standing beside her with a dark face and dark pits in his cheeks. He looked at her strangely, at her body and not her face. Her eyes began to burn and she could not stop the tears that came down her face.

"Now don't cry now," he said softly. "I ain't going to hurt you."

She tried to stop the tears but then her body began to jolt with sobs.

"Now don't you worry now. I'm not going to take your money. It's a good cause I think, a good cause, a very good cause," he said.

She turned and looked at the man. He was dark, a Negro she thought, but then maybe not a Negro.

"How many more you got to sell, huh? Many more?"

She began to cry harder. "I ain't sold none of them and I got to have them all gone by lunch and two dollars."

He raised his eyebrows but his eyes still would not look at her face. "Now, that's a shame now. I reckon you just don't know the right people, is that so? I bet Arnold in there ain't got one yet," and he glanced towards the restaurant. "Come on, you and me will go in there and sell him one."

They went in the restaurant and Cary walked slowly behind the dark man who went over to the man behind the counter.

"Arnold, how about getting a dime out of the register for this child. She has some mighty pretty flowers there." Then he turned and looked at her. "Come here and show Arnold what pretty flowers you have there."

She looked at Arnold and when he smiled at her she walked over and lifted the lid on the box.

"Now ain't they pretty. I think I'll buy one to put in the window yonder. Don't look like them are going to bloom by themselves."

A man at the bar laughed and Arnold went to the register and got a dime and handed it to her. He took the flower she handed him and went and wrapped it around the stem of one of the paper plants in the window.

When she put the dime in the box and heard it roll under the flowers, the man that had brought her in turned and spoke loudly.

"Arnold's poor old flowers ain't going to bloom by theirselves so why don't everybody buy a flower for him. Only a dime for a flower for Arnold's window."

As each dime hit the box she handed Arnold a flower which he took over and twined around the dusty green stalk of the plants. When she left the store she turned and looked in the window where all the red flowers hung on the plants, their wire stems bent awkwardly around the stalks. The plants looked even deader to her now.

"Now ain't they pretty to look at?" the man said. She couldn't answer him as she looked in at the plants.

They went down the street and into more stores, until she only had four flowers left. They had reached the end of the street and there were no more stores left.

The man said, "Well now, we got four left. Where shall we sell them?" The dark centers of his eyes shook back and forth while he looked at her body as he spoke. He seemed to be thinking, and there was a long silence before he spoke again.

"I know where to go. We could sell twenty more there if you had them."

"I don't need to sell but these four. We didn't make no more than twenty apiece."

The man looked straight at her body and didn't seem to be listening to what she was saying.

"Come on. Let's go in here." She followed him into a strange door that moved around in a circle and she walked into a little section. For a moment, when she stopped inside and the glass behind her bumped her, she could see the man in the glass section in front of her. Then she had to run when the door moved again and the man pulled her out on the inside.

"That was fun, wasn't it? That there's called a revolving door."

On the inside she saw rugs on the floor and dark furniture with a few dim lights over them for people to read papers on the sofas.

She started to walk towards the people but the man put his hand on her shoulder. "Don't go over there," and his eyes got shiny. "Them people ain't got no money. We don't want to bother with them. It's the ones upstairs who got the money, the ones that got the rooms upstairs."

She looked at him — he was no longer looking at her but was

looking up the stairs. Then she pulled her shoulder from under his hand but he didn't seem to notice her as he began to walk up the stairs. She followed him up the dark stairs until they stepped into a hall with a bunch of rooms with numbers on the doors. He knocked on the doors one by one but no one came. She had begun to follow him but walked slower and slower when she saw no one was coming to the doors.

"Maybe we had better go someplace else. I don't think no one's here. I don't like this place," she said and turned to walk away.

"Wait!" he said and his voice was loud in the silent hall. "A few of them may be out but I bet someone's here who'll buy them all at one shot. The people that live here have lots of money. They won't think nothing of giving you a dime."

She began to walk down the hall not liking at all the dark wallpaper and lights on the walls. The door knobs were shiny, but the numbers on the doors were tarnished and crooked. He walked by two doors without knocking and came to one where he stopped. On a chain attached to his belt he had a key which he took to unlock the door.

"This is where my sister lives. She'll buy them all because she has more money than she knows what to do with."

They walked into the room and there was no one in it. He began to walk through the door into another room calling a name. The name was Elsa.

"I know an Elsa," she said.

The man acted as though he didn't hear her and came across the room towards her.

"Elsa is out selling flowers too. I bet she's already sold all of hers."

The man spoke again, still not listening to Cary. "She'll be back in a minute. She always goes out at this time. You and I will just wait a minute and she'll be back and buy them all."

Then he looked at her and didn't say anything for a minute.

"We'd better go back. I don't think I ought to be here," Cary said.

"Now you wait a minute. She'll be back and buy them all."

Cary didn't like the way he kept saying the same thing over and over.

"I hear you're selling them to get a bathroom," he said. "Now that's a nice thing. Them outdoor johnnies are bad in cold weather and they ain't sanitary. It's not nice for little girls not to have a bathroom." Then he looked straight at her and said, "You ever seen a bathroom?"

"Once at my aunt's," she said. She didn't like to talk about the bathroom like this.

"Do you know how to use a bathroom? I bet you would like to use a bathroom now. I bet you ain't been to one since this morning."

When she thought about it, she did want to use a bathroom. He walked over to the door of the bathroom.

"Here, you go in and use the bathroom here. My sister won't mind."

She stood watching him and he said, "You can close the door; I won't look." When she saw the man's eyes looking at her, she turned and ran to the door. She ran into the hall and hit her side on the wall as she turned to run. When she got inside the revolving door, she pushed hard but it would not move. Then it began to move fast as it had when she had come in and she thought the man was behind her. When she got to the sidewalk, she was afraid she would feel the hand on her shoulder. For a moment she felt his hand, but when she began to run down the street she was free and she ran until the people were behind her and in front of her and she was back on the main street. Suddenly she stopped; she saw Elsa.

Elsa turned her head when she saw her but she did not walk away.

"There ain't enough people in this town. I got five left and there ain't no one left without them."

"I ain't got but four. I don't think there are no people left either."

Cary heard her own voice, but it seemed like a strange voice, not hers, that had answered Elsa.

They walked down the street back towards the bus and she knew Elsa didn't know what had happened.

"Elsa, did you go in the buildings to sell yours?"

"Go in the buildings?"

"Like the big ones with the numbers on the doors?"

"Did you go in there? You went in a hotel?"

Cary began to walk in front of Elsa and did not answer.

"You better not have," Elsa said. "That's where those sorry women go and men pay them to get naked."

Cary turned quickly and looked at her saying, ". . . to get naked?"

"Yeah, they give them money to let them see their business."

Cary remembered how her body had begun to shake and she couldn't talk to Elsa anymore.

She thought of this now as she sat with her breakfast cold in front of her. Her face and eyes burned when she thought of how stupid she had been and how it was too late to do anything about it. She got up and scraped the food in the bag in the corner and put her plate in the sink before going in the bedroom and looking around for her dress. She found it on the dresser; it had been washed and the little tear in the back stitched neatly together. When she saw that the dress was clean she went into the bathroom and washed up, drying with a damp towel she found on the floor. After going back out into the yard and sitting on the steps, she could hear the green flies buzzing in the grass across the yard. The swarm would rise into the air and settle back down again. She sat there until the sun was hot overhead before she heard the car pull up in front of the house. She started to walk away from the steps but Sam was already around the house.

"Hi! Didn't have any trouble getting the car but I have to have it back by four or a little after," he said.

She stood and looked at him but did not speak.

"Where was it you wanted to go?"

She thought about the little albino in the ditch, but when she looked at Sam in his clean shirt she knew she could not go there.

"Oh, let's just ride around nowhere in particular until we think of something," she said.

They got in the car, Cary getting in on his side, crawling across the seat, and opening the window on her side. Sam started the car and they turned around in the street and headed back towards the highway.

"Have you ever been up on Piney Hill?" he said.

"No, but I know it's back of the farm," she answered quietly.

"There's a road up there, you can see our whole place from the top. Want to go?"

She nodded her head and watched the white line on the highway go beside the car. They came to a winding dirt road; then through a long stretch of pot holes under the tires with a strip of broom sage and scrubs down the middle. The short trees thumped against the oil pan of the car and it groaned as it made the slow trip upward.

"Nobody hadn't been up here in a long time. The road didn't used to be so rough."

Beside the road was broken-down barbwire fence around neglected pastures filled with rocks and bitterweed. The bright yellow flowers stretched to the top of the hill and the air was heavy with their dusty scent.

"We're almost up there. See, there's where the rocks are you can go out on to see from."

He stopped the car and pulled on the emergency brake, letting the car sit for a second to see if it was going to roll. Then he got out and ran to the edge of the rocks.

"Come here, you can see good today."

Cary walked out on the rock beside him, braiding her hair as she walked. "See, there's Johnny's horse over there, see. And there's her colt, she's on the other side of her. Can't see her too good from here," he said.

"Point out your house from here, it's hard to tell," she said quietly.

He turned suddenly to Cary as she spoke. When she felt the wind blow her dress between her legs, she wrapped her toes over the top of the rocks. Her hair blew in dark streaks in front of her eyes when she looked down. Then her eyes rested on her legs that seemed too dark and thin.

"There, over there," Sam said. "It looks so much neater from up here. Everything is in squares and all."

Cary walked out to the edge of the rock. She turned and looked into his face and realized he had been looking at the stitched-up tear that was in the back of her dress. She turned quickly away, looking back toward the farm.

"There's where our house was, I bet. See, the black place in the trees. Funny it seems so far away," she said, then turned and looked again into his face. "You know, not just far away, like it was a long time away too."

When her head moved her long braid fell over her shoulder and she saw Sam watch it drop. "What's it going to be like now, Cary; I mean what are you going to do?" he said.

"I don't know, like I told you, go to school I guess." She turned away suddenly feeling resentment as he questioned her again. "I don't want to go to school, but I don't want to do anything."

As soon as the words were out, she was sorry she had said them.

"You ought to want to do something," he said.

Then she looked into his face, her face beginning to burn. "You talk, that's all; you talk!"

"Well, you don't have to get mad. I just think you ought to want to make something of yourself. You won't ever have anything if you don't go to school."

She stepped back and slipped from the top of the rock and suddenly his arms were around her. She shoved him backwards and pulled from his grip.

"You think I don't know anything! You think I'm too dumb to know why you wanted to come up here where there's no people, saying the road hadn't been used thinking I didn't know you and Mollie Stallings had been up here."

"What's the matter with you?" he said as he quickly started back towards the car. "If you think I'd want to bring someone ugly and skinny like you up here for that, you're crazy."

He walked over and got back in the car and she watched him slam the door. "You better get in; it's a long way down," he said sharply.

She got in the car, but he did not start the engine. Then he spoke quickly, "I didn't mean what I just said. I'm sorry I said that." She was still silent so he spoke again, "Do you really want to go right now?"

"No," she said finally.

She sat there for a moment before raking her nails up her arms again.

"Did you get into some cow itch?" he said as he reached over and touched her arm. When he touched her skin with his hand, she whirled in the seat and snatched his hand, squeezing it between both of hers. A sharp smile was on her face and the corners of her eyes seemed to turn up as Sam looked at her in confusion.

"You said I was ugly," she said, as she stared at him.

"Oh, I didn't mean anything when I said that. You just made

me feel bad and I had to say something. I said I was sorry about that and I mean it. I just got mad, that's all, because I didn't think you'd act like that." He watched her eyes and they seemed to dart back and forth across his face. "I never thought you were ugly," he began again. "I always thought there was something about the way you looked."

"What was it? What was it about the way I look?"

"Oh, I don't know," he said as he slipped his other hand over hers. "It's like you look wild or something, like you are that way. Like it feels strange to me to know you're sitting here . . ."

"Do you mean I'm wild, like I'm a crazy wild person? Do you think I'm crazy?"

"No, I don't mean that at all. You're not crazy. It's just you're different from Mollie, she just, well, I don't know."

She pulled his hands towards her and said, "You mean she doesn't fight you back when you take her out here."

"No, well, I mean yes. Anyway sometimes it was her, not me. You know, don't you?"

Then she looked down and saw she still held his hands; he pulled her forward. Her body felt light and agile as he pulled it towards him, but in her back he felt a slight stiffness. When he looked quickly into her face, she tried to speak but couldn't. As he snatched quickly at her back, she felt the stiffness disappear and she closed her eyes and he pressed her lips to his.

He held her awkwardly against him until she pushed him away and looked at his face. Her eyes were dull now and she shook her head and put the back of her hand against her lips.

"I knew you'd pull away," he said as he released her. "You make me feel like such a fool . . ." He turned around and started the motor quickly. Then she pressed her face against the window and felt the glass thump against her forehead as they drove down the hill.

Before they got to town, the sun had seemed bright across the fields, but when they reached the house the sun could not be seen

for the trees and houses. The houses formed a gray wall and a
heavy shadow across the street, leaving even the splotches of light
tinged with gray as the factory smoke settled across the rooftops.
The children were off the street and sat in rows on the bottom of
steps watching the cars go by as the people got off from the mill.
A lone lightning bug flickered in front of Cary's eyes, lifting up
and down in the air until one of the boys from the steps across the
street began to run after it.

Then the bug rose high into the air and the boy reached up
with his hand and began to leap uselessly after it, landing in soft
thuds on the ground.

"We can go back inside the car if you want to."

"No, leave me alone," she said hastily, "I want to stay out
here."

"Well, I just thought because of all the kids . . ."

"No, I want to stay out here where there are people around."

Cary watched the little boy disappear around the house and
the lightning bug still flashed in the air.

"Do you give Mollie money?" she said quickly.

"Give her money!" he said sharply. "She's not a damn whore."
Then he stood up beside the steps and said, "Do you really think
that? That I'd go out with a whore?" His voice had been loud
and in the silence that followed she could not look up at him.

Then she tried to speak, "Maurice . . . the one that came
today . . ." and was silent again.

"Maurice who? That nigger blacksmith? What about him?
He's sorry as hell."

"I don't know," she said and dropped her face into her hands.
"I don't want to stay here," she said, jumping up from the steps.

Sam started backwards as she spoke again. "Take me back out
to the highway and drop me, please."

"What for? If the mill is getting off it's already after four. I
better go anyway."

"Please take me anyway."

He turned and walked towards the car. "Well, come on then."

When they got to the highway, she turned to him and said, "Let me out over there by the dirt road."

He stopped the car without speaking and she got out, standing at the top of the ditch with her back to him until he drove away. Then she walked down into the ditch and stood in the soft sand. The little white boy was there scrambling for a field mouse, and he looked up into her face when he saw her walk towards him. She ran down the ditch and scooped up the mouse into her hand, giving it to the little boy. She watched his parched lips stretch into a smile and his pink eyes shut into slits as he closed his hands around the mouse.

Chapter Thirteen

EACH MORNING after that she would start the trip to the ditch, walking down the highway in the late August sun. The pavement was hot to the bottom of her feet as she alternated between it and the sharp gravel and fescue on the shoulder of the road. She watched fescue scratch her legs, leaving little white streaks in her brown skin. At the end of her walk she would come to the ditch and stand for a moment cooling her feet in the soft topsoil that had washed from the garden into the ditch. In the bottom of the ditch she always found the little boy, his legs sprawling from the loose legs of his shorts. He would look up into her face and smile, exposing strange dark creases between his teeth. The rest of him was pink and white, a softness that glowed pink each time a blade of grass brushed his skin. He leaned against the side of the ditch and watched Cary as she chased the field mice.

One morning she scooped up a tiny mouse and held him cupped in her hand, his tiny head through her fingers. The little boy looked at its black beaded eyes and tipped his head to one side. Then he placed his finger lightly on the mouse's head, quickly taking it away with a soft giggle in his throat. Suddenly Cary pulled open the front of his t-shirt and dropped the mouse down his chest. As she sat back and laughed, the little boy squirmed and pounded at his chest until the mouse ran out his sleeve. The mouse tumbled on the ground, righted itself, and scurried off into the grass. She stopped laughing as the little boy's bottom lip dropped exposing the red inside of his gums. He was clutching at his chest and tears were gathering in his eyes.

"Oh, I'm sorry, Jasper. Jasper," she said as she lifted his shirt. She let out a short gasp as she saw where the mouse had run up his chest; his skin was dotted with red spots of blood.

"Oh, Jasper! Jasper, I didn't know he would hurt you. We used to put them under our shirts all the time because they tickled. I didn't know he could hurt you."

"O.K., O.K.," he said in a feeble voice, looking up with a light smile on his face. "Don't hurt much, Ka."

"I won't ever do like that again. You can be sure of that, Jasper. I won't never let nothing hurt you like that again."

"Ka, let's go get turtle shell."

His eyes began to widen as he spoke and his nose flattened at the corners when he smiled. She dropped her hand to help him up and he rose slowly from the ground, the top of his white tufted head coming just below her shoulders. The front of his t-shirt stuck to his chest and little drops of blood spread into the cloth. When they crossed the little patch of dried garden, Jasper kicked the oversized cucumbers into the air, but the dried vines snatched them back. After they crossed the smooth yard, he crawled between the piles of rocks that held the house off the ground. Cary stooped and looked under the house where his white body glowed like a light in the dark. Then he emerged back into the daylight, his eyes squinted and dusty cobwebs draped across the top of his head. In his hand was a cigar box with a rock on top of it. A thumping was heard from within, shaking the rock off the top. He set the box on the ground and the lid rose up, a turtle crawling over the top. On its back was written "Jasper" in pink nail polish. Jasper laughed as the turtle stumbled out and fell on its back, its feet waving in the air. When he reached out and touched its feet, the scaled claws of the turtle tucked back inside the shell. Jasper watched the shell rock silently in the dirt and said, "Ka, make him come out again." When she looked into his face, she saw a trace of the same expression it had had when the mouse was in his shirt.

She turned the turtle over but its legs stayed in the shell as it rested flatly in the dirt.

"Come on out, old turtle. Jasper wants to see you." She knew those words would make him laugh, and when she heard his soft giggle, she smiled and said, "Well, Jasp, I guess we'll have to put him back in the box where it's dark before he'll have the nerve to come out again."

She placed the turtle back in the box, and in a few minutes he was thumping at the lid with the back of his shell again. Jasper began to laugh aloud, then suddenly he flipped the lid from the box. He pinched the head of the turtle between his fingers and pulled him from the box. The turtle's neck stretched out into a thin wrinkled cord as it dangled hopelessly in the heavy shell. When Cary grabbed Jasper's wrist and squeezed it, the turtle fell with a thud on the ground, rolling over on its back. He placed his other hand down on his wrist which blazed red with white stripes between where her fingers had been.

"Jasper, why do you always do that! You hurt him and he'll probably die."

Then Jasper stood up, still holding his wrist, and squealed loudly with tears streaming down his cheeks. Cary watched him squeal, his thin little voice filling the air until finally a colored woman walked out on the back stoop, with her fists pressed into her hips.

The colored woman said, "Lawd, Jasper, what you hollering about?" When she saw Cary on her knees in the yard, she screwed up her face. "You done here again. Hump, what's a white girl doing messing around colored folks' places."

Cary stood up, her face burning and tears filling her eyes.

"I come to see Jasper." Then she stopped and looked at the

little boy with the spots on his shirt now faded into dark brown. "Me and him get along fine usually, but he always wants to hurt things."

The colored woman began to beat the dust out of a rag in her hand on the side of the house, sniffing as the dust rose into her face.

"Jasper ain't got good sense. You could have told that he ain't got biddie brains in his head and there ain't no sense in the world messing with him trying to get him to act as you please because if he ain't got a mind to do it there ain't no one to talk to him." Then she muttered as she went in the house, "Lawd, the first time I seen him the day he was born, that youngun done took enough out of this woman to last a hundred years."

Cary looked down at Jasper, whose expression had not changed. Then she looked over at the grass and saw the turtle struggling away, its legs reaching far out of the shell as it bumped along. She ran and scooped it into her hands, giving it back to Jasper.

"Look at the old rascal, thinking he could run away. Here, you keep him, Jasper." Then she paused and said, "and be nice to him so we can play with him again and he won't die."

Jasper held the turtle against his chest; it had gone back into the shell except for one leg with its claws stuck in Jasper's shirt. Cary turned and walked back across the field, but she did not turn to look back at Jasper. She stepped across the cucumbers that were rolled from their dents in the soil and were bleached yellow on the bottom side. As she walked onto the highway, she thought of his expression when she handed him a field mouse or put a lady bug on his arm. He always smiled and laughed as he felt the animals against his skin, and he had squealed with laughter the day she wrote his name on the turtle with her mother's nail polish. But then she thought of the little mouse he had flung against the side of the ditch and the lady bug that had not even bitten him, he had mashed to a pulp one day on his arm. She could hear his squeal, not strong enough for a human squeal, more like a bug or a bird, the same as it had been today when she made him let go of the turtle, and the sound was still in her ears.

As she walked in the edge of the fields, the heat becoming unbearable on the highway, the sun rose full overhead. A persistent hollow sound was in her ears. The squeal of Jasper had faded but was replaced by a sound that rumbled up and down like an annoyed voice. It was no one's voice she knew, yet it had the motion of her mother talking, only talking to her as she had before her father died, scolding and complaining. Cary stopped and sat in the dirt behind a tree, pressing her hands to her ears, but the voice grew louder. The shade relieved the burning sun on the top of her head, but she began to break out in a sweat. She shook her head as the chills ran up her back but she could not stop them or force herself to open her eyes and relieve the shaking inside of her head.

Then suddenly all the undesirable things she could think of began to rush through her mind when she tried to think of something else. They returned before the other thought could form and tightened in her throat. She thought of smashed tobacco worms oozing green blood into the dirt, of having to step on them and feeling their gristly bodies crush under her feet. She tried to make herself laugh and forget this thought, but her stomach began to rise and stop her mind from thinking of something else. She bent her toes and twisted her feet in the ground, but the feeling would not go away. Then into her mind came the thought of earthworms. Even though she knew the thought was coming, she could not prevent it. She struggled, pressing her nails in the dirt, but the thought came anyway, then came the maggots in the fly trap that crawled in among the dead flies. The glass jar had hung in front of the stable and Johnny had put it there after he ordered it from a catalogue.

"You'll see, it'll catch hundreds of them in one day. More flies than you ever dreamed were around here," he said to her when she stood beside him with her fingers on her nose as he cut up a fish and put it in the bottom of the jar.

"I don't see how anything could stand that smell, even a fly."

"I've seen a fly that could stand something even worse."

Her face had flushed as she looked away from him. "Why did you say that? That doesn't sound like you."

"What doesn't sound like me?"

"Talking about things like that."

"I was just answering your stupid question, and besides, I talk about what I please. You don't have to act so god almighty, you've heard much worse."

"I didn't ask you a question, I just said something."

"Well, I don't give a damn what you did, question or not; I couldn't care less about you. What makes you think it matters what people say around you?"

Then she walked away and leaned against the post of the stable. "You didn't have to say that either. I know you don't care less but you didn't have to say that." She could not keep her voice from trembling and he noticed it, looking up.

"God damn, nobody could know how to act around you. Half the time you act scared of people and the rest of the time you act like you're so mad you'd fight anybody. Not that I care but I couldn't say anything that was right around you if I thought all day."

He went back to the fly trap, finally, hanging it on a nail while she stood motionless by the post. Almost instantly the flies that had buzzed around him while he worked began to light on the top of the jar and go in, slowly crawling down the sides of the jar until they pounced upon the fish at the bottom. Most of the flies remained on the fish, but a few began to fly upward, beating their bodies on the side of the jar, trying to find the way back out after discovering they were trapped. Then they fell into the bottom of the jar and lay on their backs, trapped in the sticky fish blood, their legs kicking in the air.

"See, look at that. They can figure out how to get in but they can't get back out," he said excitedly. Suddenly his face dropped as he looked at her for she had not moved at all when he had spoken.

"What is it with you?" he said, the color returning to his face. "What the hell do you expect? Do you think people are even going to want to be nice to you? Nobody on earth owes you anything."

She turned sharply to him. "What does anybody on earth owe you? You think I give a damn about you? I just get tired of your telling me you don't give a damn. Get it through your head that I don't care!"

"I don't have to get anything you say through my head." His eyes glistened with anger and red splotches appeared on his neck. She looked straight into his face as he spoke. "Nothing, nothing about you means a damn thing!"

"Look what happens to you. You get mad and you can't even make sense. You just say things to me because you know I won't hit you like Sam does."

"Sam never beat me at anything!" His eyes began to darken and his hand was clutching the shoulder of her shirt.

As soon as his hand touched her shirt, she began to laugh and her laugh grew louder as he looked into her face. He slapped her in the mouth with the back of his other hand and her head hit the cedar post behind her. She dropped to her knees and the blood fell in the dust, rolling into little balls in the dirt. Then the blood stopped and only the taste was left.

She looked up and saw his legs were still in front of her and she began hitting them with her fists. As he walked backwards she followed him on her knees, beating his legs until her knuckles were raw from the rough denim of his jeans. When he turned and walked quickly away, she fell forward on the ground and beat her fists in the dirt and cried until he got to the house and slammed the screen.

As she sat under the tree now thinking of this, she beat her hands into the ground beside her, clutching at the dirt with her hands. She felt she wanted the ground to rise up and resist her. It was solid and hard as she beat against it and her nails could only scratch the surface. Nausea rose again in her throat as she thought of the trap after she went back a week later. The sight of it pressed on the inside of her eyes until she squeezed them shut. The dead flies had risen in a heap on the bottom, the fish completely covered except for the smell that was all around the stable. The flies no longer flew in for the fish but lighted atop the decaying flies. Among the stack of bodies was an occasional honey bee or wasp that had gone inside. On the top of the heap the living flies rolled over the body of a bumble bee that was still buzzing, flicking the flies from its body only to have them crawl on again. As she looked closer at the bottom she saw tiny white worms crawling through the mass of dead bodies. Then she had turned away and shrieked, pressing her eyes into her hands.

Johnny had come to the door of the stable and said, "What is it?" His voice was soft as he walked over behind her and said, "Did you hurt your eye, Cary? What is it?"

She had swung around into his face. "You make me sick, you hear!"

Then he had looked into her face but the anger did not rise again. "I thought about what I did and I was sorry. I didn't mean to hit you."

"Oh, that's great, you're sorry. You are not; you just think you ought to say that because you feel like a coward for hitting a girl but you'd do it again without even thinking about it."

She watched the anger begin to rise in him again but he

clutched his fists and pressed them against the sides of his legs. "Well, I'm saying I'm sorry. That's all I can do now . . . and that's all I'm going to do."

She turned away from him and pointed at his fly trap. "That is so bad! So sickening! Have you looked at that thing up close?"

"No, what is it?"

"You just look!"

He walked up to the trap and turned his face away suddenly and looked back at her. His mouth was open and his bottom lip dropped as he shut his eyes. Cary looked at him a moment before turning and going into the stable. A few minutes later she heard the roots in the ground outside cracking as a shovel broke through. She looked out the window of the tack room and saw Johnny digging a hole in front of the stable. He had taken down his fly trap and it was sitting beside him. Then he turned it up and emptied its contents into the hole throwing the bottle aside and raking the dirt quickly over the dead flies. Cary felt the horrible smell brush her nose for a second in the inside of the barn as she watched Johnny fill the bottle with dirt and throw it on the compost pile. He began coughing and ran to the rain barrel, plunging in his hands as she turned away from the window.

Cary thought of Johnny now as she looked out into the road. Her nausea had finally passed and she felt a soft breeze brush her face as she sat in the shade. She thought again of Jasper and of the little mouse that he had thrown against the side of the ditch and how it had lain stunned for a minute before it wobbled away into the grass. She remembered how she and Johnny would catch the mice in front of the hay baler and put them in a shoe box.

"They don't really hurt anything, do they Johnny?" she had asked.

"No, I don't see how they could, they're so little. They aren't really like rats or anything." Then he shook the box and they began to scratch around on the inside. "Boy, you've got a bunch of them. Where are you going to turn them loose?"

"I don't know. I guess I should find somewhere they can get something to eat."

"I'm sure a mouse could find something to eat anywhere. You better set them out away from the crib because Mama gets mad as hell when they get in the corn. She has to lock the cat in there sometimes."

"They do make a mess of the corn. I guess they don't know what they should or shouldn't eat. How come there are so many out here? They always hide in the hay."

"Oh, they're just eating the seeds off of it. I think they just must eat seeds and bugs."

When she opened the box, they tried to run over the top so she closed it again.

"They've got pretty little shiny eyes. I'd like to keep one but I don't guess it'd ever be still and let you pet it the way they jump around all the time," she had said.

"Yeah, they're just too little. I like a dog or something big you can really make a pet out of. Course they have to be smart too. You can't really pet a horse like you can a dog because they're not smart enough."

"You can make a good pet out of a biddie, and they're little. I used to always be able to tame the sick one that I had to feed by hand. They liked me better than the other chickens."

Then Johnny laughed and said, "Yeah, but they're not wild animals. They like to be petted especially when they're babies, but you just try to do that with a rabbit or a squirrel when they grow up. They don't like you anymore when they don't need you."

Cary remembered looking at him when he said "they don't need you," thinking of all the wild animals she had raised and how they would scratch her and run from her when they grew up. And she and Johnny had taken the box to the edge of the woods and opened it, watching the little mice run and tumble over each other as they scurried off in the leaves.

They had walked back up the path and met Sam coming down. "Where have you two been? Mother said for you to get up there and help stack the hay in the barn."

"We set some mice loose in the woods," Cary had said.

"You did what?"

"She caught a box of mice and wanted to find a place to put them out."

Sam had turned in the path and started walking with them. Then he said to Johnny, "Well, I could have expected Cary to do something like that."

"I didn't see any reason to kill them either. They don't hurt anything."

"Mother would be real glad to hear that, since they almost ruined a whole crib of corn."

"Well, you don't have to make so much out of it. We turned them loose in the woods," Johnny had said.

"That's one of the stupidest things I've ever heard you say," Sam had said as he walked away up the path. Cary had looked at Johnny when he watched Sam walk away. As he looked down and began to shake his head, she spoke to him.

"I'm sorry, Johnny. I didn't even think about him getting mad over something like that."

He looked up quickly at her and said, "Cary, you don't have to be sorry. If I want to turn mice loose in the woods, I turn them loose. I don't take orders from him. He just likes to think he sounds like Daddy used to and it makes him feel big. He wants me to feel like I'm acting like a girl or something." Then Johnny paused and said, "Then he wonders why my horse won't let him touch him. I hope it bites his head off."

Johnny turned and started walking towards the barn and she watched him a moment before she followed.

"Johnny, wait. I'll go with you and help you."

He stopped and looked back at her. "O.K.," and he smiled at her. Cary remembered running up beside him and walking back to the barn. She got up now and started back down the highway towards town, looking over the edge of the ditch for a mouse. When she saw one, she jumped down and scooped it up and tried to hold it in her cupped hands. For a moment it quit moving and she could feel its warm fur and its heart beating hard inside of it. Then she stooped down and watched it jump from her hand and run off into the grass.

Chapter Fourteen

THREE DAYS after she had left Jasper with the turtle in his arms, she went to see him again. She only had three days left before school started. When she walked down into the ditch, he looked up and smiled as always.

"Hey, Ka!" he said in his thin little voice, dropping his face. He began touching the dew drops on the grass, knocking them off into the dirt.

She sat down beside him watching him touch the grass. His legs stuck out awkwardly to the side and there were dark spots and scratches in his white skin.

"Jasper, how did you hurt your legs so?"

He stopped touching the grass and bent over and looked at his white skin. Then he placed a finger on one of the scratches and his skin twitched beneath his own touch.

"Brair, Ka. Brair where turtle go and get chigger."

"You mean that old turtle got away from you?"

"Gone, Ka." Then he looked up at her face, the large pink circles of his eyes quivering. "Look and look but gone, Ka."

"Well, we'll find you another one, even bigger. That one's always going to have your name on it anyway so when someone sees it they'll know who to bring it back to."

While she spoke his eyes had stopped quivering and settled back in their sockets and a white haze seemed to slide over them. His head dropped back down as if it had been released and swung slightly on his neck as he began to touch the dew drops again. He raised his hand, the drops clinging to the end of his fingers a second, before falling off in narrow streams that slid slowly through the fine hair down his leg.

"You shouldn't do that, Jasper, the dew infects things. You are going to make your legs worse."

The thin little shoulders began to shake as he pressed his head against his knees.

"Oh, Jasper. I didn't mean to make you unhappy, Jasper, don't cry." She stopped and thought a second. "Jasper, I'll take you somewhere new if you'll laugh again. I thought about it today and I'll take you to a special place and show you something you've never seen anything like."

He looked up at her with tears in the corners of his eyes and running in the crease beside his nose. "Okay, Ka, won't cry."

She took his hand and they walked down the ditch, his small white body in the shade. The ditch came to an end where a wooden bridge crossed over it and the fescue and the topsoil that had washed down clogged the opening underneath.

"We'll have to go over the top, Jasper. You tell me when the sun gets too hot and we'll find some shade for a while."

They walked along the shoulder of the road while the little colored children in the yards stopped their play and lined up on the edge of their yards. They didn't speak or move their eyes from them as they passed. The air got hotter as they went along and Jasper became more and more irritable, constantly snatching his hand from hers. When they stopped in the shade at the edge of the woods, Jasper said, "Ka, how much more we got to go?"

"Not much more, Jasper. We can cut through the woods now where it's shadier." Then she looked across the field to the railroad tracks that went by the Strawbright farm. She thought quickly of the pennies that she had left under the cross ties. "Jasper, you wait here in the shade and rest. I'll be right back."

Cary ran across the field and dropped to her knees beside the cross tie, reaching under for the pennies. She felt the cool pennies under her finger and lifted them out in her hand. When she put them on the iron runner, she held her hand steady until they balanced on the track. She stood up a moment, looking down at them, before turning and running back to Jasper. He sat under the tree with his legs straight out in front of him with a little swarm of gnats hovering over the sores on his legs. Cary stooped beside them and brushed the gnats out of the sores, crushing some of them on his skin.

"Jasper, you ought to try to keep the bugs out of them."

He looked up at her and, as the sunlight through the tree hit his face, his large red pupils faded to pinpoints and two wrinkles appeared between his eyes.

"The train will come while we're gone and I'll have a present for you on the way back," she said.

A faint smile crossed his face as he said, "present," then he batted his eye shut as a gnat flew into his lashes. Cary reached over and pulled his fist from his eye and picked the wiggling bug from the corner of his eye, watching the lash begin to open and close quickly and his eye become red and watery.

"I got it." Then she stood up still holding his fist and lifted him to his feet beside her. "Come on now. Let's get going again and you listen out for the train."

They walked into the woods and as they finally were surrounded by trees, the little streams of sweat on Jasper's forehead began to dry. His nose and cheeks were flushed a deep red, and the tops of his arms were still shiny with sweat. They walked down the creek bed, dry but for a thin and crooked stream down the center. The ground was soft near the edge of the trickle of water and moss grew bright green with red stalks reaching fragilely above the mother plant. The pale green moss grew up the side of the creek bank, and through the woods the straight brown trees had a pale touch of light on the side where the moss climbed up the trunk and looked like snow on the bank as it caught the sunlight through the trees.

"Jasper, look here! Look here in the water! See that shiny stuff. You don't find that many places. That's real gold!"

Jasper looked into the water, finally dropping to his knees beside the stream and lowering his nose directly over the stream. "Ka, what gold?"

"You've got to look good, Jasper. See the light shining on it? It's that real shiny stuff in the water and it's worth a lot of money."

But Jasper had stood back up and started to walk back down the creek bed. He stopped and turned when he realized she was not with him. She looked into his blank face that he tipped up at her. Since she could not look back at the gold at her feet, she started down the creek bed after him. When they got deep into the woods, the water gathered in pools and the bright green moss had become dark and damp. Overhead in the trees the wild orchids hung gracefully over the limbs, their long orange tongues like flakes of light in the trees.

Jasper stopped and looked up. "Look Ka!" and he pointed at the flowers above him. When he turned to her and began to laugh, Cary's face felt warm. She put her hand on top of his head, but at the touch of his slick skin and the soft bristled hair, she took her hand away, for the skull felt as though it would collapse.

"Look up there, Jasper," she said quickly. "See them blue flowers. They're called iris."

"Let's get some, Ka."

"Oh no, Jasper, we can't do that. I dug up a bunch of them one time, roots and all, thinking I could put them in my garden but they all dried up."

"I want some."

"But they won't live, Jasper. They get all ugly when you try to take them away from their home because it's wet and damp here."

He turned to her and his white face appeared strangely dark. The smile was gone and he balled his little fists.

"It's just like a wild bird, Jasper," she spoke again. "They aren't tough like an old turtle and they won't live if you try to take them away."

Jasper snarled and made a clicking sound in his throat. As he began to walk down the creek bed towards the spring, she called to him.

"Wait for me, Jasper. I want to show you something you've never seen before."

Jasper kept walking in front of her until they came to the terracotta pipe at the spring.

"Oh look," she said. "They've spread all over the place since last year and gotten bigger too."

The coral mushrooms rose under the pine straw, in some places just a lump with a touch of color at the top, but in others a great colored bulb above the ground. Cary bent down and pressed her hands gently around one. But she took them away quickly as she realized they felt like the top of Jasper's head. She stared at the bulb a moment seeing that she had broken away some of its soft pink tentacles with just her touch. It leaned on its side slightly and some of the short roots had pulled from the ground.

Suddenly the pink bulb was smashed in front of her, and as the bare foot was lifted the odor of the crushed plant rose into her face like the scent of decay. She looked up into Jasper's face, but he turned it away from her and began running around under the trees, smashing the mushrooms and kicking them until they rolled over and over with a clump of brown short roots dotted in the color of the uprooted bulbs.

"Jasper, stop it. You're ruining everything." Her lips felt dry as she spoke. "Jasper, why do you always have to be like that? Stop! Quit, please!" she cried.

Then she turned and walked away, the little boy still kicking and spinning under the trees until all of the plants were dislodged. She walked a short distance, hearing the fast pat of his feet behind her, but she did not turn around.

She left Jasper standing in the yard of his house and he watched her with sad eyes when she walked away. Neither had spoken during the long trip back in the hot sun which left Jasper burned red all over and his eyes swollen half shut. As she walked down the yard she stopped; she had to turn around and look. When she looked at him a deep pain spread outward from the center of her chest. The little boy still stood where she had left him. Behind him was a row of little colored children, their brown skin splotched with bright colored clothes. Jasper appeared like a little ghost before them, his body almost transparent in the bright sun. But as she looked at him, his head began to blur and soon she could no longer see him. The smashed mushroom rose in front of her eyes, its pink softness crushed out of shape in front of her. She turned her head and began walking, but she never knew where she was going until she caught her foot in a dead cucumber vine in the garden. Pulling her foot from it, she looked straight ahead and saw the road was there. She walked quickly down the highway, raking her nails up and down the skin on her arms. While she walked beside the road, the cars brushed by, blowing the short hair around her ears into her face. She realized suddenly that she was walking back towards the Strawbrights' place instead of towards town. She was tracing the same path that she had taken Jasper down today, and looking down in the fine sand she saw that their footprints were still there, Jasper's tiny prints weaving in and out and on top of hers. She stopped under the tree where Jasper had sat down in the shade and watched the gnats that had circled around him circle around the rotten persimmons on the ground. As she looked up and across the field to the railroad tracks, she felt the tiny bugs begin to bump and tickle her legs. She walked slowly across the field and stooped again by the iron rail. The two pennies lay beside each other, bent smoothly around the runner. She held the pennies to her lips and touched her tongue to the smooth copper. The copper taste ran between her teeth and into her throat. As she sucked her teeth her mouth began to feel as though it was lined with metal and the taste seeped through her skin.

She stood up and walked back across the field, stopping in the middle of the tall grass when she heard noise coming from where her house had been. She felt the pennies begin to get warm in her hand, and as she stood without moving she began to hear a voice. It was her father's voice, but she could not see him in her mind.

"I guess just about the dirtiest thing in the world is money. You know a million people must have handled it."

The pennies slid from her hand into the grass and she started walking back towards the spring, her throat heaving dry, and chill bumps breaking out on her arms and running down her back. As she walked into the woods the light around her began to die, and only the faint sparkle of the gold could be seen in the stream at her feet. Then she cupped her hands down in the spring and felt the cool water run over her wrists. She lifted her hands and drank, her eyes becoming wet when the cold water ran down her throat. She looked up quickly and the water splashed from her hands back into the spring as she turned around.

"Cary?"

She moved away from the spring and climbed to her feet. She did not speak as she looked at the boy beside her.

"I haven't even seen you since you left here."

She reached behind her until her hands felt the rough bark of the tree. The moss began to crumble at her touch and she heard it fall in the leaves. She looked at his feet then leaned her head back against the tree.

"I just came back here once. That was today," she said quietly, her eyes darting up the trail behind him. "I hear you building."

"Yeah, we're putting your house back. Sam and I. I saw you come across the field. At least I thought it was you and had to come and see if it was."

Cary turned her face away quickly, but Johnny had already seen the tears begin to run down her cheeks.

"Cary, what is it? Is something the matter?"

She shook her head and said, "The water was cold." Then she paused and closed her eyes. "I did a stupid thing."

Johnny began to move uncomfortably but did not speak. Cary bit her bottom lip and started to speak, but her voice was weak and her hands began to tremble.

"You remember when we came down here, you and me and Sam," she said. The tears flowed faster from her eyes but she kept talking. "Then we found the gold in the water and the mushrooms."

"I remember. But I guess it's not gold."

"Look at the mushrooms. He smashed them all."

Johnny began to frown and looked on the bank where the mushrooms had been. The air still smelled of the crushed bulbs that were scattered in the brown straw, their roots upturned. Then Johnny turned back to her and said, "They're all torn up. Did Sam do it, Cary?"

"No, no, not him," she said, shaking her head violently. "Jasper, the little boy we saw by the road, the albino nigger . . . I showed them to him and he did it . . . I didn't know he would . . . I didn't know at all."

"Maybe they'll grow back, Cary."

"I would fix them but they won't live. I can't make them live; they'll just dry up," she said, not listening to him.

"Cary, Cary please don't stay down here and look at them."

She looked up at him and the tears stopped coming from her eyes. "Why?" she said weakly.

"I don't know . . . I don't know how to tell you why. Just don't. Please don't." He turned his face away from her and looked at the scattered mushrooms again. "Just wait until I come and tell you if they come back. I'll come and look and I'll ask Sam if they will or do something. Just don't come back here." He looked up suddenly and they heard Sam calling him from the house. He reached over and pushed awkwardly against her shoulder. "You run home. Don't let him know you're here. If you don't go quick, he'll come down here; I know he'll come looking for me."

Cary began to walk backwards until she felt the cold water of the stream hit her feet.

"Cary, you understand? You do, don't you?"

Her body trembled and tears came to her eyes again as she shook her head. Johnny turned quickly and walked back up the path as Cary started running down the stream. The pebbles in the water hurt the bottoms of her feet, but she did not stop running until she came to the edge of the highway. She walked slowly down the pavement; it still felt warm under her feet. The light began to fade overhead and she saw the headlights sweep under her feet and dash across the trees at the edge of the woods. Each car that went by lighted up the land like a streak of lightning; everything was distinct for a second before it faded back into darkness. When the trees lighted up she saw an opossum amble between the undergrowth, its coarse hair silver for a second. Then it flipped over on its back and its legs stiffened it into a little corpse. When the car had passed by, taking a whining jeer and laughter with it, the night was dark and silent again. Then she thought of all of the animals that were in the forest that she could not see and when the next car passed by, the opossum had ended its bluff and disappeared. She thought of each house that she passed and each car that went by with other people in them and they had their own life and their own thoughts.

Another car went speeding past and she felt a quick shiver when her clothes were sucked into the wind. She began to think, going on down the road, how the driver in that car could have killed her if he had wanted to because she was all alone and unprotected and he was driving in a car. When she reached the end of her street, she stopped and realized that she had planned her own funeral again — walking down the highway — and was watching the stream of people that were going to see her body in the casket, and she was looking at herself too, lying there in a white dress with her hair spread across a satin pillow. She saw Mrs. Strawbright weeping, her big body dressed in her navy blue Sunday dress, and Sam and her own mother, red-eyed, and Johnny. She began to run down the street to her house, dodging in and out around the bushes and jumping to walk down the brick wall in front of the houses. She laughed as she jumped to the ground on the other side of the wall and felt the air cool and wet in her face as her hair blew under her chin.

Stopping on the steps of their house, she heard the soft droning of a man's voice. When she pushed open the door quietly, she saw the glimpse of a broad male back that hid the other figure in the bed, his plaid shirt off his shoulders and dangling from the waist of his pants. When her mother's white fingers came over the shoulders and pressed into the dark skin, Cary pushed the door to and ran into the yard. She ran around to the back yard and stopped beside the rain barrel, clutching its rough, rusty rim with her hand as she felt her legs begin to sway underneath her. Holding onto the barrel she watched the last long red streaks of the sun reach around the house like thin fingers. She walked across the yard between the red fingers until they faded and fell behind her. At her feet she saw a dark odd shape. As she went to her knees, her hands touched the dry, stiff feathers of the black bird. All that remained of it was a gray and black shell with tiny holes pecked to the bone. When she picked it up and held it in her hands, she could not stop from crushing it between her fingers, and the slow snap of the dry skin and bones began to bring back the lost screech of the bird the day it had disappeared into the grass.

Part III

Chapter Fifteen

THE TREES had already bloomed in the Strawbrights' orchard, and when the pink petals littered the ground it was not like litter at all but a soft sprinkle of color under Cary's feet. Where she stepped the petals soaked into the damp ground, spreading in a bruised film like small flakes of flesh. She felt the hard green knobs on the tree, the last clinging petals flaking away beneath her touch. Then she saw the cold and slick baby fruit, tufted at the end. The late blossoms that clung tightly to the stem crumbled between her fingers, and she could almost feel the fruit burst out. Around her feet the petals leaned and slanted across the ground, balancing against the grass blades, and she felt that she should not walk across them. She scooped up a handful of loose petals and walked away to the outside of the orchard where the color was not before her eyes. The smell of the ground rose up wet, seeping slowly into her clothes. She placed the petals on her tongue one by one, blowing them into the air with a short sucking sound.

The winter had been mild, and when the first spring day had come everything blossomed with ease and the ground popped with green plants. Across the road the rye fields lay green and tender, their baby shoots poking up red from the earth, peeling from the core into pale green stalks. The fat starlings sat along the barbwire fence, their square bodies swaying back and forth until one bird would flap its wings and steady the row again. Then the row of birds swooped into the air and leveled out in the pasture towards the fresh scent of horse manure. Cary watched them settle behind the horse, pecking into the smoking manure for the whole seeds. The horse lumbered up the hill, its tail swinging sideways, breaking into a fan of loose stiff hair, then settling again behind it. Its neck bent downward as it grabbed the seeds on the tallest stalks of grass, snapping them from their cores while it walked to the fence.

When Cary saw that the horse was coming to the fence where she stood, she snatched a handful of rye shoots and held them over the wire. The horse hesitated a moment, stopping in front of Cary with a lazy snort, then reached out, wrapping the grass into its loose lips. It stood munching the grass, gazing absently at Cary while a thin green slime dropped from its lips.

Cary touched the short hair on the side of the horse's jaw. When the horse felt her touch, it rippled its skin, jerking its head back. Cary's hand stayed outstretched until the soft, velvety nose of the horse began to rub against her fingertips, finally rolling her fingers into its lips. The cool brown eyes of the horse watched her, a soft blue spot flickering in the center, as she wiped her sticky hand against her jeans.

Cary watched the blue fleck become cloudy in the horse's eye. She moved her hands back and forth quickly in front of the animal's eyes until it started backwards and snorted at her. Cary looked at her hand a moment, then remembered the words her father had said: "A blue-eyed horse is blind." But then the horse looked upward and its eyes were black from the shadows of the tree. Cary held her cheek against its nose and saw a tiny image of herself in a blue shirt in its eye until it tossed its head away again.

The horse rubbed its nose on its front leg, twisting the nostril out of shape. On its back lay loose clumps of winter hair that fell away as it moved. The wrens flitted noisily around in the grass under the horse's feet, flying up with sprays of brown hair in their beaks. Cary thought of the birds lining their nests with the horse's hair, twisting it down into a whirlpool and laying eggs there. She remembered the time she found an old nest and took it apart. The bird had made it of leaves, and sticks, and a piece of string. In the bottom was a caterpillar leaf and some horse hair wound tightly around a piece of paper, and when she took the paper out and unrolled it she found it was the corner of a dollar bill. While she thought of the bird nest, the horse began to chew at the hair on its shoulder, the loose fur sticking to its lips. On the ends of the hairs were tiny white specks.

"Don't do that." She pulled the horse's head away from its shoulder. "You got nits in your hair and they'll hatch in your stomach." The horse looked blankly at Cary, pulled its head away, and began to chew its shoulder again.

A sharp whistle went through the air and the horse's head lifted up, its breath coming in short puffs. Its ears moved back and forth and a stream of mucus ran from its nostrils. The horse's eyes rolled around and a semicircle of white formed on one side of the brown center. Then the whistle sounded again, longer and louder, and the mare threw her head back with a heavy snort. Her feet pulled from the ground with short mud sucks when she wheeled and galloped down the pasture. As she ran and stumbled, stiff-legged at first, brown and green clumps of mud and manure came from her feet and bounced across the ground.

The thick buttocks of the horse swung from side to side as she ran irregularly through the pasture and across the dikes. She snorted and whimpered through her nose when she saw the boy in the shade on the deep end of the pasture, his blue shirt loose and in folds across his chest. He had thrown his books on the ground, and the white pages rolled back and forth when the wind lifted the covers. The horse ran to him and pressed her head against his blue shirt, nudging the boy heavily and lifting his feet from the ground.

"Old girl, old fat lazy girl, you need to get out, don't you? Huh, do you girl? Where's the stallion, girl? Where's the stallion? He's getting too big to stay with his old mother now, huh?"

Cary watched Johnny as he gathered up his books and swung over the wire into the pasture. He rested his books on the mare's withers and jumped onto her back, his legs dangling below her belly. She turned her head and nipped playfully at his legs before he turned her head with her halter and punched his heels into her flanks. At first she began to buck and twist, jolting him around on her back before she galloped up the pasture. She stopped suddenly at the top of the pasture throwing Johnny against her neck. He looked up and saw Cary standing by the fence.

"You out of school?" he said quickly.

"Two of the teachers didn't come so we got out early." Then she looked at him and added, "We don't have but four."

"Where you been lately?"

"Just living in town, going to school; we didn't go anywhere last winter. I just sat in the house and read books and had a pet bird but it died. I don't like it there."

"You know that half-breed girl down near Ellis Grove?"

"Yes, I've seen her I think."

"Well she goes to the regular county school where we go and someone told me unless you were more than half you didn't have to go to District School."

"I heard that before. But it doesn't make any difference to me." Then she looked at him and said, "Except you know at District they're blacker than tar. Not nigger black, just black like about the color of a buckeye and shiny."

"What are you out here for now?"

"I come to ask your mother about work with the eggs and all.

We need the money, Mother says." She heard her words and was surprised that she had said them so easily.

He slid from the horse's back and pulled the barbwire apart and stepped through.

"Hold it. Don't move anymore," Cary said. "You're caught."

He stopped bent between the wire while she took the barb from the back of his shirt.

"Didn't tear. It's O.K."

When he stood up his face was flushed red. "Want to go up and ask her now?"

"No, I'll wait here a while I think," and she turned and looked back across the pasture. He turned and began to walk away and she listened to his footsteps in the soft ground as he went up the path through the orchard.

She looked at the cedar post under her hand; the thin skin scaled off like paper and the weatherbeaten wood showed through the frayed bark. Then she ran her fingers across the gray surface; she felt something soft and powdery that crumbled away. On the tips of her fingers she saw the fine gray-green moss that had clung to the post during the winter. When she lifted her fingers to her nose she smelled the dusty, piercing odor of the crushed plant that went up her nose like pepper. She stood there a moment, digging her nails into the gray surface until the red cedar wood showed through, filling the air with its strange living scent. She picked the flake of cedar wood from under her nail and holding the chip under her nose, began to run up the hill to the house. The horse snorted and jumped backwards when she ran, but she didn't look back, flicking the tiny chip into the grass beside the path.

When she reached the top of the hill near the house, the freshly plowed garden stretched out before her. Two starlings scurried in and out of the upturned clods, making black dashes in the dirt. Around the edge of the garden the ground swelled and

cracked where the moles ran their veins outward, crawling from
the plowed earth. The air smelled of rotten potatoes the plow
had upturned from the dead garden, and they lay in broken
chunks across the ground. On their sides were white patches
where the moles had eaten and the plow had slashed across. She
put her foot on a zigzag mound leading from the garden, and
when she pressed her weight downward the mound folded like
dry ashes beneath it. She followed the mound with her foot,
sinking lightly with each step as she walked, the soft earth seem-
ing to float downward. The mound went into the grass, the brit-
tle stubbles of last year's dead grass snapping as she continued to
walk down the mound. Suddenly her foot arched and the dirt
did not sink, leaving in the air the pale squeal of the mole.

The sound went through her like a needle and she jumped
from the mound to the shallow ditch beside the garden. Then
she looked up into the sky; it was moving in a confusion of colors.
A grayness hung in the air between her and the pink, orange
streaks of the clouds, but they moved in and out in color shafts
passing her eyes too quickly to come into focus. The sun rolled
through them, a bleached orange hole in the sky that opened and
closed like the pupil of an eye. It slipped out into the thin gray
air and glowed orange and pink, still dancing in the center. As
she turned away the spots dotted before her eyes, blotching
around in the sky, surrounded by colorless rays like the streaks of
the clouds. She closed her eyes and the sun spots faded to pale
green and floated there like bubbles. When she held her body
still, she heard the bugs moving through the grass. Chills started
running rapidly through her body traveling in a circle and running through again. In her ears the voice began to swell up,
scolding and complaining, then mixing with the night sounds.
She dropped to her knees, pressing her face against her legs, but
she knew she could never make the voice go away. The stubbles
stuck in the calves of her legs, pressing into her flesh the coarse

dirt at the edge of the garden. In her mind she wanted to sink, like in water, to rest suspended but still sinking and never reach bottom. Then she thought of the mole path, the soft dirt folded beneath her feet and the shriek, the shriek of the little animal, where her feet did not sink anymore. She wondered if the little animal was furry and soft and if he would have stayed there all right if she had left him. She wanted to take back the touch, to stop on the mole path before she got to the end, to open the mound, and see him, but if he were crushed, No!

She heard a voice, and as she opened her eyes and looked up, the weight of the red sunlight pressed against her forehead. On the other side of the garden she saw Sam; his face was turned towards her and he rested his weight on one leg and had his hands in his back pockets. When he began to walk across the garden, she sat up quickly, stretching her legs out in front of her and leaning back against the ditch.

"Cary, what in the world are you doing sitting out here on the ground?"

She didn't speak as she looked up at him.

"I didn't see you all winter. I thought I was bound to run into you when I was in town at one time or the other but I never could see you."

He waited a moment, looking puzzled by her silence, then spoke again. "I went by the house to see you since you didn't have a phone but there wasn't ever anyone there." Then he paused and said, "Mother sent me to ask if you would come out here and stay, but when school started she said to just give up for a while and ask you when I ran into you, but I never did. I didn't even know where your mother worked."

"She sews in Gertey's store. Puts in hems," Cary said absently. Then she folded her hands together on her stomach and began to make a squeaking sound with them. "What if I told you I was there all the time when you came by?" she said.

He was silent for a moment before he said angrily, "Well, you could have come to the door and told me you didn't want to come or something. I was just doing what Mother told me to do."

Cary looked at the grass beside her hand a moment longer and jumped to her feet.

"I'm sorry. I didn't know why you were there," she said quickly. Sam looked at her but did not move. As she looked at him his body began to look strangely small and helpless. His hands hung loosely at his side and his eyes were quiet as he looked straight at her. She turned away without speaking and began to walk across the garden.

When she left Mrs. Strawbright's kitchen, it was beginning to get dark, and the air was blurred with dew and the dizzy flights of the night bugs. Cary had begun to walk from the house. She heard the people moving around in the house behind her as she left the porch steps, so she started running across the garden where she could not hear the sound. Just as she got across the garden she heard Mrs. Strawbright slam the front screen and call to her.

"Cary, won't you let me send Sam with you? I hate for you to be walking on the highway this late."

"I've done it before, Mrs. Strawbright. Don't you worry none; I'm not afraid to go by myself."

"Well, you be careful. If you call me from somewhere when you get in town, I'll rest easier."

"Yes, Ma'am. I'll see you tomorrow."

Cary started down the path on the other side of the garden through the orchard. When she heard the screen shut again, she went back to the edge of the garden and looked at the mole mound. A light smile crossed her face as she saw that the mound continued from the spot where she had pressed her foot on the mole. It had headed underground back towards the garden through the soft soil. Then she turned back down the orchard path and walked around the edge of the pasture to the road.

Chapter Sixteen

AFTER HER FIRST day's work, Cary lay in her bed, listening to the uneven breathing of her mother which rattled dryly across the pillow. Cary was on her side with her ear to the pillow and could hear the slow steady beat of her own heart. Her legs felt tired and numb and seemed to gradually disappear from her body. When she rolled over and looked at the ceiling, she saw the slow drag of the red dots that used to pour across like a swarm of round birds and now only spilled slowly and wearily before her. She reached to her side and without looking away from the ceiling began to peel the paint from around the window sill, listening as it cracked and splintered and hit lightly on the floor. She thought of lying in the grass under the apple trees looking up into the blossoms that dotted together into a mass of unreal pink with the blue of the sky between the gaps. She remembered that the ground had smelled damp and clean, but now she could only feel a coolness deep within her throat as the dry smell of the sheets filled her nose.

She squinted her eyes at the ceiling and the dots began to increase and break apart, speeding before her eyes like the snowflakes of the winter before that fell around and sideways, somehow resting across the ground in a dizzy white. At first the flakes were red, but as she thought of the snow they became white. The sky was white and the earth was white as the flakes continued to spin, hiding every brown twig and wrapping every leaf until the snow began to pile on them in slanted stacks and bend them beneath its weight.

She was walking through the woods following the dotted tracks of a rabbit until they circled back. Then she walked deeper into the woods on the untouched snow, the cries of the birds ringing from the trees. She brushed away the light snow from a rock beside the creek and it fell like dust and dissolved in the water. She watched the water trickling around the clumps of snow, pulling them spinning into the current, as the spring bubbled quietly above, sending a steady stream of clear water into the creek. In front of her the snow lay smooth and she tried to think of the round clumps of color the coral mushrooms had made before Jasper destroyed them and how they would be lying now, the snow spread over them.

When her legs dropped over the side of the bank, her jeans slipped up, the cold air chilling her skin. She looked down at the smooth brown skin of her legs that looked hard and tight beside the snow that surrounded her. Swiftly through her mind ran the colors of skin, and when she lay back and looked at the sky that had grayed because of the pure white earth, the snow fell into her face until she closed her eyes. When her eyes closed her body dropped and got lighter and smaller and the smooth skin of her legs was gone and she saw the whole dark body of Jasper's mother, standing on the porch of her gray house, her skin wrinkled and brown and rough and little Jasper beside her, white and soft. Then Jasper walked across the ground to her as if the earth below his feet were hurting him and the wind and air were too strong for him to bear. The sun flashed from behind the clouds and Jasper turned away from her and ran to the shade tree, but then the bugs swarmed through the air like the sound of machinery and motors and he waved his spindly little arms hopelessly above his head, but the bugs clung to his skin and stung until tiny red bulbs covered the surface of his white skin and he disappeared.

His mother slammed the door of the house and Cary looked away just before he vanished and when she turned back he was not there. His mother swung out a wash tub that steamed in the air and water rolled over the edge, pink with the stain of tomato skins. She poured the tomato scraps and the boiling water from the tub and the ground steamed and the water splashed back at her legs. Cary heard a slow moaning cry that began low and ended in a squeal like a pig as she rubbed the water away from her legs. But as she walked by, Cary, who lay on her side on the ground, saw the wrinkled brown skin was still brown all over and there was no mark where the water had been. The sun came from the clouds again and the legs were white and pink and her mother was there and Jasper's mother had disappeared, and before Cary was the pulpy woman, her legs planted solidly on the ground with the heavy flesh around her ankles slipping over her feet like cloth. Then Cary raised her hand and pressed against her nose until it burned and she saw before her only the needle-sharp veins in the back of her own hand that ran from a point on her wrist outward to her fingers like blue branches in the brown skin. They began to swell and tighten beneath the dark skin and fly up and down until they became slick brown wood and she felt only their movement up and down. She beat the soft pulpy legs in front of her, but they did not move and, even though she could see her fists hitting them, she could not feel them beneath her blows. She felt herself fall backwards, but she kept falling long after the ground should have been reached. But the ground was not there anymore anyway and she was waiting for something to snatch her and then the picture before her eyes was no longer light but the heavy box of the room. She looked for her hands and they were pounding up and down on the body by her that struggled and made short cries each time her fists hit it.

"Cary, stop! Quit that! Stop, are you having a nightmare? Stop! Oh!"

Her mother held Cary's wrists but her hands still pounded up and down. She pulled quickly from the grip of the hands and flung herself facing the wall and everything was silent and black as soon as her body stopped moving.

In the morning Cary saw the first light of the sun fall through the window, for she had been awake for an hour in the gray light before dawn. The yellow-white beams slid around the shades and through the pinholes in the hem around the brown paper, burning them into orange circles. Her eyes felt tightly laced across her forehead and she lay still, her body still sleeping below her while her mind raced back to the night before. She lay there trying to remember why her mother and Jasper had been in her dream until her mother began to stir beside her. Watching the woman move around forced the dream from her mind, so she got up and crawled over the end of the bed. When she stood in the center of the room her feet were cold, until she stepped onto the scatter rug beside the bed. She pulled her pajama top over her head and undid the side button, letting the pants fall around her feet. As she reached for her underclothes on the chair beside the bed, her mother looked dumbly at her, and Cary felt her mother's eyes resting on her body. When Cary began to dress quickly, her mother spoke.

"You have really developed since last fall."

Cary snatched her dress down around her legs and turned to face her. Her skin burned but she could not speak as she looked down at her mother, the woman's heavy breasts hanging off the sides of her chest and her hands folded on her stomach that rose up from beneath the sheets. Cary turned away from her quickly and a moment of horror fled through her body as she was aware of the looseness that had replaced her own firm chest. Her mother spoke again and Cary almost felt a moment of relief as she heard her words.

"You almost beat me to death last night. You must have had some crazy kind of nightmare about somebody after you, pounding and beating me like a crazy man . . ."

"I don't remember it," Cary said hastily. "Well, I kind of remember it but I couldn't have told you what I did. I just remember you were in a dream," she added.

"Well, I'll be a few bruises the better for it I can tell you," her mother said as she slowly sat up in the bed and dropped her feet heavily to the floor. She hung her head over and looked down at her knees that stuck out of her nightgown. Her hair was short and curled into a thick mass of brownish yellow fuzz. She turned over her hands and looked at the pin-pricks in the tips of her fingers.

"Mother?"

The woman on the bed looked at Cary and began to pick the crust away from her eyes.

"I've got something to talk to you about," Cary went on. "Mrs. Strawbright says she needs me more than just part-time because they are going to take on a hundred more chickens as soon as it gets a little warmer."

"Well, I don't see why you couldn't take on some more work. She's always been more than generous about paying."

"But it's not just for work after school. She needs me for the morning feeding so I would have to stay the night there."

Her mother began to frown slightly and shake her head. "Well, now I don't know about that, her having just those two boys and all. That won't look nice."

Cary's face began to tighten and she turned and looked out the window. Then she began to speak slowly, "But I don't like it here. I don't have anything to do and in the summer there are lots of things I can do there."

Her mother's eyes opened wider now as she looked up at Cary in surprise. "Well, you do get uppity for no calling. I certainly haven't asked much of you and fed you all winter. I'm trying to look out for you like your father would have wanted me to. Since he's not around to keep you, it's my job to do it until you're old enough to leave."

"Why do you keep me? Because you like having me here?" Cary asked sharply.

"I keep you because you're my daughter." Her mother brushed her hair back from her face and reached for the bedpost.

As Cary heard the woman's words her skin felt cold and wet and her body began to tremble. Then she walked to the window and said slowly, "I won't be here anymore after today."

Her mother rose slowly from the bed and began to shuffle into the kitchen. Her nightgown stuck in the sweat on her body and began to come loose from her flesh as she moved towards the stove. Cary went to the dresser and ran the brush twice over her hair, stretching a rubber band around it. She picked up her school books without speaking again to her mother and walked out the door toward the corner to wait for the school bus. Since she was early she sat down on the curbing and began to flip through her books, looking aimlessly at the pictures of good posture and poor posture, then let the book fall shut in her lap. When the bus came she got on and fell into a seat behind the driver as the bus began to move. In the back the other students rested on their knees looking over the backs of their seats at the dark girl in the back corner who was reading aloud from a love magazine.

" 'Stephany had never thought of her husband's size as a disadvantage but she now felt the eyes of those around her and overheard their snickers. Once she even heard a man make an obscene remark and had seen her husband's face contort for he too had seen it.' "

The girl flipped the page and one of the other students rose from her seat and sat beside her, peering over her shoulder.

" 'Now Stephany thought about his size when they walked together down the street and as she looked down at him with his head bowed she thought he looked smaller than ever . . .' "

"That story isn't as good as the one yesterday about the girl at the party in the made-over wedding dress . . ."

"Wait; I read it last night and it gets better." Then the girl continued to read.

" 'At night when they lay together in bed she knew her husband now felt he had to struggle to prove his manhood. He was no longer the gentle little man she had loved but a wild jungle beast and their marriage bed was a scene of rape.' "

The girls gasped at the word and told her to read softer as the boys began to turn around in their seats, craning their necks to hear what she was reading.

The bus jolted to a stop and in front of them Cary saw the bright orange bus that belonged to the white school. The two round red lights in the back began to glow as the students poured from the door. She saw Johnny and Sam step from the bus and swing their books around to their hips and begin to walk up the hill to the school. She watched them walk up beside each other, glad that she could look at them without them seeing her. Then Sam turned and looked at the bus a second and nudged Johnny, saying something to him. She leaned back behind the pole beside the driver's seat until they began walking back up the hill, talking to each other. As her bus finally started moving again, she felt that she was in a deep dark shadow and that no one could see her unless they pulled away a shade of dark green leaves that seemed to be in front of her. In the back of the bus the girl's voice was still reading the story.

" 'And she looked down from the big Italian's apartment and to her surprise saw her husband, walking alone like a stray dog down the hot summer sidewalk, and she could not turn away until she felt the now familiar hand of the big man she had so detested on her shoulder . . .' "

Chapter Seventeen

When Johnny came back from the lower pasture, Cary saw him lean his post-hole digger against the barn. Then he took a few steps forward and turned and went back, taking the digger and putting it inside the tack room. She began to walk towards him to head him off on the path so he wouldn't know that she had been watching him. They met as she walked around the grapevine and he looked up at her and began to smile.

"Hi! You ready to go anytime?" he asked.

"Yeah, soon as we eat lunch I guess we can leave. I've finished up what I had to do and the rest I can just put off."

"Well, I've finished all I can do. That ground down there is nothing but mush. Everytime I dug a hole, the slop just slid back in anyway."

"Is Sam still down there?"

They had begun to walk towards the house and Johnny stopped for a moment just as she asked about Sam. "Why do you want to know?" he asked.

Then they began to walk again as she answered, "I just wondered, since your mother mentioned him, what you had planned to do."

"Well, I didn't ask him."

"We can at lunch."

Then Johnny was silent, so she wondered if she should have mentioned Sam. While she and Johnny were eating lunch, Sam came in from the porch.

"Sam, you just turn back around and go right back out and get that mud off your shoes or leave them out there," Mrs. Strawbright said.

Sam turned in the doorway and stood between the screen and the frame as he slid his boots off and let them drop outside. Then he walked across the kitchen in his socks and sat down at the table, resting his elbows there, dropping his head and clasping his hands across the back of his neck. His hands were tanned a deep brown and, as he bent his head over, the dark tan on his neck broke at the place where his shirt hit into a lighter brown that went down his back.

"We couldn't get much done, Mother. It was too wet down there," he said as she walked over to him with his plate.

"I didn't expect you would. It poured all night long."

Then she looked over at Johnny who looked down at his plate. "Johnny," she said sharply, "did you say anything to Sam about taking off this afternoon?"

He didn't look up from his plate and began to shake his head slowly.

"Well, you say something to him now. If you are going to get to take off, then he is too."

"I don't care if he takes off. I just forgot to mention it." Then he turned towards Sam. "Cary and I are going over to see Sloan's harness horse and I thought you might like to take the car and go on into town or something while we are there."

"I'll just go on over there with you. There's nothing else I want to do in particular; I just want to do something besides work on that fence for a change." Then he looked at his mother and said, "With the ground wet as it is, we won't be able to stretch any wire for a few days, Mother."

"Well, it can wait. We haven't got to race with the devil everytime we do something." Then she turned and went back to the sink, clasping the edge of it and looking out of the window.

They finished the meal in silence and Cary glanced up and saw Johnny looking at his mother's back. His eyes were clear and still and his face did not move at all as he slid his plate away from him. Then he got up without speaking and walked out on the porch.

Then Sam said softly, "He doesn't want me to go, does he?"

Cary looked up quickly as he spoke and said, "I don't see why not. We're just going over to see the harness and sulky and I guess he's hoping to get to ride." She got up from the table and said to Sam, "Come on, let's start on over there. I don't know how far it is, but we might not catch him at home if we wait longer."

Sam got up and followed her to the door. "We will see you after a little while, Mother. You know where to reach us if you need us for anything."

"You just go ahead and have a good time. I don't see any reason why I should need you and I'd much rather see you all go somewhere together than work here all the time."

When Sam and Cary got on the porch, Johnny drove around and stopped at the bottom of the steps. Cary got in first and Sam got in behind her.

As Johnny turned the car into the highway, they could hear the hot sticky sound of the tar under the automobile tires and little popping sounds under the wheels until they reached the asphalt section of the main road. After about a half hour of silent driving through the country, Johnny slowed down the car and turned down a dirt road by a mailbox with "Sloan" written on the side. A cloud of dust rose from the tires and wrapped the already powdery yellow bitterweed by the side of the drive.

"It didn't even rain here. The dust is still on the flowers,"

Cary said, but neither of them answered as she spoke. The road began to smooth out and they reached the end of the fence, turning in under the two tall shade trees in front of the house. Johnny was the first from the car and immediately saw Billy Sloan on the porch.

"Sloan, what are you up to?"

"Hey, look who's here. Come on up."

Cary and Sam got out of the car and followed Johnny onto the porch of the house. A dusty looking boy sat on the floor in a tangle of thin straps of black leather.

"You're just in time, Strawbright. Hey, Sam."

Sam nodded at the boy as Johnny began to speak. "You getting ready to take the horse out, huh?"

"Yeah, I thought I would as soon as I soften up the kinks in this stuff."

On the floor beside him was a can of the saddle soap that he was rubbing into the leather with a sponge. Cary walked closer to the leather until she could smell the clean odor of the soap.

"You don't know Cary I guess. Cary, Billy Sloan."

"Hi, I've seen you somewhere, I think. Do you ride?" he asked.

"Yes," she replied, "but I've never had a harness on a horse except to work it."

"Let's go ahead and get Smokey out. I've got a pretty good track scraped off around the pasture that you can really open him up wide on."

He gathered up the harness and they went down the steps and walked towards the barn. Billy pushed back the sliding door on the side shed and walked into the darkness. After they heard a clatter in the darkness, he emerged from the shed between the shanks of the cart, pulling it across the drain ditch outside the barn.

"Hey, that looks sharp," Johnny said, turning to Cary. "You see, Cary, he made it out of two girl's bicycles. He just had the

metal part in the center bent in and welded and used the back
wheel off each of them. It wouldn't be any trouble for us to make
one. All the building you have to do is to make a seat."

Cary walked up and put her hand on the seat as he lowered it
to the ground. "It looks lighter than anything," she said.

Billy answered, "Yeah, a person could pull it with no trouble."
He turned to Johnny. "I thought about slanting my eyes and
starting a taxi service."

Johnny laughed and said, "Some coolie you would make,
Sloan," as he looked at the skinny tow-headed boy who stood
with his legs bent like a horseshoe and his pants piled up over his
bare feet.

Billy grinned and his gums began to show over his teeth. He
stepped out of the shanks of the cart and started around the barn.
"I'll go get Smokey. He's right out back of the barn."

Cary turned to look at Johnny, who was suddenly silent.
"What's the matter?" she said.

He blinked his eyes and turned to her. "I was just thinking
how great it would be to make one of these for the colt. You and
I could work him out with this long before he is big enough to
ride."

"Oh," Cary said and turned away from him.

Then Billy appeared at the side of the barn with Smokey. The
horse threw his head up, peeling his lips away from his teeth and
lifting Billy from the ground. As the horse held his head up,
Billy laughed, his feet off the ground and the halter rope wound
around him. Then he handed the halter rope to Sam and he and
Johnny began to put the harness on him. Cary watched them
untangle the black leather and begin to buckle the straps around
the horse.

"Get the loop under his tail first or you'll never get the other
part hooked up," Billy said. "Uh-oh! Wait a second; I forgot to
unhook the reins."

When they finished putting the harness on, Billy took the cart and rolled it behind Smokey who was shaking his head, flapping the blinkers around his face. They slipped the shanks of the cart through the loop and strapped the cart to the harness. Billy snapped the reins in the loops on the bit, saying, "I'd better work him out a little first and loosen him up. Then I'll let you all take him around. By the time I get all that harness stuff untangled, he's already mad at me." He climbed into the seat and, just as he took the reins, the horse bolted away towards the track. Billy took him to the dirt track around the pasture and gradually loosened the reins until the horse was in a dead trot. After taking the horse around three times, he stopped, jumped out, and handed the reins to Johnny. As Johnny left with the horse, Sam and Cary went to the inside fence and sat on the rail waiting for him to come around. Cary looked at Johnny when he came into the turn by them, but he didn't look up. His eyes were on the feet of the horse that came up almost into the bottom of the cart seat.

"Billy will never get him out of that," she said.

"Yeah," Sam nodded, "I guess you know him pretty well by now."

Then she turned to Sam and said, "What do you mean by that?"

Sam looked over his shoulder at Johnny, who was on the turn on the far side. "Well, he'll go home and that will be all he'll talk about until he makes one for himself."

"Well, I would too if I could."

Johnny came by in front of them and this time he looked up and smiled. "Cary, you'll love this," he called.

When Johnny came around for the third time, he pulled the sulky up about ten feet from them.

"Come on, Cary. Give it a try!" he called.

She climbed down from the fence and walked slowly towards the sulky. When she got to the cart, he picked her up and put her in the seat. Then he handed her the reins, holding for a moment to her hands, saying, "Be careful now. Just keep him in at a trot. Don't let him break because he might throw you out; he broke with me on the last turn when I let him get too fast."

She looked at Johnny for a moment in silence before saying, "You think it's all right for me to try this?"

"Sure it is. It's not hard and I don't see how you'll get hurt with us all here."

"I wasn't worried about getting hurt." She sat back in the seat and put her feet into the brace when Johnny stepped away from the cart. When she straightened the reins in her hands and jiggled them on the horse's rump, he began to move away at a quick trot. She held him down until she began to feel secure in the cart. The wheels banged against every rock on the ground and she felt her weight toss about on the seat. As the horse began to trot harder, she saw his back legs come up closer beneath the platform of the cart until it seemed they would crash into the back of her legs. When she hit the first curve the cart swung to the side sliding her across and lifting one wheel, but when the horse went back into the straight stretch she slid back to the center and gripped with her feet before she went into the next turn. Going by the boys, she tried to look up, but they were past before she took her eyes off the horse.

On the third trip around the horse reached a peak that left the ground and the rocks a blur beneath. Suddenly the speed seemed to be broken for a moment and the cart jerked upward and came down in uneven rhythms.

"He's broke, Cary! Pull him in hard," someone called.

She pulled in on the reins and the horse stumbled a few steps throwing her forward on the edge of the seat before he settled back into a trot. She held him in tightly until she got back to the boys.

"I guess I let him get too fast. It sure is rougher than it looks from the fence," she said breathlessly.

"I just think he's not over being a saddle horse," Billy said. "I can't keep him from breaking either. You did all right. Smokey's not used to girls."

Billy looked around and asked, "Where's Sam? Didn't he want to take him around once?"

Cary looked back at the fence, noticing for the first time that Sam was gone. Johnny said, "He went down to look how you had some wire strung on the fence posts or something. He doesn't care anything about horses."

Climbing back into the seat of the cart, Billy said, "We better keep him running or he'll tear the cart to pieces."

Cary hopped over the side to the ground and Billy slapped the reins against Smokey who jolted forward, sliding Billy back in the seat. Cary climbed back onto the fence beside Johnny asking, "Why did Sam run off? I think he would have enjoyed riding."

"Because I rode first, I guess."

Cary slid from the fence when the cart went past again and turned to face Johnny at the edge of the track. "I'll be back in a minute." Before she could see the expression on his face, she turned and ran towards the back pasture. As soon as she got around the edge of the barn, she saw Sam down at the bottom of the pasture with his arm resting on a post. She crawled under the fence and began to walk towards him, hoping he would not turn around. When she got to the fence beside him, he jerked quickly away from her, trying to relax against the post, but his body seemed rigid and uncomfortable.

"Why aren't you up there riding?" he asked awkwardly.

"Because I came to see what was wrong with you," she said quickly.

"Well, nothing's wrong. I can just think of things I'd rather do."

"You mean you wouldn't like to ride the sulky?"

"Oh, I wouldn't mind. I just don't see much point in it."

Cary reached down and pulled a seed stalk from the grass by

the fence, listening for its squeak as it slid from the plant. Then she said, "I'm glad I rode it. I've never felt anything like that before. It really feels faster than it looks when you're just watching."

"Johnny is always trying to do something that makes him feel like he's not just living on a farm. Everybody notices that and they talk about it too. He could go to the State Fair anytime and see that the professionals have those sulky horses and not a bunch of homemade carts."

Cary wound the grass around her wrist and slid the seeds off between her fingers. "But you just get to watch them. It's different when you get to do it yourself."

Sam turned from the fence post and started walking back towards the barn. Cary walked behind him until she heard the sound of the horse trotting in the corral, then she ran to the edge of the fence beside Billy. She felt Sam walk up beside her and rest his elbows on the fence. When she glanced sideways at him, she watched his eyes as the horse went by, but they did not follow the red flash of the sulky.

Then he turned to Billy and said, "You should have put another strand of barbwire over your stock wire, Billy, because the cows are going to reach over to eat grass and push it down."

Billy didn't turn away from the horse and said, "Think so? I'll watch out for it."

"You wait and see. Even if they have enough grass on the inside . . ." And Cary walked down to the gate of the corral where the sound of the sulky rose above his voice.

Cary and Johnny drove into the driveway in late afternoon of the next day and pulled the car up beside the barn. The trunk was wired shut to hold two bicycles which they had bought at the junk yard.

Johnny turned to her and said, "Now all we have to do is get someone out here to weld those two things together. Wish I had thought about it and we could have dropped them by on the way."

"I know one blacksmith it's not going to be," Cary said quietly.

"Oh, do you mean Maurice?" Johnny said, then thought a minute. "But there again I don't know of anybody else around here that could do it. Come on, we'll take them by to him and then tonight you can get started on the sanding and I can work on the seat."

Johnny turned the car around quickly and Cary felt a collapse within her chest and was unable to answer him. She glanced sideways at him, but he wasn't watching her as they rode back down the dirt drive. The dry dirt from the road slid in the window until her nose and throat were clogged. She felt inside that she was being swept along and could not resist the movement.

The car turned in beside a car graveyard and Cary saw a thousand bits of glass sparkle in front of them as they headed down the overgrown road. The sun was bright in her eyes, and she turned her head and held her hand up to the side of her face. Under the tires was the sound of crushing tin as they rode over beer cans and bits of the crushed cars. As they moved further down the road the vines that covered the cars began to thin and there were flashes of color over the heaped wrecks. The rust that had turned the cars into a soft brown beneath the green gave way to the flashing chrome and tin of the newer cars, but their doors and windows were broken open in the same frightening way.

"I hate those things!" she said finally, and her voice rang through the silence so that Johnny started forward in the seat.

"What things?" he said, and then when she didn't answer he replied, "Oh, you mean them, the cars?"

"I hate those car graveyards!" she said, almost as loudly.

"Well, they have to put them somewhere, but I guess they are sort of gruesome."

"You see all those brown streaks on the seats and around those pushed out windshields? That's blood and they didn't even bother to get it out."

"Yeah, I never thought about it but a lot of people died in them. I saw one bad accident on the highway and I stopped to look but you can bet I'll never stop again." He went on to talk about the accident, but Cary had ceased to listen and wished he would stop talking.

When Johnny was silent she said, "This is just the place I'd expect to find that goddamn Maurice in."

Then Johnny pulled the car up beside a dark brown building covered with peeling signs. They got out of the car. When a man appeared at the door, she stepped behind Johnny. It wasn't Maurice.

"Help you with something," the man said. He was dark and wiped his hands on his rag of an undershirt.

"We were wondering if the smith was in and if he was if he was busy."

"You mean Maurice. He's in the back. I'll holler for him."

The man disappeared into the darkness of the shed and called Maurice's name. The sparkle of lights in the back faded into darkness and, in a few minutes, Maurice stood in the door, his shoulder pressed against the wall. He frowned when he saw Johnny and said, "You want me?"

"Yeah, I've got some welding I want you to do, right now if you could."

"What is it?"

"I'll have to explain it when I show it to you but I want you to weld the center bars on a couple of bicycles to make a cart."

"You got them with you?"

"They're in the car."

"I can do it now I guess. Jack, get them out for me." Maurice turned to the dark man who had been at the door and he walked by them towards the car. "Is it like what I did for Sloan?"

Cary stepped behind Johnny as Maurice walked by. "Yeah,

that's it. I thought you must have done Billy's for him," Johnny said.

"It'll cost you ten dollars," he said dryly.

"That's O.K. I've got it. I thought it would be about that."

Cary heard the rattle as the bicycles hit the ground, but she did not turn around. Then Jack rolled them by her and into the shed. Maurice turned to follow Jack into the shed and, as he turned, his eyes met hers before he disappeared. Though he was already gone, she turned away quickly.

Johnny took her into the shed and she saw Maurice lift the bicycle up on an old automobile wheel before he began to saw the bars with a hacksaw. The inside of the shed was dark and gloomy, the floor covered with automobile parts that were showered with steel filings.

Maurice walked away from the tangled pile of bicycles and bent over with his back to them. Then he pulled the dirty shirt he had on over his head and wadded it in his hand, throwing it in the center of a wheel on the floor. When the shirt had gone up his back, she saw streaks of skin that were pinched together. His face shield clattered to the floor and he bent slowly to pick it up; she began to feel a tight, aching feeling down the inside of her legs. She stepped away from Johnny and sat down on a stack of tires on the floor, pressing the palms of her hands against her thighs.

Johnny looked down at her, but her eyes were on Maurice who turned and walked back to the bicycles. When he started the torch again, flashes of light went across his dark chest and light went under his chin, darkening the pits in his face that blurred beneath the shield. She watched the muscles move beneath his dark tight skin and the long scars on his arms that seemed to resist the movement of the muscles. He cut off the torch, and the sparks bounced and died on the floor as he began to tear the bicycle with quick flashing movements of the saw, letting the scraps fall flatly into the dust at his feet.

As she listened to the monotonous sound of him working, his movement was strange and animal-like; he seemed to devour the bicycle before him. Johnny had not moved at her side, and it seemed for a moment that all the life had left him. Her eyes began to feel heavy and she jerked backwards each time the torch flashed again and the sparks spread and disappeared like fireworks. The monotonous sounds in her ears began to build up, and before she could move or run, the voice came back to her again. She didn't have to think this time; it was the voice of her mother . . . over and over . . . "No man as little as you . . . near 'bout black as a nigger . . . look twice . . . look twice . . . man enough for any woman." As the voice reached a screaming pitch within her, she looked up and in the sparks saw Maurice's eyes, but they did not look at her, at her breasts, as they did at her mother's.

She felt her arms start to reach for Johnny but then she ran and was outside. In front of her the heavy clumps of cars seemed to mock her with bats and birds slowly flying in and out of the dangling doors. She looked frantically all around her but no one was there. Then she screamed shortly as two hands grabbed her from behind.

When she heard Johnny's voice call her name, she began to cry and laugh at the same time. As she spoke, her words were broken and jumbled, "It could have been him, Johnny . . . Johnny, it could have . . . it's so ugly . . . and I feel uglier . . . and I see him . . . Johnny!" She screamed his name and he led her to the car. She lay face down on the seat beside him and couldn't stop her body from jolting.

Then she looked up at Johnny. His eyes were frightened and his right hand gripped the steering wheel tightly, the skin on his knuckles stretching thin and white. "Cary, please tell me what's wrong. You have to tell me something."

She began to speak again and her chest trembled violently beneath her. "I want to kill him, to beat him and claw him, and cut him up with a knife and beat him until he is not there anymore, that's what I want when I see him there tearing up that thing. I want something to fall and crush him but . . . but then I want someone to crush me. I want someone to hurt me — that's what I wanted!"

"Who, Cary? Do you mean Maurice? I don't understand."

Then she dropped her face on the seat. "I wish I was dead. I wish I could die right now. I hate myself worse than I hate him. Everytime I see him I think of him with her and how he could have been my father and how . . . and how she and my father must have been and I hate her."

Johnny frowned and tried to put together what she was saying. "Cary, what do you mean? He wasn't your father."

She began to breathe deeply and her eyes grew calmer as she heard him speak. "I know, I know," she said softly, "but it wouldn't have made any difference to her. He could have been."

She was silent now and Johnny began to speak. His voice was close and she could feel his hand on her face. "Do you mean he knew your mother?"

She felt her face burn as she looked up, but she could not see Johnny's face. "I saw them together, at our house. She must have known I saw him because I never saw him there again." Then she saw Johnny's face as he turned and looked down at her.

He said, "You mean she . . ."

Johnny shook his head and sat back in the seat, silent for a moment. "You'll be all right, won't you, if I go and tell him that I'll come back tomorrow and pick up the sulky."

"Yes," and she sat back up in the seat and watched him bang his fist against his leg before he disappeared behind the door.

As they rode back towards home, Cary sat with her elbow on the door and her fist bumping monotonously against her chin. She looked out the window with the fields bobbing up in front of her eyes until she began to feel nauseated. When she took her elbow off the bumping door, the fields smoothed out and they had begun to pass the unpainted houses in the Negro section. Then she saw a group of small Negroes in a field. A gray and broken tennis ball wobbled over their heads until it came to a dead stop in the dust. A small boy picked it up and hurled it back up sending a spray of dust into his eyes.

When he dropped to the ground with his fists in his eyes, Cary said suddenly, "Stop, Johnny!"

"What?" he replied as he hit the brakes of the car.

"Stop a minute and let me out. I'll be right back."

Johnny stopped the car and she opened the door before it stopped rolling and stepped out on the ground, leaving the door open. She ran down into the ditch beside the road where the grass was tall and stung her legs. As she climbed over the side of the ditch, the little Negroes stopped playing, the one with the sand in his eyes walking towards her. His cheeks were wet with tears, but he smiled at her with his head cocked to the side. He stopped about ten feet in front of her and turned his head further to the side. When she walked up to him, he looked into her face silently.

"Do you live around here?" she asked.

He turned without speaking and pointed to the brown house behind him.

"Do you know a little boy named Jasper, a little Negro boy with sort of pinkish skin?"

He still did not speak and stepped back into a group of little colored children that had gathered behind him.

Then Cary turned to the largest boy in the group and asked again. "Do you know a little colored boy named Jasper? I know you would remember him because his skin was white."

The little children began to look at each other, but the largest boy looked straight at her and replied, "He's gone."

"Oh, they moved away? But weren't you here when I used to come to see Jasper before?"

"Mama said you had no business here."

"Then Jasper was your brother," she said quickly. "You're the right one then."

"But he done gone somewhere."

"Well, where is he? I'm not going to bother him. I just wanted to know about him and how he was getting along."

"He done went to the spring in order to get away from the bugs."

"Which way is the spring? Is he down there now?"

The larger boy was quiet and the little children ran away. Cary watched them as they all hid behind trees in the yard and peeped out at her. The boy kept looking at her and shuffled his feet in the dust.

"Well, if you won't tell me, I'll go see if I can find him."

"No! No!" the boy cried and jumped in front of her. Then he stepped back and looked at the ground. "I mean he ain't down there now. He just went down there one day."

Cary began to grow impatient with the child. "Then why did you say he was there?"

"I didn't say he was down there. I was fixing to tell you what happened to him."

Then the child was silent again. "O.K., now tell me where he is," she asked again.

"He's up yonder under that tree where Mama put him." Then the boy turned and pointed at a tree that stood behind the house. He went on, "She won't let none of us go round there and she would beat dickens out of me if she knew I told you he was yonder."

Cary looked at the tree. It stood in the shady part of the yard where the branches of all the tall trees were intertwined. The dirt was beaten smooth under the other trees but here there was a tangle of weeds and vines. Her heart seemed to drop inside of her as she turned suddenly back to the little boy.

"You mean he's dead! Jasper's dead?"

The boy began to cry and started to run, but she held his arm. "What happened to him? Did he just die?"

The boy whimpered and tried to pull away from her. As she held tighter to his arm, he began to talk, "He went down yonder, to the spring, and I seen him there but he was in the water. He done fell in I guess. He was in the water and didn't none of us do it. Mama beat us to death because she thought one of us done it, but it won't so. He done it when he won't with us. Didn't none of us do it."

She released the little boy and he ran back to the others that hid behind the trees. She heard the porch begin to rattle as their mother walked out and looked across the field. Cary ran back down across the ditch and climbed into the car.

"Hurry, Johnny! Hurry, let's leave!"

He started the car, and as they moved down the road she pulled the door shut.

"What did you talk to them little niggers about?"

"They killed Jasper."

"They killed who?"

"Jasper, the little albino. Don't you remember him? The little white nigger."

"Aw, they wouldn't have killed him. He couldn't live long anyway."

"He drowned in the spring and I took him to your spring once. You remember I took him to the clean spring on your place to show him the gold in the water and the mushrooms and he stepped all over them? Do you think he might have fallen in his spring looking to see if gold was in the water?" Her speech was hysterical again as Johnny stopped the car by the side of the road. His hands were trembling and he rested his forehead on the steering wheel. Then Cary jumped as she heard his voice loud after the long silence.

"Why don't you stop it? Why don't you?" She looked at him blankly and did not answer.

"You don't have to go back home anymore. You don't have to even see your mother. And that little boy . . . that little boy couldn't even see those mushrooms like you did. Don't you know that?"

She turned her face away from him and pressed her hands together but still could not answer.

"Why didn't you tell me about Maurice before I took you there? If I'd known about your mother sleeping with him, I wouldn't ever have let you go there. And then you make me stop where that albino lived and you'd already found out a long time ago that he just would hurt something you loved. You just sat right there and let me take you there."

Cary yelled back at him, "I'm sorry. I shouldn't have told you about anything."

"Dammit. That's not what I meant." Then he moaned and leaned back in the seat. "I don't mean to sound mad at you. I just want to tell you something" — then he paused and said — "but I'm not sure what it is." He started talking slowly again. "You just don't show things like those mushrooms to a little kid. They don't know no better than to tear them up. Any little kid would tear them up and not think nothing of it."

Cary looked down at her lap and spoke, "I just had been saving them to show somebody and I thought . . ." She stopped talking as her mind began to cloud up.

"I'm sorry he died." She jerked her head up quickly as Johnny spoke. "I am."

He started the car motor again but did not put it in gear as the car began to vibrate. "We'll go the other way home, O.K.?"

"Why?" she said as the car began to roll forward.

"Oh, I don't know. There are just a bunch of farms with some ponies and they probably have some little colts."

Cary looked out of the window as the fields began to move by again. "I bet those little colts aren't much bigger than dogs are they?"

Johnny turned to her and smiled, his eyes flickering with white dashes across them. "Not much, they're just little balls of fur with legs."

The white fences of the pony farms began to go by the car windows as Cary said to Johnny, "Can we stop and watch them? I mean for a little while."

He pulled the car off the road and stopped the engine. "Sure we can. Come on." Cary followed him to the fence as the little ponies looked up and began to move towards them.

Chapter Eighteen

WHEN CARY WALKED into the hen house that evening, the chickens hopped from their nests and ran back out into the lot. She reached in the nests and clutched the rough brown eggs between her fingers, laying them in the bottom of the basket where they wobbled and bumped against each other. Through the plastic paper on the window, the sunlight came in filtered streams, catching the dust in the air. The dust flakes began to swirl when she passed by, rushing and disappearing into the air beyond the sunbeams. As she placed her hands in the nests, she felt the warm excelsior where the heat from the hen's underside remained in the curled wood shavings.

She stopped, setting down the heavy basket, and remembered standing behind the smoke house with the warm chickens pressed against her side. She was waiting with a white chicken under each arm for Papa to come for them. Johnny and Sam and the Negro tenants had handed their chickens over first and gone back to work, but she had held hers until last, feeling their warmth sinking into her side and their soft white feathers under her fingertips. Papa had come around the smoke house and, without a word, taken the chicken from her left side and walked back around the shed. She had held the other chicken against her chest and rubbed it under its red comb until it clucked and hummed deep in its throat. She ran her fingers up the smooth feathers on its throat, clutching her hand around its full puffy craw. When the squawking began behind the shed, the chicken began to squirm in her grip, its yellow claws digging into her arms. A thump came from behind the shed and then the clatter of wings on the ground. When it was silent again, Papa walked around the barn and took the chicken from her. He looked down at the jagged scratches on her arms and said, "You know better than that. I told you to hold her feet."

She had seen the lines deepen in his face as he looked at her scratched arms and clutched the chicken by its feet, carrying it upside down and flapping around the shed. She had begun to run, but she could not outrun the thump behind the shed. The squawking had stopped when she reached the corner of the house, and the only sound was the feeble beating of the wings in the dust.

Cary's nose began to tingle with the smell of wet feathers and scalding water, and she rubbed her nose with the back of her hand. She thought of the stacks of chickens, picked clean and pink, stacked up, lifeless and all just alike and how you no longer cared that they were dead then. She wondered why she had thought of that, as she saw the white chickens peeping curiously at her through the door. They began to walk slowly in, reaching with their orange claws stiffly outspread and grasping and piercing the wood shavings on the floor. When Cary began to shell corn she had tied in her apron, they rushed in the door, dragging their beaks across the floor in search of the grains.

She took each ear and rolled it under the palm of her hand then tossed the cob towards the stack in the corner. Listening a moment for the rattle of the corn grains as they went down the chickens' throats, Cary picked up the egg basket. She went out and latched the door and the soft clucking and scratching of the chickens was still in her ears as she walked up the path to the house.

After she put the eggs away, she went upstairs to her room. "Cary!" She turned on the steps and looked down at Johnny. "Are you O.K.?" he asked. She cocked her head to the side and stared at him. "What are you looking like that for? You know what I mean. You're not still upset about what happened today are you?"

She smiled at him and said, "No, I'm fine," and turned and ran up the steps to her room.

The air was eerie-feeling in the room, as if she were outdoors. The curtains drifted back and forth as if she were in a soundless vacuum, because the wind was blowing noiselessly. Just as she walked to the window the lightning flashed and she jumped back. For an instant she could see the bright green of the trees, then everything was black again. She began to undress, putting on her nightshirt, but did not take her eyes from the window while she slowly buttoned it down the front. The thunder rumbled over and over in the distance like an enormous pile of falling rock going down a slope, stopping and quietly rumbling as it settled to the ground. The wind began to pick up and the curtains blew straight out from the window, stiffening there a moment, before they were sucked through the window. Then the trees rattled as the first drops slashed through and fell with thumps in the dust. The few pellets of hail that came with the first drops clattered on the tin roof of the barn. In a few seconds the rain fell thickly, and a sheet of water poured from the gutter and splashed on her window sill. She walked over and watched it make spots in the dust on the sill, then soon it was washed clean and the water began to come in. She pulled the wet curtains in and shut the window. The lightning flashed through the glass and she blinked her eyes and started backwards. The front of her nightshirt was wet now and clung against her skin that browned the white cloth in spots. She jumped as she heard the wind suck a door shut downstairs and the glass prisms around the bottom of the living room table lamp tinkle against each other, and she wondered how long she must have been standing at the window. She clutched the front of her nightshirt and squeezed it; a few drops of water fell to the floor, and when she let it go, it slowly untwisted.

She turned around in the room; the air felt hot against her face. A dusty moth bumped around her light bulb and she looked away, seeing a mass of black bulbs bounce in front of her eyes. The rain got harder and the lightning lit up her whole room as she pulled the cord cutting off her light. When she went back to the window to look through, wiping her breath away from the glass so she could see, she felt the dry dust in the floor under her feet. She opened the door and went into the hall and heard Johnny and Sam and Mrs. Strawbright shutting the downstairs windows. Then she pulled her door to silently and went down the stairs into the kitchen and onto the back porch.

She took the night latch off the back door and stepped out quickly into the rain. In an instant she was wet all over and the water ran thickly down her legs. The rain barrel wobbled beside her because of the sheet of silver water that poured into it from the gutter, running over the sides and under the steps. She ran through the mud to the barn and stopped under the shed where the ground was dry. When she turned back to the house she saw the light in the window with the sparkling prisms and pink flower on the white globe go out as instantly as the lightning. For a moment she was frightened as she stood in the dry shed, but when she stepped out into the rain again and the lightning lit up the ground around her, she only thought of running across the garden to the orchard.

Wet plants slapped against her legs, and she felt better when she was walking through mud on the path away from them. She started running again and did not stop until she was under the umbrella tree beside the new tenant house. The little white house set exactly where the black hole had been, and as the lightning flashed again, lighting beneath the house between the rocks that held it up, it looked as if it was not connected to the ground. The rain only trickled slightly through the umbrella tree that was thick with leaves, and the moss under her feet was damp. She looked down and saw that the moss was growing there now across the three little graves and grew in white splotches up one side of the tree. When she began to walk out from under the tree, the rain hit her face again and she could still feel the moss under her feet, soft and wet, that grew all along the path to the spring. She passed through the woods by the spring without looking down and walked towards the creek bed.

When she looked across the flattened broomsage, she saw the bend in the creek where the dead animal used to be. Then she went to the edge of the bank, but the water had risen over the top of the bones. When she went down the side the bank crumbled and she stumbled over into the water. Her hands reached through the water and suddenly she felt vines and slime and bones wrapping around her legs like something alive with a thousand hands. She jerked her feet from them and rushed from the water towards the bank.

The bank was slippery and covered with wet plants and she moved on her stomach, getting mud on the front of her nightshirt. She stood a moment on the top of the bank letting the rain wash the mud from her clothes, but the slime clung to her legs and she rubbed them until they burned. The water rolled over and over moving quicker than her eyes could follow, and the rain fell in quick stinging blows, stopping and slashing across her body again as the wind broke through. Too many things were running through her mind for her to understand. She turned and watched the trees behind her, waiting for the lightning to flash and light up the dark black shafts.

She waited, watching the dark trees while the rain blurred her eyes. She trembled and knew she did not want to see the straight empty trees but wanted to see a person come between them. The thunder rolled over and over and she looked at the black trees until her eyes burned. Quickly and gone again the lightning came, and the dark shafts of the trees came and left as quickly. Her body shook more when she thought that she did not come out there to be alone but for someone to come to her. She heard the thunder still rumbling like the voice that scolded her in her mind, in the distance, speaking again and again but without words.

The rain began to fall steadily again, swallowing the wind that had blown in the lapse. Behind her the water sloshed along monotonously and the trees in front of her rose in black shafts again as the lightning flashed. She felt her heart beating all through her body and deep in her throat as she started to scream, but then she stopped. Listening to the pounding noises of the water and the thunder she knew how small her voice would be. Then she started running back up the path, the ground passing swiftly under her feet and the rain tossing her off balance. When she slipped back through the door, she pressed it shut until the night latch clicked. Leaning back against the door she waited until her heart and breath grew quiet again. Although the rain jarred the door behind her back, the house was still and quiet around her. She looked up the dark stairs, lighted only by flickers as the lightning broke apart, waiting until she could walk quietly back up the stairs to the dusty room and no one would know that she had left.

When the sun came through the apple prints on the curtains of her room, the design faded to a washed-out pink. The curtains hung in place as stiff as a sheet of glass in front of the open window. Cary felt the hot stillness of the day outside as the sun came in, in white-hot shafts. In the air was an odor of evaporation of wet dirt as the sun parched the earth after the storm of the night before. Cary lay in bed and felt her body begin to sweat and heard the dry irritating sounds of the flies hitting her window screen. Her nightshirt had dried and her bed was filled with grit from the mud she had gotten on her at the creek the night before. She threw the sheet off her body and began to bang her feet up and down until she felt she had the energy to sit up on the edge of her bed and get up. She went to the window to push open the curtains which felt strangely hot and soft beneath her touch. On the ground below the window, the water still stood in puddles and flashed back at her like reflections from a mirror.

She moved her face slowly from side to side and the puddles faded and flashed, then faded again. As the light hit her eyes in flashes, she felt she was remembering something, but it would slip away each time before her memory could grab it. Something would spin and flicker before her eyes, then fall away and tumble to the ground. Outside a bucket fell beside the steps and she heard heavy footsteps on the porch, and the soft thump-thump of the bugs against the screen. She put on the same dress she had worn over to the Strawbrights' when she started work, leaving a stack of new dresses in the chair. When she walked into the kitchen, Mrs. Strawbright turned away from the stove and her eyes dropped from Cary's face to the dress she had on.

"Didn't you see the new dresses I made for you? I was afraid they might not fit since I was just guessing."

Cary looked at her a moment and turned away, because she could not find an answer. Then she said, "You hadn't said anything about it, Mrs. Strawbright, so I didn't know what to do." She stopped suddenly and said, "Why did you make them for me?"

Mrs. Strawbright turned away from her and Cary heard the slow scrape of the spoon in the bottom of the oatmeal pan. "I thought you needed some new things. They aren't anything fancy, just some sack material. I've had the material lying around for a long time and a lot of time at night for sewing this winter."

She put Cary's plate in front of her on the table and Cary sat down and began to eat. She looked up as the back screen slammed and Johnny walked in from the porch. His hair was uncombed and he began to tuck in his shirttail when he saw Cary.

"Mama, I wish you'd tell Sam to go in through the barn instead of the gate. He left it open last night, or at least somebody did, and I found the mare and the stallion both loose down near the spring. Just lucky they didn't wander off or go out near the road or something."

The back screen slammed again and Johnny turned around. "Sam, did you know the horses got out last night?"

"No. You find them?"

"Yeah, I found them without any trouble but it could have been bad. You forgot to latch the gate."

"No, I didn't either. I didn't even go out there last night."

"Well, who did?" Then he turned to Cary and said, "Did you?"

"No!" she said quickly and turned back to her breakfast. After she finished, she went out of the kitchen down the path towards the chicken house. Ahead of her she saw Otis. He looked up when he saw her and looked quickly back to the ground.

"Hi, Otis," she said.

The old man looked up at her and a weak smile crossed his face. "Hey, Miss Cary. You staying with the Strawbrights now?"

They had stopped and were facing each other in the path.

"Yeah, she's taking on more chickens you know, and she needs me in the morning to do the feeding like I did when Papa and I were here."

The old man nodded his head that trembled slightly on his neck when he tried to hold it steady again.

"I knowed you was here. I seen you running around in the rain last night."

"What?" she asked quickly.

"I seen you out there last night." Cary looked at the old man and turned away as his head began to wobble more. "The way them horses was dancing around in that thunder they could have trompled you to death out there."

"I didn't go near them. I thought I left something down at the creek."

"Them horses was cutting up and squealing in that thunder."

"Did you know the horses got out?" she said.

He looked up quickly and a white rim formed under the bottom of his eyes. "No! No . . . they get out? I didn't know that they got out."

"Yeah, but Johnny found them. It could have been bad though. Somebody forgot to shut the gate."

"Oh, oh . . ." he muttered as he started back down the path. Cary stopped and turned and was surprised as she found herself looking into the eyes of the old man again. His face was twisted and his chin tottered up and down a moment, until he forced his old body to turn around and walk back up the hill.

Chapter Nineteen

SCHOOL had let out and the hot sticky June nights were short after the long hours of day. Sixteen days had passed without rain since the thunderstorm, and the baby plants cracked the earth like broken scabs. Cary had not been in town or seen her mother since spring. She lay in her bed at the Strawbrights', listening for the heavy drunk June bugs that hit against her screen, feeling in her eyes their cool oily blue shell that always felt soft and moist when you caught them to tie a string on their legs. The droning of the bugs outside and the lone fly that swooped around her room, occasionally trapping itself in the folds of her bed sheet, rose to a machine-like sound of trees falling under a chain saw. In the distance over the sound of the bugs, she began to hear a familiar sound approaching and it moved with such force and speed that she could only wait, for once it had been thought of nothing could stop it. Tonight it seemed to come closer than before and instead of being only a complaining sound, she could hear words for the first time, over and over . . . "Dry June . . . good crop . . . dry June . . . good crop . . ."

She had always wondered about the words of the complaining voice and what they would be when she someday heard them. The voice was her mother's but she would never have spoken those words. In the same distance that the voice had come from, she began to hear the sound of hooves pounding in the soft dirt, snorts, and whinnies; and the sound of thunder somewhere far away. Then she heard the sound of a screen door slamming and footsteps on the porch that stopped a moment until the hooves were quiet. Then as the door slammed again, she felt her body jump, but it did not resist sleep and the air became silent.

Each night after that, the same maddening rush of sounds from outside filled her room. She no longer thought of the voice, because the outside sounds never left it the silence it needed to creep into her mind. Everyone was always asleep before her, because she had to dry the tubs full of eggs and stack them in the crates. Then in the bed each night, the same noises that hurt her forehead and could not be muffled under her pillow came again. Always she heard the sound of thunder, but no rain slashed through the trees and the sky did not flash with lightning; the June just went on, thirty days without rain. She heard the short panting of the horses as they moved restlessly around, and their breath sounded almost human. Then she heard the wood fence creak, and a short squeal, feminine and pathetic. She sat up in the bed and her eyes were open with fright. The horses coughed and whined slightly as before, but the pounding of their hooves in the dirt had a different sound. Before, the animals were moving restlessly because of the heat and the storm in the distance she thought, but now there seemed to be something all wrong in the air. She got out of bed and left her room, walking down the dizzily quiet staircase to the door. The house was black dark, but outside the moon lighted up the porch and she could see the green leaves of the plants in the cans on the gray railing.

As she walked towards the barn, she stayed in the shadows, afraid of the yellow-white paths of moonlight across the sand of the yard. Close to the corral the noises grew louder, and just before she reached the slatted gate a chill swept through her body and the sound in the corral became all human. The gate was unlatched and stood slightly ajar, making everything suddenly all wrong. She spread her long hair across her chest and leaned slowly around the edge of the barn, expecting something to rise up scorching into her face. Instead, the bright moonlight from the clear area hit her face with a cool burn, and before her she saw the old man, Otis, with his back to her. The top of his hair and his shoulders were white with the moonlight, his body naked from the waist up. His old shoulders looked crinkled and child-like in the light, as if they had never grown. In his hand flashed a sheet of tin, the white light flickering through the nail holes. As she watched, the thin old shoulders began to tremble violently, finally the tremble descended into the arm where the tin folded and unfolded.

Suddenly the air was filled with the memory of the thunder all the nights she had lain in bed and waited for the raindrops that never came. The sound grew louder and was no longer like thunder but was the clattering of tin. From the dark under the trees on the other side of the pasture, a huge white creature rose up, and Cary saw Johnny's stallion come out, snorting and whinnying, its body twisting beautifully beneath the slick summer coat. The noise stopped and the horse walked towards the old man, its nose bouncing along the ground in the direction of the tin. When the pink, whiskered nose got about three feet from the tin, the old man began to shake it again. The horse flung itself backwards and fell on its side in the grass, its four soft unshod hooves pointing upward. Then it pushed itself up again on its front feet and crouched in front of the old man with its eyes rolled back deep in its head. The old man walked towards the horse and Cary saw the dark genitals drop lower. The old man began to laugh, a light shrill laugh like that of a woman and the horse walked backwards, its back legs bent up under its chest and its eyes on the tin in the old man's hand. Otis shook the tin once more, but the brassy sound left instantly as the horse bolted forward, dropping the old man who slid his face under the tin. The horse pawed a moment at the tin and the old man groaned beneath it, until the hooves stopped. Then the horse whirled and dirt clumps went into the air. Cary stepped back and pressed herself against the wall as the horse rushed against the gate, pushing it open with its shoulders. The gate swung open quickly then flung back against the horse's rump as he stumbled once and galloped off into the darkness.

Cary stood there a moment and then turned and looked at the old man under the dented sheet of tin. The mare had walked over and was sniffing over him gently, but he did not move. Cary heard the limbs breaking in the woods towards the highway and turned away from Otis and began running after the stallion. In the dark woods, every way she turned branches caught her clothes or she battered against a tree. The tears streamed down her face as she pushed forward with her hands outstretched. The horse was getting farther from her and she was not sure if she could still hear it. She fell forward in the pine straw, her foot wrapped in a honeysuckle, and as she hit the ground she heard a deep thud in the distance. When she got to her feet and pulled her foot from the vine, walking forward slowly through the trees, she began to hear voices and the motors of cars. Her legs were stinging and she felt the slow trickle of blood each time a blackberry vine pulled across her flesh. Between the trees light began to appear, not the moonlight but the headlights of the automobiles on the highway. She heard the ripple of voices as she began to walk from the trees across the ditch beside the road. In front of her were the silhouettes of people moving about and leaning against each other and the long thick clump of a tractor-trailer truck.

Somehow she felt the smell of blood in her nose, and she walked straight to the white blood-spattered mound, twisting in the ditch on the other side of the road. The dark genitals of the horse lay still across the dirt in the bottom of the ditch, and his legs twisted and wrapped beneath his belly, his front leg bending in three places. Cary walked to his head and went to her knees in the dirt. She felt the air darken behind her as the people closed in around the top of the ditch and she bowed her head, pressing it against the soft head of the horse. She began to talk softly to him as she felt the slow smooth breath trickle from his nostrils and the blood with it that went across her cheek. His bristly lip moved slowly against her neck, and she closed her eyes in the warm hair on his head. Above her she heard the people begin to move, voices, then silence before the air cracked.

The horse coughed, and the lips were still but for the warm flow of blood. She lay there with him until someone lifted her away, then she sat back, feeling the blood, now cold, trickle between her breasts. She looked up into Johnny's face; his mouth was open and his eyes were dry as he ran his hand slowly up the clean white fur on the horse's jaw. He touched the sticky blood on the horse's lips, then pulled his fingers away slowly as the flesh stuck to them a moment before pulling loose.

Old Otis was sent to the state hospital; the side of his face had been smashed under the tin and he could no longer talk. He made sounds like an animal and could not look at anyone in the face without his head wobbling out of control, so Dr. Jason sent him away. Mrs. Strawbright had his house cleaned out and a new tenant moved in with his family. She burned his clothes and brought his goat up to the main barn and put it in the corral with Johnny's mare. One evening when they were all sitting on the porch — Johnny, Sam, Cary, and Mrs. Strawbright — the laughing sound of the goat cut through the air.

"Why are you keeping that goat, Mama?" Johnny said angrily.

"Well, I don't know. Didn't really know what to do with it. I reckon a dog or something will get it before summer's over."

"You know I've been figuring about old Otis and something I heard at school." It was Sam who had spoken and who looked around for a response.

"What," Johnny finally said and his voice trailed off.

"You know he was scaring the horse with that tin, getting him all excited. Well, he was just one of those sex nuts."

"Sam, hush that!" Mrs. Strawbright said.

"Well, there's no reason not to talk about it. Cary knows what it's all about and so does little brother."

Cary sat still and felt her body sway as her muscles tightened and she tried to make him think that she did not hear him.

"She told me what he did, wiggling that tin and getting the stallion all excited, didn't you, Cary?"

"Yes," she said simply and Johnny turned and looked at her.

"Well, she didn't stop him," Johnny said angrily.

"Johnny, I told you not to bring that up again. I doubt very seriously you would have done a thing either or could have or would have known what to do or anything. At least she had enough concern to go see what was wrong with the horses," Mrs. Strawbright said.

Then Sam said, "Well, look, that's not what I was getting to. You know that old goat; well, I heard at school that a lot of guys in the war used to use . . ."

"Sam, shut up that talk!" Mrs. Strawbright said loudly and stood up. "Where is your mind, talking that way?"

"Well, I was just trying to figure the crazy mess out. I was just wondering, that's all. He was trying to do something, that's for sure."

"Sam, I'll just tell you about that old man. I don't know much, where he came from or anything, but I guess I know as much as anybody does. Your daddy hired him years ago, and in two years he was just like a mule too old to use, only you couldn't take him to the ditch."

Then she sat back in the chair. "Years ago when he first started shaking, he was carrying up the eggs for me, and I could smell licker on his breath too, and he missed a step and broke it must have been a hundred eggs on the porch. Well, he just got up and ran instead of helping clean it up and left me there to shoo the chickens away from pecking those busted eggs. They got in them anyway and for months they were busting their own eggs and eating them no matter how much you fed them and I asked your father about just letting the old man go on relief . . . but anyway what I'm getting to is, I went out to the barn later; I hadn't seen him since the busted eggs; and walked in the stable and heard someone crying like a little baby and over there in the mule stall, just about buried in straw and manure, was old Otis, his legs sticking out from the heap like two toothpicks. Well, I thought it was the craziest thing I'd ever seen and then the night the horse got killed I found him back in the same place before I pulled him out with his head all smashed and took him to Dr. Jason's. He was just crazy as a tick, that's all there was to it. He thought someone was just going to kill him for what he'd done so he thought he was hiding; he was just that crazy."

Sam began talking again. "But that don't explain why he was laughing and getting them excited. He had a reason and Cary said he was laughing . . ."

Johnny had not listened to Sam but stared at his mother and said, "I would have killed him if I'd found him. I don't care how crazy or not or what." He stepped back and leaned against the porch rail.

"Johnny, you just have got to forget the whole thing. I know it doesn't seem fair at times, but it's part of growing up to get over being mad and to forgive and forget. You should find it in you to feel sorry for someone like that."

"I don't care if he was a sex nut or crazy or what. He killed my horse and he was old and stupid and not good for a damn thing and that was the best horse I've ever seen. He wasn't, was he? He wasn't good for a damn thing!"

Cary looked up at Johnny and saw the light from the inside window catch in the pocket in his cheeks. His eyes were wet and a narrow streak of light ran sideways across the center of them.

"Grow up, little brother," Sam said.

Johnny pushed himself forward from the rail, straightening his arms.

Mrs. Strawbright reached up and held her hand between them. "Sam, that was uncalled for, completely uncalled for."

Cary heard Sam and Mrs. Strawbright continue talking, but she did not take her eyes from Johnny, who slowly began to settle back against the rail. Then he swung over the side of the porch and dropped over the side of the rail to the ground. Cary looked at Sam and Mrs. Strawbright as they watched him disappear across the yard. She jumped from her chair and ran down the steps after him. When she got to the corral, she saw him leaning across the gate looking at the goat that watched him back with her head cocked sideways and her chin whiskers curling towards her neck. Cary walked behind him, and her body began to shake until she had to clutch the gate against her with both hands.

Then he said, "That goddamn goat! I'd like to take that goddamn goat and beat . . ."

"It wouldn't do a bit of good."

"Dammit, whose side are you on anyway?" and he turned and clutched her shoulders tightly. "Goddamn, I thought you'd be the one person . . ."

"That's it, that goat; that stupid goat . . ." and her voice trembled as she dropped her face. "You'd kill that goat then you'd look at it and it would be all bloody too and wouldn't have done anything but then you'd think that you had killed a poor dumb animal and you'd keep thinking. You would have hurt an animal because it couldn't protect itself, and all the time it was the people, the people were the ones you wanted to get and they won't let you . . ."

He pulled her quickly against him and she felt his heart beating against her cheek as she reached up to touch the cloth of his shirt. She opened her eyes and looked at the cloth in her fingers before she clutched it in her fist and his arms tightened around her. He twisted his fingers through her hair and she felt the sharp pull on her scalp that brought tears into her eyes. Then he released her suddenly and stepped backwards away from her. As she stood there she grabbed sideways for the gate and tears ran down her face onto her lips.

"Cary, I didn't mean . . . you." When he spoke, she looked up at him. He turned his face away, and as she watched him disappear around the barn, she could only think of the old man and how he had crawled under the straw and how if now she had to crawl under it she would smother. She only wanted to lie with her arms and legs outstretched on the grass somewhere where it was cool and wet and forget everything, but her body would not let her be still. She turned and tried to make this feeling leave her, running her fist along the gate until she felt a splinter go into her hand. Then she beat it deeper and deeper until the tears that fell were now from the pain that ran up her arm and deep into her shoulder.

Chapter Twenty

THE FIRST GARDEN was ripe now, and Cary sat on a milking stool, pulling it down the row behind her as she picked snap beans in the garden. She reached under the leaves that fell like green lace over her arms. When she put down her pan of beans, lifting up the leaves, she saw on the underside, in furry yellow rows, the eggs of the beetles. The yellow- and red-spotted beetles opened their wings like tiny flower petals when she lifted the leaves, and rose into the air leaving the eggs on the plant. Then she folded the leaf and felt the soft yellow eggs crush and pop between her fingers.

"Beetles have just about taken these, Mrs. Strawbright."

"Yes, I know, Cary. Just a bad year I guess, but we've already gotten most of the good out of them anyway."

"Want me to dust them anyway? They're budding a little still."

"No, they're not worth it. Why don't you take the afternoon to pull them up and get some late ones planted?"

"Oh, but I told Johnny I'd help him with the seining down at the minnow pond."

Mrs. Strawbright stood up and dropped the last three squash she had picked into the tub beside the row. "No, you let Sam help him. I doubt you'd be much help and I don't want you messing around those two boys down at that pond. They're liable to drag you off into the water over your head and that seine is too heavy for you to handle."

"I used to help Papa do it when he went to get the crawfish out, Mrs. Strawbright. I can do it."

"No, I'd rather you get these plants up. You let them do it. The two of them can get along fine."

Cary clutched the bean plant that she was picking by the stem and pulled it until the root broke from the ground with a loud pop.

"Aren't you going to finish the row first?"

"It's easier this way. I can pull off the beans after they're up," she said and threw the plant between the rows. She worked slowly down the row and stopped and watched Mrs. Strawbright as she left the field with the tub resting on her hip. Cary quit working and began to crumble clods in her hands. When Mrs. Strawbright had disappeared into the house, she began to throw the clods at the rain barrel until one whanged against the side and left a dusty spot. Mrs. Strawbright's face appeared at the door a second, then she went back into the kitchen.

When the face had gone, Cary began to look at all the emptiness around her and began to feel completely left out of everything. She could see no one and could not hear Johnny and Sam from where they were working putting up posts on the lower side of the pasture. She thought of the time only a few years ago when they had brought the stallion from the Creek Farm and Johnny had given them twenty-five dollars to let him use the horse. She had watched them unload the stud from a covered truck, and she could still see the big white horse with his pink-tipped nose. They had brought him down the ramp and he fell and fought his way down instead of walking. Then when they went to drive the truck away, the horse had twisted in her father's hands sending one sharp hoof out which hit dead center in the headlight of the truck. The horse snatched his foot from the rim of broken glass, and little red trickles went down his ankle when he slammed his foot in the ground.

"Crazy bastard! I couldn't stop the crazy bastard," her father had said.

Johnny said, "Lead him on it, see if he hobbles."

"Hobble hell, he'll drag me if I give him an inch."

The horse beat the ground with his front foot, reaching out towards her father's legs, and the halter twisted back and forth across the horse's nose as he tried to pull from Papa's grip. A thick foam hung on his lips and as he slung his head the foam broke into the air like little soap bubbles.

"Goddamn albino! Why did you get a goddamn albino!" her father said more in contempt than for an answer.

Johnny answered him anyway, "Because we are sure to get a palomino; with a chestnut mare it's a hundred per cent."

"That's what you read, little brother, we'll see," Sam said.

"Well, that's what they do at the palomino ranches; they ought to know."

Then they went toward the barn; the horse was leading her father, who stumbled along by its front feet. When its head went up into the air, her father's feet lifted off the ground. Cary followed them, keeping a safe distance behind the hooves of the horse, watching its jittery side steps. Then her father stopped and turned to her, the horse yanking him off balance again.

"Be still, damn you crazy son of a bitch! Cary, you get on back to the house!"

She stopped and slid her hands into her back pockets. "Why?"

"Because I said to, that's why. You got no business out here."

She stood there a moment and looked at all three of the faces impatiently waiting for her to leave.

"Why can't I see?"

"Goddamn it, will you get back to the house!"

She looked at the faces a moment longer then turned and ran out of sight on the other side of the barn. She could remember now the coughs and snorts of the horses and the shouts of the men. "We are going to have to hobble her if she doesn't stop kicking . . . Goddamn, she is going to tear him up, lost another load . . . Johnny, keep her head up so she can't kick . . . If he keeps on losing his head . . ."

And she had sat in the shade and watched them put the stud back into the truck. The mare nickered shrilly to him and he answered, his voice echoing deep inside the metal walls of the truck. Cary looked up at the mare now. The horse had her head over the fence, her ears firm and forward, her shoulders pressed against the gate. Cary gathered up an armful of the bean plants she had pulled up and walked out to the corral. When she dropped them over the fence, the mare raised her head from the grass and crossed over to her, dragging her nose along the ground. Then the horse munched noisily on the bean plants, her ears flicking backward and forward under a little cloud of gnats.

Cary heard Johnny and Sam drop their shovels in the barn and the handle of one slide down the wall and hit the floor. A few minutes later they came out through the stable, Johnny with the seine over his shoulder.

"Come on, Cary. We are going to get on it early so we don't have to worry about keeping them alive till morning. We can take them in this afternoon."

They walked past her, but Johnny stopped and turned to her, saying, "Come on, let's get going."

She walked off down the hill after them, picking the sticky bean leaves off her shirt, rolling them into balls. Flicking one into a spider web, she saw it hang suspended for a moment then fall out, pulling half of the web down. She ran by them, and when she got to the pond she heard the sound of the frogs as they plunged into the water.

That night they had loaded two barrels of the little fish into the trunk of the car. The thin little shiners rolled over and over each other, swimming thickly in the water. When Johnny started the motor, the surface of the water began to ripple and slosh over the edge.

"Johnny, wait! They're all going to slosh out." Cary turned and ran into the barn, coming back a few minutes later with two blocks of wood in her hands. She put one in each of the barrels and the water slid over them, gradually stopping until it was calm but for the scurrying of the fish underneath.

"Hey, that's great! Where did you learn that?" Johnny said as he looked over into the barrels.

"Papa told me about it."

"Johnny, we better get going. He closes a little before dark," Sam said.

"Yeah, Cary, feed the mare, will you?"

"When we get the money, we'll buy you something, Cary," Sam said as he shut the door of the car.

Cary watched them leave, then walked to the house to change her wet clothes. She passed by the garden and saw the row of beans still there. A sudden fear seized her that she must get them all out of the ground before anyone saw them. She started pulling up the plants, and when she pulled the last one she rubbed her sore hands together. Then she ran to the barn and got a hoe and reached into the seed barrel for the sack marked "bunch snaps" and put it in the pocket of her jeans. She scooped up a bucket of fertilizer and went back out into the garden. After she had put the fertilizer in and smoothed over the row for the seeds, her nervous haste left her. She opened the bag of seeds and put them back in her pocket, taking the hoe in one hand and going down the row chopping shallow holes and dropping seeds.

"Eena, mena, mina, mo . . ." and she dropped four seeds, two in each of the holes she had just chopped.

"Catch a nigger by the toe . . ." then she reached out with her foot and kicked the dirt over the seeds.

"If he hollers, let him go . . ." and she pressed the dirt over the seeds, making a print with the back of the hoe.

When she walked to the next mound, the words "Eena, mena, mina, mo" went through her mind, but she had not said them. She stood still a moment and realized that the voice was Papa's. The voice seemed to hang in the air and then was completely gone. When she looked all around her and saw that no one was there, she began to laugh. The laugh felt dry and uncomfortable in her throat, and she could feel a tight ache from it as she went down the rest of the row. After each step, she felt a little dizzy, as though she were hungry, and when she gathered up the tools she began to feel nauseated. By the time she had gotten to the barn, the air was dark as if night had come suddenly. She put the hoe in the corner and listened for its clank as it hit the wall and fell against the fertilizer barrel. She lifted the lid on the seed barrel and dropped in the bag after twisting the top into a knot. She threw the bucket into the corner and, when it hit, she heard a swishing sound.

In the next moment she had screamed and she began to cough and strangle. The top of her feet burned and she lay on the floor with the back of her head against the barrel. She reached down and began to rub the top of her feet until they were sore. As she looked to the door, she saw the shiny black body of the snake that had run across her feet wrap around the corner, oozing along until the end of its tail disappeared from the light as if someone were pulling it by a string from the other side.

Cary sat there looking at the strange light where the sun made its last dots on the floor, and she could hear the even wobble of the bucket in the corner. Her body was still shaking violently, and she held her arms around her knees, but she could not stop it. She looked up and saw the air hanging with dusty spider webs and the wall crested with dirt dauber nests. Her shoulders trembled, grating against the rusty fertilizer barrel when she closed her eyes. Only the hum of the bucket in the corner could be heard, and when it stopped it was like the sound of a door closing, locking. The cold sweat seeped into her clothes and she twisted her body to make it run, but it only soaked and soaked until her clothes felt inches thick and they were tight and she could only tremble within them. Her body seemed to be made of bars with openings all around that could be pierced between the slats into her open sides.

Like the cage bars of the mad squirrel. She had locked it in a box. It seemed he was no longer a thought but a scratching in her mind. It had been in the chicken box, here in the tack room, foam bubbling over its lips, and when someone came in the room it threw itself against the bars, then sprawled back inside. Deep in its throat she had heard it cough and wheeze, and when Papa went into the fields she would go where it was and watch it every day, running a stick down the bars until it grew weaker from its lunges and only tossed on the floor.

She remembered when she had taken Johnny in to see it jump at the bars, but he had gotten angry and said, "You're crazy . . . Why do you want to see anything so miserable . . . ?"

"I didn't do it to him; I didn't do it; it's just that way and I didn't do it . . . watch . . . he wants to tear me up . . . every day he sees me and wants to tear me up, but he can't get out . . . don't go near . . . he might reach through the bars . . . he might think you are me . . ." She didn't look up as she spoke and kept watching the animal in the cage.

"Why don't you kill it . . . nothing inside of it but poison and rot . . . it could kill you . . . if it bites you, you'll go crazy like it . . . Why don't you drown it or do something . . . It's not right to let something like that live," Johnny had said to her.

She turned and looked up at Johnny and could remember his face now when she had said, "But he's not like the others, the ones in the trees. He would hurt me if I let him." Johnny had looked down at her in silence, and she could hear the thumping and rattling of the bars behind her.

"Johnny!" He had turned from her and started towards the door where he had stopped without turning around. "Johnny, I didn't mean to hurt him. I really didn't think about him as being anything living. I didn't mean to hurt him."

Johnny had walked from the barn, and as she looked at the door now she remembered how it had swung shut and the dust had fallen and the spider webs moved silently in the air. She felt her clothes dry stiff against her body as she stared across the tack room at the empty cage where the squirrel had been. She had watched the squirrel that day after Johnny had left, and it had grown weaker and weaker until it was only a shriveled little rat-like animal, helpless and twisted in the bottom of the cage. She remembered how it had quit moving, but she had been afraid to touch it even then as it lay with its mouth open and the foam drying on its lips. Now Cary tried to remember how she couldn't move towards it or do anything and Johnny had left her alone. She wanted to get up now and move from the barn, but her body seemed to be dead around her.

"Why do you want to see anything so miserable?" Again she could hear the words Johnny had said. She didn't want to see it miserable. When she looked at the cage, she was glad it was empty. Her side began to ache as she stood up and walked to the door, her hands pressed against her ribs. She found herself walking towards the spring, the light dimming overhead and dotting in thin spots at her feet while she walked through the trees. When she got to the spring, she stopped and looked at the straw beneath the pine trees where the mushrooms had been, but the straw lay smooth and flat across the ground. On the bank beside the stream grew two thin white skeletons of the mushrooms, their color faded to white and their tentacles short and darkened. Water ran by them where they grew on the edge, their roots showing on top of the dirt. She felt none of the excitement inside that she had when she saw them the first time. Their bright color in the straw was only a faint image in her mind. The dirt broke away slowly from beneath them, but she no longer wanted to look at them until they would finally tumble away and fall into the water. In the faint light they looked almost like the frail little face of Jasper, blank and expressionless and without life. As she walked back up the path towards the house, she felt strangely calm and her anger seemed to have left her. The trees moved by her face and only blurred beside her as she looked behind the house at the thin orange breaks in the dark sky. Her mind seemed to be free as her eyes moved across the dark frames of the trees again, each tree making a fresh picture before her.

She stopped as she heard the car doors slam behind the house and waited until she could see the two boys walk around towards the front of the house. In the dim light she recognized Johnny's thinner form run to the edge of the drive. She started running across the pasture towards him as she heard him call her name above the singing of the bugs at her feet.

Chapter Twenty-One

THE NEXT DAY they began planting the late tomatoes. Cary put a bucket under the pump and lifted the lever up and down until finally a thin rusty stream fell in the bucket. The chunks of iron rust rattled into the pail like hailstones on tin before the clear water began to flow in a hard solid stream. She emptied the rusty water and began to pump harder until the bucket filled up.

"Cary, for Christ's sake, hurry up with the water! I'm out," Johnny called from the garden. He held the dripping tomato planter in his hand and the last three plants lay crooked in dry holes. Sam stood beside him with a handful of plants wrapped in a wet newspaper, holding one ready to drop in the shoot.

"Will you wait a minute? The rust will clog the planter up."

"Come on, come on," he said, swinging the planter in his hand.

She hurried up the row, splashed the water and stumbled, wetting the side of her jeans. Johnny began to laugh at her, and when she got in front of him with the water, she put her hand on the bottom of the bucket and threw the water at his chest. He dropped the tomato planter and held his arms away from his wet body. Cary felt a hollow feeling in her chest as she looked up at him and dropped the empty bucket at her feet.

"Gaaa . . ." he cried as the water ran down his legs and his clothes stuck to him. He looked at Cary and in an instant had grabbed her around the waist and thrown her over his shoulder. She beat on his back as he carried her down the row towards the pump. He dropped her on the concrete slab and held her by the hair as he pumped the cold water over her head. When she grabbed his leg, he fell off balance in the muddy water under the pump. He still held the handle and the water kept pouring across their heads and shoulders.

Sam called from the field, "When you two decide to stop horsing around, you could come out here and finish planting this stuff."

Johnny looked at Cary. The water had sealed her hair in black streaks across her face. She peeled her hair away from her eyes and he laughed as she got her hands tangled in it.

He reached down for her hand and yanked her roughly to her feet. "I'll get you for that. You just wait," he said. Then he looked at her and laughed. "When you least expect it."

"Cary!" She looked across the garden to Sam who had called her. "Go up to the barn and get that other bunch of plants."

She turned to Johnny and said, "Be back in a minute," then walked around the field to the front of the barn. A truck was sitting in front of the door and she heard a voice inside and the sound of the mare moving. She stopped short in the door when she saw the dark image of Maurice trying to tie the halter strap to the door.

"What are you doing here?" she said quickly. Maurice jumped forward, dropping the lead rope, as the horse bumped against the wall of the stall.

"Mrs. Strawbright told me to shoe this bitch animal but I ain't 'bout to mess around her back feet no more what I ain't got nobody holding her head," he said angrily, watching the horse roll her lip up at him. "She'll kick you winding with two feet off the ground. She's going to have to get somebody else to do it."

"I'll hold her," Cary said, then walked past him into the barn and took the horse by the halter, rubbing the horse's nose when it wrapped its lips around her wrist and began to run its clasped teeth up her arm. "She just knows you're scared of her."

Maurice walked back behind the horse, watching its back foot rest sideways, then stopped and looked at Cary.

"I've got her, Maurice. Go on and get it done," she said, feeling her heart tighten when he seemed to notice her presence for the first time.

He squinted his eyes at her and then lifted the horse's hind foot onto the forked iron rack. Cary watched him clip the broken hoof away, the gray chips falling into the straw, then rasp across the foot with a big iron file. The mulatto's legs bent together at the thighs and he stood on the sides of his feet as he swung back and forth with the file. When he set the horse's hoof back on the ground again, he stood up, stretching his shoulders backwards. He threw his file into the box and took one of the shoes off the bar across the top.

"You're black as tar," he said suddenly to Cary.

Cary turned and looked at him with a frown. "I get like this in the summer," she said nervously. "She's quiet now. Do you still need me to hold her?"

"You stay right there till I'm done, you hear, or she ain't going to get shoes."

Then he laughed and smiled crookedly at her, his lips peeling away from his dark gums and stray yellow teeth. On his lip was a white sore and the whiskers bristled around it.

Then he spoke again, "You're part nigger, that's what you are."

Cary tightened her grip on the halter and pressed her knuckles against the side of the horse's head. "My daddy was an Indian."

"Indian, nigger . . . there ain't no difference."

"I'll go get Johnny to hold her. I've got to carry Sam some plants."

"You stay there. I'll be done in a minute."

He turned and lifted the horse's foot, pulling it between his legs, and began to tack on the shoe. She turned her back to him and began to brush the gnats away from the horse's eyes while he bradded the nails. Suddenly she jumped forward and the horse threw up her head, knocking over the forked stand. Maurice had run his hand under her arm and across her breast.

"Liked that, didn't you?" he said as he started walking towards her.

"You get away, you dirty . . . get away from me!"

"I knowed who your pappy was; I knowed him and I knowed who your Mama was too."

Cary walked back from him and glanced sideways at the horse that had backed out of the stable. She looked at the door of the barn and her eyes blurred with tears when Maurice stepped over to block the door of the stall.

"Your Mama liked black men . . ." Then he began to laugh. "Yes sir, the blacker the better for your Mama."

"You get away from me; you're crazy!" She started to rush through the door of the stall but he put up his hands, and she felt the hard rough palms hit her shoulders and push her back against the wall. Maurice turned suddenly and saw Johnny standing in the door with the horse.

"Did she get loose . . . ?" Johnny stopped and glanced at the two of them. "You son of a bitch, Maurice; get your hands off her." Johnny let go of the horse's halter and ran towards him. "You dirty goddamn bastard; get out of here!"

Maurice jumped around quickly and grabbed the file from his box. Cary watched Johnny step in the door of the stall and clinch his fists, his eyes following Maurice who hopped around on his bent feet. Johnny edged inside a few steps and looked quickly over his shoulder and back at Maurice again.

"You getting quiet, ain't you, white boy?"

Johnny watched Maurice wave his file feebly in front of him. "You bastard, Maurice! If you had any guts, you wouldn't stand there waving that file. You pick up your stuff and get out of here!"

Maurice tottered a moment with the file in his hand, reaching behind himself for the bar on the top of his tool box. He began to go out with his back to the door, stumbling and falling backwards over the sill.

"I didn't mean to start no trouble. I just made a mistake. Don't you mention this to nobody, hear?" he cried as he climbed back to his feet and began to move sideways towards the door of the barn. "Don't you tell your Mama!"

Johnny walked over and grabbed the forked rack, throwing it through the stall door in front of Maurice. Maurice bent over with his eyes on Johnny and picked it up, tucking it under his arm. He stiffened up again, the file still in his hand. Then he backed out of the door and threw his tools with a clatter into the back of his truck. The mare walked back to Johnny and pushed her nose against his chest and he caught her halter, watching Maurice's truck flash by the door. When he looked over for Cary, he saw her balled up in the corner of the stall with her face in the straw. He led the horse up to the stall and tied her halter rope to the door frame, where she stood beating her unshod foot in the dirt.

"Cary?"

"What!" she said shortly, her voice muffled in the straw.

Then he went and stooped beside her. "He's gone."

"I don't care if he's gone or here or what," and her body drew into a tighter knot.

"Did you say something to him or what? I didn't know he was in here."

"No, I didn't say anything!" she said angrily, then rolled over and looked into his face. The straw had left creases across her cheeks and she squinted as she looked back in the light. Then Johnny's face began to come clear and tears rose in her eyes when she realized he was looking at her.

"He knew her and he came to our house and slept with her. All the time she was making like he was just there to fix her coffee pot. I knew he did it. He just said that she liked black men." Then Cary rolled back face down in the straw. "She's a dirty bitch!"

"Cary, I told you not to worry about that anymore. You should never have gone near him."

"I didn't think about it. I didn't. He was scared of the horse and I was just going to hold her for him." She pressed her face deeper in the straw and her back began to jolt back and forth.

Johnny took her by the shoulders and lifted her up, but she was limp and fell back against the wall of the stall, her head falling forward from her shoulders.

"Come here, Cary."

She looked at him and her eyes were glassy and wild. "No!"

"Please let me hold you."

"No!" and she pressed her head back against the wall, jarring the tears from her eyes.

He reached out and pulled her to him and she fell heavily against his chest. She balled her fists in front of her face and pressed her eyes against them. He began to pull her hair from the inside of her collar and spread it down her back.

"Your hair's still wet."

"Sam's going to come in here. He's going to catch us."

"He's out in the field; what if he does?"

"He'd say something."

"I don't care if he would say something. Now dammit, quit pulling away. You don't want to."

She pushed back from him and looked into his face. "What do you expect me to do? Like I did last time and have you push me away and go off and leave me? I'm not going to do that again. I'm never going to let anyone do that again."

Then Johnny looked steadily into her eyes until she turned away and screamed, "Why do you look at me like that? God!"

She pulled from his grip and leaned back against the wall, blinking her eyes that were sore when her wet lashes hit her bottom lid. "So dirty and grubby . . . thinking he could . . . oh, goddamn, I hate him! I hate her worse!"

She felt Johnny's hand go over hers and grip it until it hurt. Then she realized that she could not speak anymore. When she looked at his face, he was no longer looking at her, so she looked back down at the hand that was still gripping hers tightly. She touched the back of his hand, running her fingers over the veins then pressed the palm of her hand against it. He looked up at her.

"Cary!" and his arms were around her tightly and she felt her body go against his chest. Her arms reached around his back and she knew that she had reached for him too. She put her face against the top of his shoulder and closed her eyes, afraid to open them because as long as she kept them shut she felt that she did not have to speak and he would not go away. As he held her tighter, her body stopped trembling. When they lay sideways in the straw, her body felt warm; the wet clothes coming unsealed from her flesh. He kissed the side of her face. She opened her eyes and saw at first only the color of his eyes and his dark skin. His hair grew blond in the front and fell loosely over his forehead. She watched the dark rims of blue that circled his eyes and drifted into paleness towards the center. When she began to run her fingers up the side of his face, he reached around her neck and pulled her face slowly towards him and kissed her. When he kissed her, she was no longer afraid to run her hands up and down his back.

He held her head back and brushed the hair from her face before he pulled her back to him and held her arms against her side. He released her suddenly as he heard the wash tub on the back porch clanging and his mother's voice calling them to lunch.

She watched him stand up in front of her, and when he held his hands to her she grabbed them and he pulled her to her feet.

When they stood in the door of the stall he put his arm around her shoulders and pressed her against his side. "Let's go to lunch, huh?"

Chapter Twenty-Two

CARY WALKED in the powdery topsoil, feeling the heat of the day still in the ground as the wet sand on top rose around her feet. The sky was beginning to darken, and each time she looked up the orange streaks of the sun pulled thinner across the top of the trees. She stopped and walked into the shadows beside the spring where the hum of the nightbugs surrounded her feet. They bounced against her legs, falling with soft splashes into the shadows beside the spring. In the distance she could hear the flutter of wings as the chickens were rushed into the house, and somewhere the lonely cry of a calf trembled as it ran up the hill to the barn in search of its mother. Cary began walking again, going behind the tobacco field on the path to the chicken lot.

When she looked in the lot, the door had already been shut. She took the key off the nail and went inside where the white hens hovered around a silver water container with a purple liquid in its trough. The chicken heads went up and down like a seesaw as the water slid down their throats. She walked over and put her hands into the warm nests, but the eggs were already gone. Mrs. Strawbright had collected the eggs without her, and she felt a moment of disgust with herself because she had not done her job.

Then she thought of her afternoon in town; how she had stood behind the bolts of cloth in Gertey's store, watching her mother run the needle up and through the hem of the red dress in her lap. Her mother's eyes had stayed on the hem; all of her body tight. She concentrated on the filmy red cloth in her lap as if it was almost more than she could do to keep her mind there and as if the red cloth might suddenly melt and float off into the air. Her fingers were tightly pinching into the material, and the soft pink skin drew across the bones. Then the needle had hit her finger pricking up a tiny red drop. She looked at it until tears swelled in her eyes and ran into the gray lines that sank around them. She lifted the soft red cloth in front of her eyes and looked at it until the tears ran freely down her cheeks. Cary watched her raise the pricked finger and move it closer and closer to the dress until it touched and the drop was sucked quickly into the fabric and disappeared into the red of the dress. The dress and hands and her face came tumbling down suddenly, and Cary looked a moment as her mother's body shuddered violently and colored spools began to tumble and clatter onto the floor.

Cary turned quickly and went to the door. As she looked outside at the street, she felt the laughter and movement of the people and knew she would never have to look at the pink-fleshed woman again. Her heart hurt in her chest but her eyes were dry. She looked up and down the street until she saw an old man; he leaned against a railing and looked blankly at the sidewalk. Then she ran into the street and began to walk slowly when she reached the highway. She looked around her at the shiny green and gold of the fields that almost hurt her eyes. Then she had started walking down the side road that led to the old house where her grandmother had lived and where she was as a child.

Cary stood on the bottom step of the old house; she had never seen a house come to an end like this and just stand until it fell. It seemed strange to her that a house would fall as soon as there were no more people in it, because she could never remember her father or her grandmother or any of her relatives doing anything to repair the house when they were there. Yet, since they had all been gone from it, it began to turn the color of the earth, and the earth that had been smooth in front of it had become green with grass and vines. She looked at the vines that went up the side of the house and curled into the windows and ran across the top of the steps.

When she started up the steps she stopped again as the birds began to fly through the broken windows, screaming into the air, and a brown creature ran by her feet and down the steps. She felt her body tighten to jump aside as it went by, but the animal had disappeared into the grass behind her before she could move. She wasn't frightened, and when she saw that some of the vines were bruised and broken, she knew she wasn't the only one who had been to the house. Under the porch chairs there were little white curls where the paint had peeled and fallen to the floor, and the chairs were red-brown from rust. In the row of flower cans on the porch were a few dry stalks and sticks with white rags that still held up the dead stems.

Cary sat down in the chair and looked out across the overgrown yard. She didn't know exactly why she had come there and why she didn't go ahead in the house, but she felt that somehow she must think before she opened the door. The old lady's garden, her iron pot, her wood pile; they were all out there somewhere, but she couldn't see them for the vines. She remembered her grandmother boiling clothes in that iron pot and turning them with a stick as the fire burned around her feet. She remembered when the other kids called the old woman a witch and they pretended that she was cooking up roots and poisons in the iron pot. It seemed that now there was very little she could remember, yet it hadn't been so very long ago when her grandmother was living. She remembered there was a funeral and that they got her a new dress to meet all the relatives who came to the house but that they wouldn't let her go to the grave. And that then she went to the orphanage and she wore the new dress, and when she left she still had to wear it even though it was out-grown.

On the day of the funeral she remembered all of the people that came to the house; so dark, much darker than she was, and how hard it was to pick her father out from them that day and how alone she was. They were all Indians and she was the light-est one there and not as much of an Indian as they were. She couldn't remember crying for her grandmother or her father or anyone in particular, but she could remember that she cried. She had sat down in the ditch by the road in her new dress and cried, and all she had thought of then was that she was only half Indian and she felt ashamed and ugly and that all the others were much stronger and prouder. Especially the little children that were no older than she, but she was ashamed to play with them because she didn't feel as good as they were. She could almost hear them laughing now as she thought how pale she felt then. Now when she was in a crowd, she felt she had her own cool shadow and that her expressions would not be so open on her face as the others because it was dark.

Cary stood up from the chair and it creaked back and forth loudly as she stood beside it. Then she went to the door and shoved it open with her foot. As the door swept inward it left a semicircle of clean floor at her feet. She stopped a moment to see if there were any more animals inside, but it was still and quiet. The furniture was gone except for one chair with a broken back, and the floor was covered with worn linoleum. She walked to the center of the room and dusted a spot clean with her foot, and she could see the corner of a checkerboard where she and her grand-mother used to sit on the floor and play checkers. There were a few clean squares on the wall where the pictures had been taken down, and there was only one left — a calendar with mountains and a lake and the months torn off.

For a moment she felt very frightened and turned quickly and shut the door. She felt strangely closed in inside of something that was different from the outside. When she went into the kitchen, more birds flew to the windows, bumping against the walls until they found a broken pane to fly through. In the corner under the sink she saw a stack of books. She stooped down beside them and looked at the colored covers. She knew that she had never seem them before and that they must have been behind the pans. She picked up the top book on the stack, but the name had worn off and there was only an impression of letters that she could not read. When she opened the cover, she saw a drawing on blue paper that was light around the edges and dark on the part that was inside the cover. It was of a tiny girl with pigtails that curled upwards standing beside a flower that was twice her height and had no leaves on its stem, only a yellow flower at the top of a stalk. At the bottom she could see where she had written her name in scattered letters and her Sunday School teacher had written, "To Grandmother on Mother's Day from . . ."

On the inside cover of the book, something was written in a handwriting that she did not know that covered in small letters all of the blank spaces at the beginning of the book. She began to read: "Green corn ceremony at harvest . . . shame is worse to steal and not be caught, a Cherokee will pay until death if he does not tell he has stole . . . the Cherokee will die slow and give birth to another . . . There is evil in an owl in the horse corral, when it cries evil will come to your baby or the owl will come out and eat you . . . an old woman if seen by herself will bring you evil and you can't run or look down to get away from her."

Cary continued to read through all of the books, and when she realized that the shaft of light that she held the book in was almost gone, she looked up for the first time in many hours at the room. Everything seemed blurred and the sun had set, leaving only a rusty glow of red inside the house that seeped in the front window and caught lightly in the silk of the spider webs. She stood up and went to the window. A light rain was falling, but the sun spotted across the leaves where the rain hit with a soft rattle. She watched the leaves tremble and straighten again until the rain became harder. Then she blinked her eyes and turned to pick up the books that were all open at her feet.

When she walked towards the door with the books under her arm, she stopped a moment before she went outside. "Shame is worse to steal and not be caught . . . a Cherokee will pay until death if he does not say he has stole." These were the words that she remembered from the book, but then she smiled and went out into the rain. She walked slowly through the wet vines and closed her eyes as the rain hit her in the face. Then she thought of the books again. "We will not be hunted like wild beasts; when we are forced from our orchards and cornfields, our unmilked cow will cry as hard as that of the white man and in the snow our feet will freeze and our poetry will sing like things of the earth, the rain in the trees, the thunder of the mountains, and the water against the rocks."

Cary walked down the dirt road back to the Strawbrights' and watched the dirt pull away from the banks and slide into the ditch. The tobacco fields bent under the rain, and she could hear the rain slash against the stalks. She walked by a Negro house where the chickens huddled together under the trees and she remembered the book — the book on the great march to the west. A woman had thrown an apronful of corn to her chicks and stared at them until someone had come to lead her away. And the white men were jealous of their cornfields and had driven them out to take their land but they had come back. Her people had to be the ones that had come back or had hidden in the hills because they were there now and there had been some very old people when she was young. It was almost dark now, and as she came to the last house in the Negro section she saw an old woman in a blue dress on the porch. She had a white cap pulled over head and her thin gray, frizzled hair puffed out around it.

"An old woman by herself is evil; don't run and don't look down," the book had said. Cary looked at her as she walked, and then she saw the old woman bend over and shove a frizzly chicken from under her chair. The chicken tumbled down the steps and began running in circles in the yard, kicking up mud with its feathery legs until it disappeared under the house. Cary began to laugh and lifted her hand to wave. The old woman kept rocking and raised her hand slightly from her lap, nodding and smiling at Cary.

Cary had crossed the railroad tracks and walked towards the Strawbrights' road, stopping to look in the mailbox before she turned towards home. The rain stopped, and she could hear only scattered drops hitting around her in the darkness.

Now she looked at where she was in the chicken house that was dusty in the daytime but dim and golden at dusk. The white hens began to nestle against each other on the roost, until the last hen flapped her wings and settled into place among the white bodies whose heads had begun to droop.

Cary walked from the chicken house, going into the feed room and stopping to listen for the chicks in the incubator. A beautiful warm peeping sound came from the box with the faint scurrying of little feet as they pressed together under the light bulb. When she lifted the lid, they began to flutter to the sides of the box, hurrying back to press against each other under the bulb again. She scooped up a yellow chick and put it under her shirt. It had squawked loudly as she pulled it from the light but began to peep quietly again as it huddled against her skin. Cary began to fill her shirt with the little chicks, until she felt the mass of soft fluff around her waist and the sharp little claws that tried to burrow into her skin.

After listening for a moment to the muffled peeps inside her shirt, she took the chicks out one by one, and they began to squawk again until they melted into the group of yellow fluff huddled around the light bulb. She dropped the lid shut on the incubator box and slipped out the door. The sky was dark overhead now. A pale green haze rose over the top of the hill behind the barn.